A
CHRISTMAS
PASSAGE

A CHRISTMAS PASSAGE

**David Saperstein
and
George Samerjan**

KENSINGTON BOOKS
http://www.kensingtonbooks.com

KENSINGTON BOOKS are published by

Kensington Publishing Corp.
119 West 40th Street
New York, NY 10018

All Kensington titles, imprints, and distributed lines are
available at special quantity discounts for bulk pur-
chases for sales promotion, premiums, fund-raising, ed-
ucational, or institutional use.

Special book excerpts or customized printings can also
be created to fit specific needs. For details, write or phone
the office of the Kensington Special Sales Manager: Attn.
Special Sales Department. Kensington Publishing Corp.,
119 West 40th Street, New York, NY 10018. Phone: 1-800-
221-2647.

Kensington and the K logo Reg. U.S. Pat. & TM Off.

ISBN-13: 978-0-7582-2580-1
ISBN-10: 0-7582-2580-6

First Kensington Trade Paperback Printing: October 2008
First Kensington Mass-Market Paperback Printing: December
2008
10 9 8 7 6 5 4 3 2

Printed in the United States of America

*For my wife, Ellen, who has always encouraged
and supported me throughout our life's passage.*
David

*For my wife, Joy, whose partnership
transcends the passage of our lives.*
George

Acknowledgments

Sara Camilli—our super-agent who keeps our thoughts, dreams, and work revealed

Audrey LaFehr—our professional and caring editor who keeps the spirit of Christmas with us

Ivan Saperstein—our high-powered, creative lawyer and advisor who keeps our best interests first

Christmas past sometimes finds those lost on Christmas Eve,
souls bereft of Christmas spirit softly touched,
sparks kindled against the darkest of inner moments,
illuminating forgotten joys from long ago,
reminding the heart of what it forgot,
but never lost.

George E. Samerjan

CHAPTER 1

MARTA

Normally quiet Fulton County/Brown Field, servicing corporate and private aircraft and a few commuter airlines, was crowded with holiday travelers this Christmas Eve morning. The modern drudgery of air travel—overbooked flights, time-consuming security checks, delays, cancellations, and general rudeness—was held to a minimum at this small facility. But this morning, with snow falling and a heavy influx of hurried, tired, infrequent travelers, civility was discarded as unceremoniously as last year's gift wrapping. The terminal was hot, damp, loud, and odiferous. At the entrance to the one row of kiosks and stores, a banner proclaimed—LAST STOP FOR YOUR CHRISTMAS SHOPPING. Marta Hood wore a pastel yellow sweatshirt and form-fitting Levis over her plump thirty-five-year-old body. Her boots, a pair of well-worn Uggs, were still wet from the accumulating snow outside. The heat in the terminal caused her to carry her ski parka as she ushered her children—

Ronny, age eight, and Nancy, age eleven, toward the gate area. Marta stopped in front of the TV monitor that served as a departure board for the airfield. She was nervous. She hated flying. With one eye on her children and one eye on the unsympathetic monitor, she searched for her flight number and gate. The title of an old movie echoed in her mind, *Quo Vadis?* "Where are you going?" She vanquished the thought and zeroed in to find the listing she needed: Blue Ridge Flight #6224 to Asheville—Gate 6.

What the hell are we doing? she wondered, as she had so often during the past weeks.

Carlisle Lane had its Christmas traditions, some that began months before the holiday season. Knute Lincoln, a retired engineer from an aerospace company, and a man with entirely too much energy to be retired, decorated his house, a red and white clapboard saltbox reproduction, with Christmas decorations after Columbus Day. Disapproving looks and anonymous notes from his neighbors had forced Knute's pre-pre-Christmas activity back to Halloween. But that was not acceptable, either. Finally, for the sake of neighborly peace, he acquiesced and pushed his luminous exhibition back to the more traditional time—the day after Thanksgiving. But the unforeseen consequence had been that Knute expanded his glittering exhibit to a much more elaborate display. His house became a beacon, an explosion of light and color that lit up the entire street all night long. He made the installation and maintenance of his extreme holiday show a full-time job. Word of the "radiant display on Carlisle" spread, and so, from

November twenty-seventh until well into January, hundreds of cars slowly made their way to Carlisle Lane for what many described as a cheerful and uplifting observance.

The journey took them past Claudia's gray Cape Cod, sorely in need of paint, but with a fresh Christmas wreath hung on her door by her son-in-law; then past the colonial of Pieter, an expatriate from Holland who in a feat defying gravity had hung Christmas lights from atop a tall ladder with a leaf rake, projecting wires and lights thirty feet above his shingled roof like a giant, incandescent teepee. Next was Steve and Stephanie's house, also a colonial, where a big menorah, strategically placed in the large picture window, tastefully signaled it was also the season of Chanukah. Finally they arrived at Knute Lincoln's Victorian and his storied display. There they stopped for a long moment as though they had arrived at an important shrine. Aware of the traffic behind, people lingered only a minute at most.

Next door to Knute Lincoln's electrified showplace stood Marta Hood's house, a contemporary knockoff of a classic Dutch colonial. But this year there were no candles in the windows, door wreaths, or the old-fashioned sleigh pulled by four life-size reindeer with a jolly smiling and waving Santa in tow. This year passers-by on the lane, out for a stroll in the chill December air, saw no warm green, red, and yellow lights gaily festooned on the Hood Christmas tree in the large front bay window. The house was unadorned. The dismal mood of it, especially compared to the rest of the lane, was striking. Inside the house, Marta's children had their holiday, and lives, dampened with anxiety. Childish anticipation of gifts beneath the tree had given way to fear of the unknown that lay ahead. Their parents were divorcing. Bitterly. The children felt helpless and afraid.

Ronny, a precocious third-grader with a knack for annoying his teachers by reading ahead in the curriculum, had been oblivious to the problems at home. Then one night, in a bedroom cluttered with war toys, tanks, aircraft, and thousands of plastic soldiers, while reading under his blankets by the light of a flashlight, Ronny heard loud and angry voices coming from the dining room.

"Mortgage . . . credit cards . . . empty bed . . . affair . . . frigid . . . let yourself go . . . overweight . . ." None of these words made sense to him as they floated up from below and through his bedroom door, but the hostile tone of the voices frightened him. He bravely crept to the top of the stairs and listened. His mother then made a sound he had not heard from her before. She was crying. There was no doubt. The instinct to help her rose in his young body with a rush of adrenaline. But fear of his father's size and short temper kept Ronny from descending the stairs. As his father's voice grew angrier, his mother's sobbing grew quieter. Then there was silence. Suddenly Marta raised her voice with a vehemence that Ronny had never heard before.

"Get out!" Marta screamed. "Get out of my life!"

Ronny clenched his fists as an abiding hatred for his father grew in his heart. He gathered his courage and stood to go downstairs. The touch of his sister's hand on his shoulder stopped him.

"No," she said softly. "Stay here. There is nothing we can do."

"What's going on?" he asked, as tears welled up in his dark brown eyes.

"We're getting a divorce," Nancy said.

"You're insane," their father said in the room below. "If I leave, I'm not coming back," he threatened. Marta then unleashed a diatribe that both children would never forget. It would be the stuff of nightmares for years to come.

"All those years!" Marta shouted. "All those years you criticized me about everything . . . the checkbook, the house, how I drove your precious car . . . even the laundry and dry cleaners. I couldn't get your French-cuffed shirts done the right way. I didn't dress to please you. I wasn't a good lover. I was inadequate. You remember that? Inadequate, you called me, like I was subhuman or retarded. You almost convinced me I was worthless. Almost. Not coming back, you say? Thank God, I say. Go to your girlfriend and abuse *her*. Get out of our lives! Get out! Get out! Get out!" Marta screamed those words over and over until Nancy and Ronny heard the door slam. Then they heard their mother sobbing. They hurried downstairs and found her on her knees in the foyer. The children embraced her and joined their tears with hers. It was three days before Christmas.

The next morning Marta hurled the gaily wrapped Christmas gifts, one after another, out of the front door. Silver wrapping and bright ribbons glittered brightly in the sunlight. The packages fluttered like wounded ducks shot from the sky. They were aimed at her husband, who had returned. He dodged the last package, but in doing so slipped and fell backward onto the wet lawn. He lay there, looking up at Marta as she stood with her hands on her hips, forbidding him entry and access to Ronny and Nancy, who stood behind her.

Knute Lincoln and his wife, Laurie, had come out to see what was going on. A few other neighbors had also gathered.

"Damn it, Marta! Have you lost your mind?" Robert, six feet, five inches tall, with well-coiffed blond hair, stood up and brushed some mud from his tweed overcoat. Breathless from dodging the gifts, he glanced at the gathering neighbors and decided not to press for entry. The words "Hell hath no fury as a woman scorned" rolled around in his thoughts. And he knew his neighbors, with whom he had purposely little contact, would bear witness against him if he got physical.

"That's it!" shouted Marta. "Go away!" She wore a pale blue silk blouse with the collar turned up, and pleated navy blue slacks. Wisps of hair fell over her eyes, and she brushed them back with her right hand, like a prize fighter clearing sweat from his eyes before launching the next set of punches. "You have any problems, you can tell it to the judge. I called Harold Buckman this morning and told him to file for divorce. Adultery!" she yelled loudly for all to hear. "Adultery with your so-called assistant."

"I just want to give the kids their presents," Robert said plaintively. He took a timid step forward. His body language, the step forward, and an incipient smile on his thin lips angered Marta. But she felt empowered.

"You think that dumb smile, raised eyebrows,

and syrupy charm works? Ha! Presents? You gave them their present last night. They heard everything. No!" she said emphatically. "Get lost!" Marta felt a surge of strength course through her body. She knew he was no longer in control of her life, and though the prospect of being a single mom was daunting, she found the thrill of her ability to confront him addictive.

"Are you saying you won't let me see the kids?"

"You got that right." Marta stepped outside, closing the door behind her. She walked forcefully to where Robert stood, stopping inches from him. She was in his face; eyes wide, teeth clenched. "Your relationship with the children will be decided in court. Harold will contact you the day after Christmas with the details. We'll be in Asheville for the holidays. Don't try to contact us there. You know you really don't want to deal with my father." She turned her back on him. Then, over her shoulder, she shouted back, "January fourth. Noon in Harold's office. Get ready to pay for your adultery, big time!"

Marta let a few tears fall as she walked back to the house, but she wouldn't let Robert see them. Slamming the front door behind her, she leaned against it with her arms across her chest. The wide foyer was dimly lit. A long, narrow table with an antique mirror stood against the wall. Memorabilia of a marriage, residue of incomplete events, was still in place. Framed photographs of birthdays, vacations, once cherished souvenirs like a gray pottery jug with the words *Current Realities* imprinted on it. . . . Marta glanced at the mini-gallery of her married life and sat down on the second carpeted step of the staircase that led upstairs to the bedrooms. She cradled her face in her hands.

Ronny, with tousled hair and his plaid shirt buttoned one hole off, sat next to her. Nancy sat on the other side. Marta wiped the tears from her eyes, and reached out to them.

"Are we ever going to see Daddy again?" Nancy asked.

"Yes," Marta said, embracing both of her children. "Of course you will. But there will be rules about it."

"Does he love us?" Ronny asked.

"Yes, dear. He's your father. He'll always be your father." She took a deep breath and stood up. "Okay, guys. Now we've got to pack. Grandma and Grandpa are excited that we're coming. We'll have a wonderful Christmas there."

"But, Mommy?" Ronny asked. "If Christmas is going to be wonderful, why were you crying?" Marta forced herself to smile. She hugged Ronny tightly.

"Someday, young man, you'll understand that people cry sometimes when they're happy."

"And you're happy now, Mommy?" Nancy asked. Marta embraced her children with even more ardor.

"Yes. Very."

"But you threw our presents at Daddy," Ronny said.

"This is Christmas, and there will be presents," Marta told them. "This year we're having a real Christmas."

CHAPTER 2

ANDY

Marta, her kids in tow, pressed through the crowded terminal toward the gate area. Outside, she observed that jumbo flakes of snow were blanketing the tarmac. De-icing equipment had rolled out adjacent to aircraft getting ready to depart. As they walked past the crowded airport bar, Marta glanced inside. Smokers sat in their special section, veiled in a cloud of nicotine-filled air, enjoying their cigarettes. *Fools,* she mused, paying for overly expensive drinks in return for refuge from the dictates of the smoke-less world. Sucking death into their lungs. Strangers brought together by a fatal, addictive habit, pausing momentarily on their journey home for Christmas. Marta shook her head to clear a wisp of melancholy. Christmas and divorce. *No,* she thought, *I will not let him ruin one more day of my life.* Ronny tugged at her sleeve, anxious to get on the plane.

Nancy watched a pretty young woman at the bar take a long, deep drag on her cigarette while the man in the expensive suit talked rapidly to her. But the young woman seemed disinterested in what he was saying. Her gaze wandered away and caught Nancy watching. The woman smiled and winked. As Nancy smiled back, Marta gathered her children up and moved away with a bounce in her step. Okay, single-mom-to-be, a new year! A new life! She guided the children briskly toward the gate.

Inside the crowded bar, in the no-smoking section, Anselmo Casiano nursed his second Rolling Rock. He had not had one of those in nearly thirty-eight years. Andy, as he preferred to be called, smiled to the notice of no one around him as he reminisced—a beer run to Xuan Loc. *Now why did I go there,* he wondered? Andy was lately aware of how often, since Maria died, he reflected on the past. They were married a few months after he returned from his second tour in Vietnam. Thirty-five years. So many plans for retirement. Gone. Ovarian cancer took her in six months. And now he was on his way to see his old army buddy George Spillers in Asheville, North Carolina. George was dying too. Leukemia. Agent Orange, George suspected. But the docs at the V.A. wouldn't admit that was the cause.

Andy's thoughts drifted back to the Rolling Rock. The images flooded in, blotting out the snowy landscape outside. A tropical sun baked the flatlands beneath the hills of III Corps. Their jeep's floor was layered with stuffed, pale gray sandbags. A fifty-caliber machine gun was locked and loaded, on its mount, welded to the floor behind the driver's seat. Wild-ass Captain José Morales, a West Pointer on his third tour, drove. Andy and George held on in the back as they sped at sixty miles an hour down the dirt road. A rooster tail of dust rose behind them. *God,* Andy recalled, *Charlie could have seen us coming from miles away.* It had been a beautiful day. Three young, stupid, and self-proclaimed immortals on a beer run to Xuan Loc because the word had come over the radio that Rolling Rock was going for a buck-fifty a case. All the way there Andy's heart had pounded wildly, yet now, in the anonymity of the airport bar, he recalled loving every minute of the adventure. The madness of indestructible warriors.

Andy sipped his beer and smiled, shaking his head. No one around him noticed. His thoughts again drifted to that day and their arrival at Xuan Loc. There was that stupid, young MP corporal facing Captain Morales down.

"Roll down your sleeves and get into proper uniform, sir," he announced moments after they had parked. His sleeves? Andy smiled, vividly recalling Morales was wearing black pajamas with infantry crossed rifles on one collar, and his captain's railroad tracks on the other. A black patent-leather gun belt was slung around his waist. There was a notch in it for each firefight he'd been through. Ho Chi Minh sandals adorned his bare feet. The "sleeves" were the least of his military-dress violations. The captain's jungle hat bearing rust stains from grenade pins around the band would have given a more experienced MP a clue as to the person he was dealing with.

All Morales said as he turned to those still in the jeep was, "Did you hear that, guys?" Spillers clutched his M16 while Andy leaned on the fifty. The captain's hand was on the butt of the .45 dan-

gling loosely in his belt. The two MPs standing behind the young corporal suddenly paled, realizing
they were in danger of replaying something akin
to the *OK Corral* scenario. The men in the jeep
were on a serious mission. There was beer at stake:
dirt-cheap cases of Rolling Rock. Thankfully, good
old steady George Spillers kept a cool head. He
dismounted and stepped between the jeep and the
MPs.

"We just drove twenty nasty clicks for some beer.
We're not here for a dress parade, Corporal." Spillers
was a staff sergeant, speaking to a corporal. "My
captain and buck sergeant are thirsty, is all." He
nodded toward the captain and Andy. Whether it
was Spillers's reasonable tone, or what the MPs saw
in Andy and the captain's eyes, or the fact that in
their line of work, these guys were already dead,
the MPs relented. A compromise was struck: thirty
minutes to load up and get out of Dodge.

Lazily, Andy's nail peeled the damp label off the
Rolling Rock bottle. He would remember the beer-
run story in more detail and reminisce tonight
with George Spillers in Asheville. He never did tell
Maria about it. He never talked much to her, or
anyone else, about those otherworldly, bloody days.
That past would be recalled fondly with George.
But it would always be overshadowed with the pain
and emptiness of losing Maria.

Andy checked his watch, then took one last
swipe into the plastic, finger-stained bowl of gold-
fish crackers, munched them down and knocked
down his beer. It was time to head for the gate. He
glanced at the snow piling up outside and won-

dered how long the flight delay might be. No matter. He had time. Nothing but time. He paid his tab, slipped off the stool, grabbed his carry-on bag, and exited the bar.

Out on the concourse, Andy nodded at a pretty, young female soldier, dressed in desert fatigues and tan boots, as she approached and passed close to him. The sight of her, and his daydream at the bar, gave Andy an image of himself nearly four decades ago passing through the Nome, Alaska, airport on his way to Saigon. But here he noticed that civilians smiled and nodded warmly to the soldier. In his day, Andy saw mostly contempt when walking through airports. He paused, contemplating catching up to her to say . . . Say what? He could not find words to connect the young soldier's present and his past. He sighed and continued on toward the gate.

CHAPTER 3

ILENA

Specialist Ilena Burton thought about the eye contact she had made with the older man on the concourse. She was used to stares and found some comfort in the nods and smiles she often received. But he had a different look about him as though he somehow understood the fear and pain of loss that dwelt beneath her copper-toned skin—a mixture of Iraqi desert sun and her Cherokee heritage.

Inside the airport gift shop, she studied a mirrored shelf of tiny glass animals, turquoise and white dogs, ceramic cats, and little clear crystal trees with red glass leaves that reflected the shop's bright fluorescent lighting. Her long black hair was neatly tied in a bun beneath her fatigue cap. She turned away from the display, deciding that nothing there was appropriate for her Aunt Bess and Uncle Benjamin waiting for her arrival in Asheville. An illustrated political multiracial poster of a soldier, sailor, marine, and jet pilot, males and females, standing side by side in dress uniforms, caught her attention. The headline on the poster read "Support Our Heroes." Ilena looked around self-consciously, hoping no one connected her with this stateside depiction of military life. *We're not that pretty, and it ain't that clean,* she mused to herself. That thought brought back the yearning she felt—a yearning to be back with her comrades in Iraq that grew with each mile she had put between there and here. Her best friend, Beth. She could see her, Kevlar vest strapped tight, behind the wheel of an ordnance-packed diesel, flop sweat dried instantly by the near unbearable heat, running "balls to the wall," as the major liked to say, up the Alley of Death, the infamous road to Baghdad airport. Why does it take testosterone-based terms to define heroism? Heroism and guts know no gender. Beth and she had seen their National Guard buddies swept away by IEDs, while in convoy, like the hot desert wind blows sweat from a worried brow. Silently, Ilena spoke to Beth. "Foot on the gas, baby, and don't slow down. Not for no one or nothing." Mad dash from one spot on the map to the next with no thought but engine RPM, fuel, tires still on, and I'm alive. For a fleeting moment Ilena thought of turning back to her unit and comrades. She felt she had somehow deserted them. But then she remembered the major, and Beth, and six or seven of her buddies insisting she take her accrued leave, as they had. So be it.

Ilena turned back to the glass shelf. Her hand shook slightly as she lifted a glass owl from among the diminutive glass animals. Somehow it seemed appropriate to the moment, with its eyes wide open, alert, wise. An offering to the gods of war? The owl is also a hunter, like the hawk and the eagle. Perhaps this glass airport owl was the one amulet that would keep Beth safe. This might be Ilena's moment of destiny to have been here and performed an act of supplication to save her friend. She would bring Beth the owl. It would keep them both alive until their tour, twice extended, would finally end.

She waited as the struggling cashier deciphered the meaning of the data on the monitor of her computerized cash register. Ilena took her carefully wrapped package and change. As she left for the gate she watched the cashier tend to a tall, imposing black man. She noted his purchase was a book, *Notes of a Native Son,* by James Baldwin, and today's *Atlanta Journal.*

Baldwin. Jerrold Baldwin had been the first soldier killed in her unit, the 444th Transportation Company. His Humvee had no armor underneath. The 444th had not been issued any Kevlar or even flack vests. An IED had disintegrated his vehicle. Unlike the author of the book the black man was going to read, Jerrold Baldwin was white, twenty-two, married to his childhood sweetheart, and the father of two babies. He had worked days at the Heritage Furniture Factory and managed a McDonald's on weekend nights. Ilena recalled he was always griping—bitter for having joined the Guard for the extra money to support his young family. He kept saying, "I can't believe I'm in the middle of a war. I'm in the National Guard. We're supposed to guard the home front." Ilena knew his wife, Clarisse, and planned to visit her on Christmas Day.

"Rest in peace, Jerrold, my compatriot," Ilena

whispered to herself with a pressing sense of guilt at being alive. "At least you're not in the middle of it anymore. I'll tell Clarisse how you were the bravest, and how you loved her and the children deeply." She sighed and walked slowly toward the gate area.

CHAPTER 4

REGGIE

He watched the crowd on the concourse as they struggled with their Christmas packages, luggage, laptops, and knapsacks. He checked his watch, an Omega Seamaster that Yvonne had given him for his fiftieth birthday. Happier times. There was a good half hour before he had to get to his gate, so he settled down on a bench outside the one restaurant in the terminal, a Jack in the Box. He'd gone through the *Detroit Free Press* on the six A.M. flight to Atlanta.

Reggie Howard opened the *Atlanta Journal*, a newspaper he had never read before, to the sports section. He was a big man—six-three, and two hundred fifty pounds. His large hands that had served him well as a wide receiver at Northern High, but not well enough to earn a football scholarship, grasped the paper and held it wide open. There was nothing about his Lions, something else he would have to get used to. Asheville had no professional sports teams. Georgia had the Falcons and the Braves. Carolina had the Panthers, but was it North or South Carolina? He wasn't sure.

Reggie closed the sports section and briefly perused the headlines. Politics and politicians. Lies and corruption. Reggie was disgusted with all of it. It didn't matter which group controlled the White House or Congress. Red States; Blue States; Liberal; Conservative; Evangelical; Catholic; Pro-Life; Pro-Choice; Islamo-Fascist; War on Terror; NAFTA; Undocumented Workers; Market Up; Market Down; Fed Raises Rates, Lowers Rates . . . words from headlines drifted through his mind. The country was going to hell in a handbasket, as his long departed father had predicted. One headline at the bottom of the front page of this newspaper caught his eye: WHITE CHRISTMAS—HEAVY SNOW EXPECTED TODAY. Reggie glanced out the nearby window that faced the main entrance to the terminal. The snow was piling up rapidly. Taxis, arriving with holiday passengers, looked like yellow cupcakes topped with three inches of white icing on top. "Just great," Reggie muttered. "Spending a night on the floors of this place. One more indignity to suffer."

It always amazed Reggie that he had blinked awake on or about four A.M. every morning for the past three weeks. There was comfort in his bed, in his house, and most of all in his wife asleep next to him. Dear Yvonne. A lover and friend. The thoughts that awakened him were always clear and deliberate, flowing in his subconscious like an underground river, coursing through his sleep, carrying the same anger and confusion in its eddies and backwaters.

He was a strong man who had spent his adult life, more than thirty years, working on three different GM assembly lines. Reggie Howard came back from Vietnam grateful to be alive and eager to live a quiet, peaceful life. Those were still the days when prejudice and nepotism in the Auto Worker's Local put up an invisible wall to keep a black man from the best jobs on the line. He had climbed up and over that wall, just as he had several rice paddies under fire. He had succeeded, for a time, in what was still the white man's world. Though his temples grayed and his step became a bit slower, he was more than capable of holding his own with the younger men.

Reggie and Yvonne were the first African-American couple to move into their neat, suburban Detroit neighborhood. It had been difficult, but he had Yvonne, and their nightly union of souls to talk each other through the trials of the day and prepare for the next, one day at a time. Their bond was the synthesis of Reggie's urban Detroit upbringing and Yvonne's experiences growing up in the sleepy craft-paper mill town of Prentiss, Mississippi, where her parents had settled. Their marriage was a true partnership. Their love was deep, abiding, and after thirty-six years, still passionate and fiery.

Yvonne was a tall, wiry, slender woman. She resembled the light-skinned women on her mother's side of the family who had originated in the hill country of Kentucky. Most had lived to well into their late eighties, some into their mid-nineties.

Reggie's thoughts drifted back to those early mornings when he lay awake beneath perspiration-dampened sheets. He had worried about the thumping of his heart and the nightly sweats. The doctor had prescribed Valium when he felt this way, but he was loath to take it for fear of addiction. He remembered several of his buddies in Vietnam who had become opium and heroin addicts over there and brought their habits home to the streets of Detroit. He had witnessed their decline into druggie hell and unable to help, wept for them.

Reggie and Yvonne always saw themselves as an independent family living within certain limits of white society, frustrated at times by affronts to their dignity. But Yvonne was there for him, and he was there for her. There were no secrets between them. Their love was a shield against a hostile world. Yvonne, he knew, was his sustenance. Many nights, when the only light in their bedroom came from the streetlamp at the corner of Holland and Stevens Streets, Yvonne stroked Reggie's hands, scarred from years of working on the line, and listened. Her counsel was Socratic. She did not preach, but rather guided his path with thoughtful understanding.

But now their love was being tested as never before. After decades of playing by the rules set by management and the union, and the culture of productive work—after prospering as a result—all had abruptly changed. And so the racing heartbeat and sweats. Confusion and anger. He remembered a conversation a few days before he left for Asheville.

He had felt Yvonne awake, as he lay sleepless.

"Up again, baby?" she asked, moving her warm body next to his.

"It's wrong," said Reggie softly. "Just flat-out wrong."

"It's temporary." Yvonne rubbed her eyes. "You've got to let it go."

"Says you."

"Says reality. You're not Don Quixote, and I'm not Sancho Panza."

"How do you know?" Reggie asked softly, half smiling at her analogy.

" 'Cause I've seen the GM windmill, and it's too big to fight. We have time left on this earth to live, Love. We can do that."

"I don't know anything but building cars. It's all I've ever done."

"You've done a lot more than that. You've been strong for us; raised two fine children with me; fought for your country; bled for it; stood tall and took your rightful place in this world. . . . And, my love, there was a time when you didn't know how to build cars." They both laughed.

"That was a long, long, time ago, baby," he said as he rolled over and pulled her on top of him. He embraced her. Yvonne stroked the back of Reggie's neck. He looked up as if he could see the stars and full moon of a tropical night sky through the roof. This bed was paradise.

"Like yesterday," Yvonne whispered in his ear. "We'll always be young."

"How'd you end up with a laid-off, broken-down wreck like me?" Reggie asked. "I remember some of those guys you dated before me. Remember that guy studying law at Howard?"

"Clarence?"

"Yeah, Clarence. He was gonna be the first black this, the first black that—"

She put her hand over his mouth. "Shhhh, you fool. Enough. You're my man. Always my man. The first Reggie. That's who I wanted and that's who I got." Reggie felt Yvonne's fingers tighten on his neck. "Don't you ever low-rate yourself. Look at our life, our family. Can't you see? Does anyone have better kids than Donald and Samantha?"

"We're selling our home," Reggie said softly, stubbornly refusing to let his sense of failure go. "And not because we want to. It wasn't our choice."

"It was a house when we bought it, and we made it a home. We fought to make it a home, as I recall. So now we're moving on, and once you get settled down in Asheville, we'll find a perfect house and make it a home again."

"I let you down."

"You haven't let me down. You've got to stop this. You didn't get fired. You didn't quit. You got laid off along with thirty thousand others. White, black, brown. You didn't let me down. Don't let yourself down."

"I don't know about going to work for Donald."

"That's your pride talking. You know what happens when your pride talks?"

"Yeah. Nothing good. I'm nearly sixty."

"Fifty-six. Don't rush it. It'll be all right."

"You say. You know I haven't been on a plane since I got back from Vietnam."

"So you're not a world traveler." Yvonne sat up and looked at Reggie. "Vietnam? You haven't said that word in a long, long time." Reggie looked back up through the ceiling to a jungle moon of thirty-five years ago.

"I ran into Ray Clifton at the tire place."

"Ray Clifton? Good Lord. There's a name from the past."

"Yeah. His paycheck went to his bar tab every week. I figured he'd be long gone. He tells me he came darn close. Scared him. So, after all these years he goes to the V.A. They tell him he's got post delayed stress." Reggie took a deep breath. "Two wives, dozens of girlfriends, a couple dozen trainloads of bourbon . . . So he goes to the shrink. Man, I wish I'd been there. He told me it was the first time since he's back that he opened up."

"You guys never spoke about it?"

"We didn't have to. We knew . . ."

"So how is he?"

"Sober. Cleaned up good. Resurrection."

"I'm glad," Yvonne said sincerely. "We ought to have him over before we leave."

"Yeah, we should. I'd like that. We were . . . you know . . ." Reggie felt the soothing touch of Yvonne's fingers as she stroked his wrist. He soon fell into a sweet, deep sleep. It was safe, like the first night back at a firebase after a jungle patrol, surrounded by trusted others, like Ray Clifton, manning the wire.

CHAPTER 5

JOHN

As Reggie Howard set the *Atlanta Journal* aside and opened *Native Son*, a Lexus, its roof covered with snow and the windshield partly obscuring the driver's view with ice, drove into the Hertz return area and skidded to a stop. As John Sullivan got out of the car, he slipped on the slick pavement, and cursing, grabbed the open door to steady himself. He carefully made his way to the rear and popped the trunk. While the Hertz attendant, wrapped in a parka, checked the mileage and gas, John hauled his luggage and attaché case out onto the snowy ground. He waited impatiently as the attendant double-checked his entries.

"Using the same credit card, Mr. Sullivan?"

"Yes," he answered curtly. "It's in my profile, isn't it?" The handheld computer slowly spit out the bill.

"We have to ask, sir." John grabbed the bill from the attendant's hands, popped up the handle on his large suitcase, and without acknowledging the attendant, wheeled it off toward the waiting Hertz bus.

"And Merry Christmas to you, too. . . ." The attendant's sarcastic words trailed off, unheard, as the snowy wind whipped around John's bare head. He stopped and pulled up the collar of his inadequately light topcoat to cover the back of his neck. As he trudged toward the bus, John's thoughts were of being home after six weeks away.

Earlier that morning, John Sullivan, a tall, blond, thirty-five-year-old master of the universe, had been in fashionable Buckhead, shouting into the Crowne Plaza Atlanta's telephone, uncertain if the person at the other end spoke enough English to understand him.

"Damn it, I ordered two eggs over easy! These are fried to a crisp. This is supposed to be a first-class hotel." He paused, listening to silence. "Do you understand? *Comprende? Verstanden?*"

"Yes, sir, I do. And I speak English."

"Good. Then let's get it right and make it fast. I've got a plane to catch." John slammed down the receiver and glanced out the window of his executive suite. What had earlier been a few flakes drifting by his window was now a steady and heavy snowfall. His chest rose and fell with rapid breathing from the surge of anger-induced adrenaline in his bloodstream. Poor service like this was simply unacceptable to John. He had grown up in cloistered privilege, educated in privilege, and was accustomed to being treated as a privileged person of importance.

Richard Sullivan had elevated his only child to

heir at his moment of birth. John's mother, the former Meredith Simpson, was a product of overly inbred descendants of early colonists and old Charleston aristocracy. Her coming out was at the lavish cotillion thrown in the Plaza Hotel in New York City. She was a member of the Daughters of the American Revolution and the Daughters of the Confederacy. But only a few short years after her coming of age, the Simpson fortunes were decimated by her father's gambling in the stock market—specifically junk-bond speculation.

Her marriage to Richard Sullivan, a self-made entrepreneur from Louisville who controlled interests in Black Angus cattle, rice, and oil wells throughout the South, saved the Simpsons from certain bankruptcy.

John Sullivan was a bright child, who quickly assimilated life's survival lessons from his father, and, when time permitted, social graces from his mother. Richard Sullivan was an imperator. In a prior age he might have been a Roman provincial governor or Saxon baron. He intuitively understood power in all its trappings and guises. To Richard Sullivan, wealth and power were inseparable—a primary lesson he continually stressed to his son.

"Benchmark, John. Benchmark," Richard would repeat. From the day John entered his first exclusive private school until he graduated with honors with an MBA from Harvard, John was taught to measure himself against the best around him, no matter the situation. Who wrote the best? Who was the best at math? Soccer? With whom did the girls want to dance? John reported to his father, and they adjusted strategies and plans for winning. There was no shame in encountering someone better at something; but there were penalties for not surpassing the achievements of others. Richard and John were a cabal of two, plotting and manipulating John's future. In the process, Meredith's role was marginalized. Secretly, she wondered if Richard were driving John too hard to mimic his life rather than allowing him to have one of his own.

John learned the lessons of power well. After he graduated cum laude from Harvard he went on to earn his MBA there, too. He plunged into the family business with focus and intelligence, anxious to please his father, and, secretly, to surpass him.

The next step in his carefully planned life was to find a wife—a suitable mate to provide a social front and bear heirs. Richard tapped Meredith to fill the role of matchmaker. A Junior League charity event at the Sullivan estate in Asheville in late June was the setting. Canopied outdoors by a pale, blue sky, the west lawn held several circular tables covered with white cloths, set with crystal and sterling-silver flatware, and festooned with fresh lilies. A string quartet played softly as the chosen mingled, champagne flutes in hand. Bored, with business stratagems coursing through his mind, John was startled by the sound of a strange voice behind him.

"Hello, John." Turning, John noticed the woman's deep blue eyes first, accentuated by dark lashes and eyebrows. Those eyes locked with his, unwilling to lose the moment. His gaze lowered to her subtly glossed pink lips that framed a sparkling smile. Her brunette hair fell casually across tanned shoulders. Two narrow white straps held her low-cut, backless dress that ended where her long, trim legs began.

John's eyes found the gold bracelet on her left ankle and felt a provocative chill run down his spine.

"I'm Anne," she said. "Anne Blakely." She extended a graceful hand. Seven months later, they married.

Two years to the day after that, Richard Sullivan died of a massive myocardial infarction in his hotel room in Hong Kong. At the wake John learned that his father had not had a checkup in ten years and had apparently suffered a "silent" heart attack during that time. He'd been too busy to look after his health, John thought, or simply believed he would live forever.

John finished packing while he waited for his re-order of breakfast. Thoughts of his father's obsession with the business and monetary success had been troubling him lately. Was he going down the same road? There was an ache inside and something disturbing that he saw in the faces of Anne and the twins, Kate and Carly, when he left on these ever more frequent business trips. The business was growing far beyond anything that even Richard Sullivan had projected. And its demands were pushing John farther and farther away from the family he loved. Even his mother, who had seemed to blossom after Richard's death, had warned him to take time to live and love.

There was a tentative tap on the door.

"Room service."

John stepped to the door in quick, long strides and opened it. A dark-haired, heavyset Hispanic woman with a broad smile nodded. She wore a starched white uniform.

"Good morning. May I come in, sir?"

"Yes. Set it on the coffee table, please," he instructed. She lifted the stainless-steel circular cover.

"Eggs over easy. I hope they're to your liking this time."

"They look fine," he answered curtly. The woman bowed slightly and presented the slender black, plastic wallet containing the bill. He opened it and signed it, but added nothing to the service charge that was included. He handed the wallet back to the woman.

"Thank you, sir. Will there be anything else?"

"No. No, thank you." John looked at his Rolex Oyster. The woman picked up the eggs cooked the wrong way, walked to the door, opened it, and then paused.

"Traveling home for Christmas?"

"What?" John asked, taken aback by the question.

"Going home for Christmas?" she repeated.

"Yes. Yes, I am."

"Well," she said with a smile, "I hope Santa brings you what you wish. Merry Christmas, sir."

"Yes," John answered softly as she closed the door. Suddenly he felt very lonely. "Whatever that is."

CHAPTER 6

AMELIA

The snow increased as the Hertz bus passed an area where a small commuter plane was parked. *I hate those things,* John thought, knowing that he would soon be aboard one and that it would have no first-class section. He shrugged at the thought, took a deep breath, and summoned the courage to prepare himself to be just another coach passenger like those he observed now deplaning into the snowy morning.

Amelia McIntosh stepped out of the aircraft onto the platform at the top of the stairs. She immediately looked skyward. Snow gathered quickly on her cheery face. She enjoyed the refreshing sensation of crisp air and an open space, especially after the heat and humidity of Florida and the cramped multi-stop trip from Fort Lauderdale.

"Some of us have a life to lead," the young man

directly on the stairway behind her muttered rudely.

"Well, yes. Of course," the perky seventy-four-year-old retired teacher replied. "I hope it's a happy one." She smiled coyly. The young man couldn't help but smile back and nod. Amelia had that effect on people. When she got to the bottom of the stairs she felt a strong hand grip under her arm.

"It's slippery out here," the young man said. "May I help you?"

"You are a gentleman," Amelia told him, "and that is a lovely gesture." She relaxed her body and allowed him to guide her to the warmth of the terminal.

"I've got to catch a flight to Birmingham," he told her. "You take care."

"I will. I surely will. Merry Christmas."

"Yes, ma'am. Merry Christmas." He nodded his head slightly and left. Amelia looked around to find the gate for her flight to Asheville. She felt a warm flush and unbuttoned her coat.

"Cold-warm, cold-warm," Amelia muttered as she recalled her life the past few weeks.

The sweltering heat and high humidity common to South Florida had abated. It was December. The hurricane season was over. A more temperate time of year had arrived. But even so the year-round residents kept their air conditioners at sixty-eight degrees.

In the wake of an abrupt, but common afternoon thunderstorm, steam rose from the hot asphalt street outside the two-story condo building at 5665 Black Olive Drive in a senior development called

Plantation Cedars. It seemed to Amelia that the short, violent downpour was a rite of ablution, cleansing the fouled atmosphere lingering between her and her sister-in-law, Jenny.

No comfort here, Amelia thought. Standing in the frigid confines of the condo that she and her late husband Joseph had purchased for his sister, Amelia shivered. She knew what was coming. Still, ever the optimist, she searched for new words, a new approach that might somehow change the all too familiar course of the conversation.

Nearly a half-century of being Jenny's sister-in-law had taught Amelia that no matter what she said or did, it was never right, never enough, never acceptable. For decades, Amelia had allowed Jenny the latitude of believing Amelia was not "good enough" for her brother. The most civil of conversations in Joseph's presence would abruptly change to accusation when he left the room.

"You're holding Joseph back. He can be so much more than a teacher," Jenny would start.

"He's not just a teacher," Amelia would answer. "He's a professor. A Ph.D. Highly respected in his chosen field."

"At a Negro college. He could be at Harvard or Yale."

"An African-American college. Highly accredited and respected. It's where we chose to teach." Eventually, the accusations grew more vicious and personal.

"He should have married a black woman," was the final blow. When Jenny said it, Amelia stormed past the other woman to the guest room. Jenny followed like a dog on scent. She was fifteen years younger than Amelia. Her straightened hair was showing gray at the roots. Her hazel eyes were sharp and focused. Today, like most days, she wore tight-fitting clothing that displayed a full, firm figure. Her body had always been Jenny's pride and meal ticket. She had taken very good care of it and used it, with what she called her "feminine wiles," to have men around, mostly white, to do her bidding. Of course, that wasn't always the case. In her younger days, she was unable to sustain any relationships because of her self-centered nature. There were three marriages and three nasty divorces. There were no children. No really close friends. Her older brother, Amelia's husband, Joseph, was her rock and her lifeline. She considered Amelia an impediment to that relationship. Now Joseph was gone and Jenny was unable, or unwilling, to accept Amelia's reaching out with an offer of friendship and family.

The guest room was painted pastel pink with aquamarine trim. Like the rest of the condominium, it was jammed with furniture, spoils from Jenny's three unsuccessful but highly profitable marriages: a four-poster bed bought by husband number one, a Tiffany lamp provided as a peace offering by husband number two, an ornate antique music box from husband number three. These trophies were visible proof of victory for Jenny. She stood at the door and relentlessly continued her attack.

"You always put your career first. . . . You never bore him the children he wanted. . . . Joseph was always unhappy. . . ." Amelia did not respond. She had, long ago, painfully learned when it was time to walk away. Confrontation was useless. And now, especially after Joseph's passing, she was tired. This last attempt at reconciliation had been a failure. Sadly, it was time to say good-bye, perhaps forever. Amelia smoothed the front of her skirt, and faced Jenny. "I'm sorry, Jenny. I'm leaving now for the airport."

"This is so like you, Amelia," Jenny said caustically. "As long as I've known you it's always been about you." The accusation was calculated to incite. The rhythm and intonation of her words were like sparks sizzling along a lit fuse, running to detonate their explosive relationship. But Amelia would not be baited.

"This, uh, coming here to try to . . . to offer you . . . I'm your only family, Jenny, and you mine. But it was a mistake. My mistake."

Jenny stepped forward.

"You make it sound so noble," Jenny said, taking a long swallow from her martini. She swished the dark green olive on its toothpick around in the oversized martini glass, then brandished it as though it were an empowering amulet. Aware that Amelia once had a bout with alcoholism, Jenny relished the act of partaking in an afternoon drink in front of her.

"I thought after Joseph passed we could try." Amelia grasped the handle of her suitcase. "I'm sorry." Unconsciously, Amelia's tone of voice had changed from reconciliation to resignation. That only served as a trigger for Jenny, a crouching beast waiting to pounce.

"Try what?" Jenny snapped. "I don't need you!"

"No, you don't," Amelia answered calmly. "Not now. Maybe someday. . . ."

Jenny laughed. "Someday? You're old. Your damned life is almost over. I'll dance on your grave."

"How cheerful of you, Jenny. It's comforting to know that at least you'll be at my funeral." Amelia, fatigued, her patience gone, looked directly into Jenny's eyes. "Merry Christmas, Jenny. Have a good life." She pulled out the handle of her suitcase and began rolling it toward freedom. Then, for an instant, Amelia thought she saw hesitation in Jenny's eyes. But like the shadow of a fast-moving cloud racing across blue water, it was gone. Amelia allowed herself a moment of satisfaction, realizing that an old and tiresome thorn in her side was finally removed.

Mercifully, the horn of the taxi sounded out front. Amelia walked past Jenny, down the thickly carpeted hallway, opened the front door, and then gently but firmly closed it behind her.

CHAPTER 7

ALL ABOARD

Passengers for Blue Ridge Airline's Flight #6224 were seated in the gate lounge, waiting to board the diminutive commuter plane—a twin-engine Grumman turbo-prop that was being refueled. The ground crew, dressed in parkas, hoods, and boots, worked slowly to ready the plane in the steady and thickening snow.

Among the waiting passengers were Marta Hood and her two children, who busied themselves with their Game Boys. Anselmo (Andy) Casiano had a seat near the plate-glass window that looked out on the tarmac. He watched the ground crew fight the storm, admiring their professionalism. Specialist Ilena Burton sat at the edge of the lounge, off by herself, as she thought about her buddies back in Iraq. Reggie Howard had begun to read James Baldwin's *Notes of a Native Son*. John Sullivan, who sat across from Reggie, noted the large black man and the book he was reading. Not someone you'd find in first class, he mused to himself, while at the same time feeling a twinge of guilt at the bigoted thought. It was his father talking. It was something that he had to rid himself of and never pass on to his children.

Amelia McIntosh, a little out of breath, rushed up to the Blue Ridge ticket counter and handed the agent her ticket. The agent, a plain woman in her late fifties, had deep lines around her eyes and dark bags under them. Her weary expression was focused on the computer monitor, informing her that there might be delays due to the snow. She kept Amelia waiting for several moments while she absorbed the possibility of overtime and unhappy passengers whom she would have to control. And it was one of the most heavily traveled days of the year—Christmas Eve day. Finally she looked up, took the ticket, and gazed beyond it at Amelia's cheery face, barely above the level of the ticket counter.

"Oh dear," Amelia said breathlessly, "I thought I'd never get here. A simple flight from Fort Lauderdale," she went on. "My sister-in-law . . . she made the reservation." The agent paid no attention to Amelia's rambling. She took the ticket and without looking at Amelia, processed it. "You know we stopped in Palm Beach, Jacksonville, and Augusta," Amelia continued. "Now what do you call that?" The boarding pass printed out. Silently, the agent stapled it to the ticket envelope.

"A puddle-jumper. That's the word I was looking for," Amelia declared. "Sometimes I forget things. She hates me, you know? Maybe with all those stops she was hoping the plane would crash or something. . . ."

The agent's disconnect, a practiced part of her

busyness act, changed abruptly at the word "crash." Amelia noticed the change in the agent's demeanor. She hurriedly plucked her ticket and boarding pass from the hands of the now rigid, cold agent.

"Well, I'm just kidding, you know."

"That kind of kidding is not acceptable these days, Ms. McIntosh," the dour agent grumbled.

Amelia paused and blinked with surprise. "Of course not," she said.

The agent glanced at the federal TSA guard nodding off in the corner, then back at Amelia.

"So tell me, are we flying, dear? I mean, it is snowing."

The agent glanced down at her computer screen. Nothing had changed. The possibility of delay or cancellation had not been posted. "We'll be boarding in a few minutes."

"Well that's good. Can you see if my luggage arrived from the other plane?"

"I'm sure it did, Ms. McIntosh," the agent answered officiously. "If you'll just have a seat, I'll be calling the flight shortly." Amelia nodded and walked toward the three parallel rows of utilitarian aluminum-framed plastic benches. She saw some empty seats next to the window but was drawn toward the young woman who was sitting alone at the end of one bench.

Specialist Ilena Burton smiled as the kindly-looking elderly lady took a seat next to her. Amelia's carry-on consisted of a well-worn Gucci handbag, a gift her late husband purchased on their first trip to Italy thirty years ago. Amelia smiled back, noting to herself that the young woman was a soldier, wearing desert camouflage fatigues, cap, and tan combat boots. She gently clutched a small, holiday-wrapped gift bag in her hand. There was a brown leather travel bag under the soldier's seat.

"Well, hello there," Amelia said as she sat down.

"Hello, ma'am," Ilena answered, and then returned her gaze to the gift in her lap and her thoughts to her friends, far from the crowded airport.

"You're a soldier," Amelia said in a matter-of-fact manner, confirming the obvious to herself.

"Yes, ma'am," Ilena replied. She surmised the woman wanted to talk. Maybe she was nervous about flying. Maybe she was just lonely. One thing that being under fire, in combat, had sharpened in Ilena was a sense of belonging to a larger human family, with all their fears and needs. "What gave it away?" Ilena asked, hoping the older woman had a sense of humor.

"Silly me," Amelia answered, grinning. "Of course you are. I'm sorry. It's a generation thing. I guess I'm not used to seeing women soldiers. . . . I mean dressed like we see on TV. In my day, you know they wore skirts or were nurses."

"I know. Women's Army Corps, Women's Auxiliary Marines, Women's Auxiliary Fleet. WACs, WAMs, and WAFs. We learned about all that in Basic Training."

"Are you going home for Christmas?" Amelia asked.

"Yes, ma'am."

"Your people are in Asheville?"

"My aunt and uncle. My folks are gone."

"Oh. I'm sorry."

"Thank you, ma'am. It was long ago, when I was very young. An accident . . ."

Amelia studied the hardened face of the soldier. *Not young now, dear heart,* Amelia thought. *Your face is young, but your eyes tell me otherwise.* At that moment, Amelia's heart reached out to the soldier, wanting to ease whatever troubled her.

"So are you, um, are you over there in Iraq?"

"Yes, ma'am. I'm on a ten-day leave from my unit. I'm a truck driver."

"Oh, I see. Well that's nice. . . . I mean it isn't, with fighting and all . . ."

The voice of the dispassionate airline clerk interrupted as it blared out over the PA system. It was loud in order to overcome announcements from other loudspeakers scattered throughout the terminal.

"Good morning, ladies and gentlemen. Blue Ridge's ten-thirty flight number 6224 to Asheville is now ready for boarding. Please line up at the door and have your boarding passes ready. It's a short walk down the stairs and out to the plane. Anyone needing assistance please step up to the front of the line." The agent eyed Amelia, who prudently looked away. "Thank you." The agent then went to the door and opened it. The clock above the Blue Ridge counter read 10:05 A.M.

An elderly couple and Marta Hood, with her two children, stepped to the front of the line.

"Would you like to go ahead?" Ilena asked Amelia.

"No thank you, dear. I'm fine. If it's slippery, I might hold on to your arm, if that's okay."

"My pleasure, ma'am."

"It's Amelia. Amelia McIntosh."

"I'm Ilena Burton. It's nice to meet you, Amelia."

Most of the sixteen passengers shivered at the blast of icy wind as they stepped from the terminal onto the slick tarmac. Their plane was fifty feet away. They noted Marta Hood and her two children entering its open doorway, being aided by a flight attendant. Heavy snow continued to fall. A swirling wind drove it around the plane, partially obscuring the tail section.

"This ain't good," Andy Casiano muttered to John Sullivan, who was next to him. Both men squinted and lowered their heads in the face of the blowing snow. Off to his right, at the main terminal section, John watched the larger jets being de-iced and wondered if they had gotten to their aircraft.

One by one, the passengers made it up the flight of eleven stairs and into the narrow cabin, where they were greeted by a male flight attendant. There were no assigned seats. Those, like Marta Hood, who had others traveling with them, sought seats together. There was a little shifting about, but for the most part people were polite and anxious to get going. Once a seat was found, carry-on bags were forced into the small overhead compartments. Finally, everyone was seated and buckled in.

Within minutes, the aircraft taxied through heavy snow on the tarmac approach to the runway. Its wheels bounced against patches of packed snow that the plows had missed.

The plane's seating was eight rows of twos on either side of the center aisle, and it was filled to capacity. Passengers fought to avoid pressing against the thighs and arms of strangers in the narrow, uncomfortable seats. As the plane taxied, the flight attendant, a man in his mid-forties, finished the preflight pitch. Suddenly the plane came to a stop.

The flight attendant glanced out a side window, then turned and walked up to the flight deck. The passengers grew quiet as everyone watched the flight attendant speak to the cockpit on the cabin phone.

John Sullivan was seated on the aisle, next to Marta Hood. She was not a good flyer and needed to have a window seat. Her children, Nancy and Ronny, were seated together across the aisle.

"Looks like a great day for Santa to be flying around in his sleigh, huh, kids?" John said softly to the children. They looked at Marta, then nodded to the stranger. They could see that their mother was extremely nervous. John noticed Marta's concerned look and leaned closer to her.

"It just takes a few minutes," he told her, "and we'll be up and above all this weather." Though not in control of his emotions himself, John made an effort to make it appear so. "I heard the snow has already stopped in Asheville."

"Really?"

"Yes," he continued. "It's one of those Canadian Clippers. It dropped lower and faster than they predicted."

"Like they're always right," Marta announced with sarcasm in her voice.

"Who's that?"

"Weather people," she said. "They're totally unreliable."

The flight attendant hung up the phone and made his way toward the flight deck. At the same time, a minor ruckus started across the aisle, with voices rising to a staccato that only children can reach onboard an airplane. Andy and Reggie slid down in their seats, awaiting the inevitable screams they knew would ensue. Ilena, who was seated with Amelia, glanced back at the source of the noise.

"Mommy," Nancy cried. "Ronny punched me."

"I did not," Ronny protested.

"Did too . . ."

"Did not . . ."

"Did too . . ."

"Did not . . ."

"Excuse me," Marta said to John, leaning across him and admonishing her children. "That's it! Now cut it out!" Ronny stared at his sister.

"She's always starting things."

Marta's eyebrows arched, and her facial muscles tightened.

"But he started it, Mommy," Nancy pleaded.

"I don't care. I said stop it. If you don't . . ." Marta reached down as if to unfasten her seat belt. The children took notice and became quiet. So did the cabin as the flight attendant stepped out of the flight-deck door, closing it firmly behind him. At the same moment, the captain's voice, loud and distorted, came over the intercom.

"Well, good morning, folks. Captain Snyder here . . . I guess I don't have to tell you all it's snowing a little harder than we'd like. Good for a white Christmas, but not so good for takeoff at the moment. The visibility just went below FAA regulations. So we're going to head back to the terminal. I know it's Christmas Eve and you all want to get home. Me too. We'll do our best to get you there. But at Blue Ridge your safety comes first. So we're going to wait it out for a while. We appreciate your patience."

In truth, the passengers, although disappointed

that their trip home was delayed, were relieved that caution was being exercised. A few people smiled.

"Mommy?" Nancy asked. "Does this mean we won't get to Grandma and Grandpa's?"

"No, dear. We'll get there," Marta answered. "We just have to wait a while."

As the plane taxied back to its gate, Andy looked out of his window and noticed that the ground crews had stopped de-icing the other planes. The flight attendant's voice came onto the PA.

"Ladies and gentlemen, please remain seated until we have come to a complete stop at the gate. And remember to take all your personal belongings with you."

"That ain't good news," Reggie muttered to Andy.

"And be sure to remember where your seats are," the flight attendant continued, "so that we can expedite reboarding."

"Well, maybe that's the good news," Andy said.

Amelia clung to Ilena's arm as they slowly followed the other passengers down the portable aluminum staircase onto the icy tarmac. The light emanating from the terminal doorway ahead looked warm and welcoming compared to the gray, windy, snowy morning outdoors. But when they all took seats in the gate-lounge area, a collective anxiety spread among the passengers. The worry about an uncomfortable flight through the snowstorm was behind them and forgotten. Now their concern was that there might be no flight at all.

CHAPTER 8

LISA BARONE

Lisa Barone, a comely woman in her late thirties, paused in the tiny vestibule of Our Lady of Mercy Roman Catholic Church. She dusted the snow from her navy surplus pea coat and bright red ski cap. As she did, a loose coat button popped off and fell onto the stone floor. She knelt to pick it up and noticed that one of her new Gortex boots was untied. Slipping off her worn leather gloves, wet from the snow, she tied her bootlaces. So far, it had been that kind of day. Nothing was going right.

Her early morning visit to her father, now living in this church's assisted-living facility, had been upsetting. Lisa chose to move him down to Atlanta from Asheville two years ago when it was confirmed that he had early-stage Alzheimer's. This way he would be close by and she could look after his needs without giving up her job at Stone Mountain Park. She was manager of the three-hundred-passenger Henry W. Grady Paddlewheel Riverboat that was used for private functions. Lisa handled bookings and catering on the riverboat and private guided tours of the park. One of her father's proud possessions was a replica of the memorial carving in Stone Mountain depicting three Confederate heroes of the Civil War: Confederate President Jefferson Davis, General Robert E. Lee, and Lieutenant General Thomas "Stonewall" Jackson. It was her gift to him on his seventieth birthday. It was on a small table he had placed near the window.

The insidious disease was advancing rapidly. He was losing it, muttering today, almost incoherently, about her mother and the accident.

"I have to make a choice, Loretta," he said to her long gone mother, thinking Lisa was her. "I'm so sorry, my darling." Over and over. "So sorry . . . so sorry . . ." He stared out the window. It was seven in the morning, and the snow had just begun to fall.

"I have to go up to Asheville for a few days," she told him. Her mother's sister, Linda, had fallen and broken her hip. Lisa was her only family. There was no point in telling her father why she was going to be away for Christmas. He wouldn't understand. But she tried. "I'm going to see Aunt Linda." Leopold Barone's eyes suddenly cleared and focused.

"For Christmas?" he asked.

"Yes," she answered quickly, so surprised she couldn't think of anything to say but the truth.

"Why?"

"She's in the hospital. Broke her hip."

"Will she die?"

"No. No, Daddy. But we're her only family and—" Leopold raised his hand to stop her.

"I don't want to know if she dies." His shoulders then sagged, and he slumped back into his chair.

He didn't speak again, or react when Lisa kissed him good-bye and wished him a Merry Christmas.

She was weeping in the hallway outside his room when Sister Mary Bernadette, the home's administrator came by. She tried to comfort Lisa. They talked for about twenty minutes. Sister then suggested that Lisa stop by the church and light a candle for her mother and father.

The snow was sticking, and by eight o'clock Lisa knew it was a major storm. She had parked her van in front of the church. There were no footprints on the steps.

As she stepped from the vestibule into the sanctuary, the vaulted structure rose over the hollowness of an interior void of parishioners. Though only occasionally revisiting her faith over the years, Lisa had been moved by Sister Mary Bernadette's kindly way and soft voice. Maybe lighting a candle or two and saying a heartfelt prayer would help. She stuffed her ski cap into her coat pocket and rustled a blue-and-red checkered bandana from the back pocket of her well-worn jeans. She put the folded bandana over her head and tied it at the neck. Dipping her fingers in the basin of holy water, she knelt, made the sign of the cross over her heart, then rose and walked quickly through the deserted church to the distant altar rail. Glancing down the rows of empty pews as she passed, she wondered how many souls over the generations had knelt in desperation, or joy, and sent their prayers skyward from these pews. She wondered if the spirits of those departed might appear to her.

The squeak of her boots on the wooden floor

echoed through the tall chamber. Alone in the quiet and peace of the sanctuary, Lisa felt a sense of self, soul, and spirit; a connection to thousands of other souls across time. Events of import and emotion had occurred within these walls—marriages, christenings, funerals, anguishing confession and silent devotion. She tenderly placed four unlit candles among the many lit ones. Then she took a lit candle and slowly lighted her candles. She watched them catch and their flames grow and glow.

"This for my mother, God rest her soul. This for my father; may he find peace. This for Aunt Linda; may she heal quickly. And this last is for my dear friend and love, Murray. May he and his National Guard unit all return safely from Iraq."

With great reverence, Lisa walked to the altar rail and knelt. Looking up at a statue of Christ on the cross, whose painted head was tilted down and to the left, she looked into His eyes seeking solace and purpose. The statue seemed to look directly down upon her, its gaze into her soul. A cold draft rustled some papers on the altar. Lisa felt the chill and pulled the scarf around her head, gently grasping the knot.

"Lord," she began, "it's been a while. I'm sure You've had Your doubts about me. I've had them about me, too. I can't seem to let go. Even after all these years; after all the logic and all the therapy, the burden of guilt will not leave. I need Your help. Your guidance. I need to do something. I feel that. Help me. Please help me to find peace."

Lisa prayed silently for the next several minutes, opening herself up to the power she felt around her. Then she opened her eyes, looked up at the statue, and smiled. Still kneeling, she made the sign of the cross and rose. The church was no longer cold, nor dark, nor unwelcoming. She walked lightly and quickly from the church and out into the winter storm that had now gathered strength.

Only a few people struggled through the snow on the sidewalks and the slush in the streets. Heavy snow had accumulated rapidly, challenging the plows that with yellow, blinking lights moved slowly through the street trying to keep up. The sky was a dark, gritty gray with little definition between it and the earth it was blanketing. Lisa pulled her ski cap out of her pocket and down over her head, buttoned her coat, and headed down the snow-covered steps to the van. She started it up, turned on the heater and defroster, then tuned the radio to a soft-rock station. Popping open the rear door of the van, she set aside the two knapsacks she had packed for the trip to Asheville. Underneath she found her tire chains and next to them the old broom she had brought along to brush off snow.

As she proceeded to clean off the van, the music was interrupted with a news bulletin that several flights in and out of Atlanta had been cancelled. The newscaster said it was likely that for the next twenty-four hours all the Atlanta airports would be closed, then went on to describe the thousands of unhappy travelers who would not be getting home for Christmas Eve.

Lisa suddenly knew what she must do. Looking over her shoulder at the church, she smiled, whispered a heartfelt, "Thank you," and hurried to finish cleaning the van.

CHAPTER 9

GROUNDED

Unaware of the decision to close the airport, the passengers from Blue Ridge Flight #6224 sat glumly waiting to reboard the plane. Engulfed by swirling snow, it was barely visible through the floor-to-ceiling plate-glass windows that faced the tarmac. Beyond their commuter, the heavy snow covered the other aircraft and runways.

John Sullivan sat apart from the others on the bench that faced the window. He glanced over at the clock above the boarding door. It was 12:42 P.M. He checked it against his own watch and realized his was still on Zurich time. He adjusted it ahead six hours. Years of extensive travel told him that they were not going to fly today. He mused on how long it would take the airline to level with their passengers. But that wasn't his worry. How to get home by Christmas Day now occupied his thoughts. Calling Anne now, without a plan, would accomplish nothing. She would write it off as "predictable" even though it was not his fault. Weather.

An act of God. But she was expecting him. John took out his cell phone and punched in "home." He got up and walked away from the area for some privacy.

"Hi, hon," he said as Anne answered.

"Problem. Right?" was her response.

"The snow. You have it up there?"

"Yes. It's stopped now. So what's up?" She sounded as he expected. Cold. Distant. Angry.

"We boarded, but came back. I don't think we're flying today. I guess I'll get their first one out in the morning. Sorry."

"Yeah. Sorry. The girls were so excited that you were going to be here to light the tree tonight."

"I can't control the weather, Anne."

"No. But you could have come sooner instead of leaving everything to the last minute."

"I don't leave everything to the last minute. You know that." There was a long pause.

"You're right. You don't. Only when it comes to your family." John felt a pang of guilt and a chill surge down his spine. Was she right? Had the job been so important that he couldn't have come home a day or two earlier? "I've got to go, John. I guess we'll see you when we see you. Let me know." She hung up. He snapped the phone shut and stared across the terminal. It seemed much emptier now. And darker.

The Blue Ridge clerk, drowning in a sea of fatigue and the frustrating inability to control the situation, was on the phone. Several of the passengers, those who lived in Atlanta, and were like John Sullivan, savvy travelers, had surrendered to the inevitability of bad weather, and left. Only eight, who had come in from other cities and were not local, now remained. They were clinging stubbornly to the hope that they might yet fly out today and be home for Christmas Eve.

Unconsciously, like a scattered, desperate tribe trapped in a strange valley, they gathered close to one another in front of the Blue Ridge counter. Besides John Sullivan, there were Marta Hood and her two children, Reggie Howard, Specialist Ilena Burton, Andy Casiano, and Amelia McIntosh.

Marta was relieved that her kids were distracted with their Game Boys but aware that they were getting hungry.

Reggie tried to concentrate on *Native Son,* but the constant noise and musical glisses of the Game Boys were distracting. He would never allow his grandchildren, Cameron and Katie, to be so inconsiderate.

Though part of the group, Specialist Ilena Burton was asleep, stretched across three seats. She slept as only a soldier can, in an intense, deep, invigorating slumber, only a hair's breath away from awaking to a critical situation without transition. The combat-zone mantra was to sleep and eat when you can, because you don't know when you'll get another chance. Her eyes snapped open at the sound of the clerk's raspy voice on the PA. She subconsciously reached for her M16, then realized where she was and sat up.

"May I have your attention? The official word is that this airport and Hartsfield-Jackson International are now closed until tomorrow morning." The clerk made the announcement with cheery finality, signaling her release from duty, and a trip home for the holiday. She was off tomorrow. There was a groan of obvious disappointment among the passengers, followed by immediate questions. Amelia looked at Ilena, who was now standing. Reggie snapped his book shut and muttered, "Damn it!" Andy looked at John, who shrugged his shoulders. Ronny and Nancy were no longer playing with their games. They were up and next to Marta, questioning their future. "Where can we go?" "Do Grandma and Grandpa know how to find us?" "Mommy, I'm hungry." "Me too."

"Blue Ridge will continue this Asheville Flight in the morning," the clerk continued. "We're sorry. Now, if you will all wait here for a few moments, we've made arrangements for transportation to take you to a nearby Ramada. An agent will be here shortly to guide you. Once you check in he will have a better idea of what time your flight will leave tomorrow. Vouchers for your meals will be supplied at the hotel. Your baggage has been off-loaded and will be placed behind this counter. Again, we're very, very sorry for the inconvenience." The agent moved away quickly, looking over her shoulder only once to see if any passengers were pursuing her. Relieved that there were none, she disappeared into the main terminal before anyone could approach to ask the inevitable and interminable questions about their future that she did not have the information or inclination to answer.

Silence reigned as each traveler contemplated missing their Christmas Eve plans. All except Amelia and Reggie took out cell phones and began to dial.

CHAPTER 10

THE OFFER

Reggie stood up and scoped the area for a pay phone—an item that was getting scarcer and scarcer as the mobile phone world exploded. Andy noticed his fellow passenger looking around and said pleasantly, "Hey, if you need to make a call you can use my phone. I'll be done in a minute." He gestured with the phone toward Reggie.

"That's okay," Reggie answered with coolness in his voice, evidence of a long-held mistrust of strangers, especially if they were white. "I'll grab a pay phone."

"You're welcome to it," Andy repeated. Reggie waved him off with a forced smile and a slight shake of his head and walked away from the group into the main aisle of the terminal.

Andy went back to his call. He knew it would take a few minutes for Head Nurse Laws to stroll down the corridor of the V.A. hospice to George's room. The level of his old friend's sedation would determine how long it would take the nurse to wake him, or if she even could. As Andy watched Reggie walk away he heard Nurse Laws come back on the phone.

"Mr. Spillers is resting quietly now, Mr. Casiano."

"It's Andy."

"Okay, Andy. I know he's looking forward to your visit. He talks about it all the time . . . when he's awake, that is." There was a touch of sadness in her voice, and finality.

"So, uh . . . I hope to be there tomorrow. In the morning. How's he, uh . . . ?" Nurse Laws knew what Andy found difficult to ask. She had been a hospice nurse for ten years, watching the last of the World War II vets pass on and the next surge of Korean War and some Vietnam vets arrive. "He's as comfortable as we can make him, Andy," she said softly. "Get here as soon as you can. There's not much time left."

"Thank you," Andy said. "Come hell or high water, I'll see him tomorrow. Merry Christmas."

"Merry Christmas, Andy."

He snapped the cell phone closed and turned away from the group. His eyes filled with sorrowful tears. As he took out his handkerchief to wipe them away he noticed the young female soldier looking at him. He smiled. She nodded and returned the smile.

There were no pay phones to be seen as Reggie approached the terminal's main entrance where the larger airlines had their counters. Most counters were closed or in the process of closing. Only a few passengers remained, awaiting transportation to one of several nearby hotels. Two large TV monitors in the main lobby, just past the now closed bar and restaurant, showed all flights cancelled. Finally, he noticed a small Southern Bell sign near the door and two unoccupied pay phones beneath it.

"Everybody in the world has a cell phone except me," Reggie mused as he walked toward the phones. "And that's just fine 'cause everybody in my world knows where I am, and I know where they are." But deep down he knew that bravado rang false. The world was changing, and he needed to change with it.

Reggie dug in his fold-back wallet for his calling card, looked down at the number, and dialed his son Donald's number in Asheville. By force of habit he looked over his shoulder to make sure that no one was watching to steal the card number. He hoped Yvonne would answer. He didn't feel like talking to his son right now. Two rings and the familiar, reassuring voice of Yvonne was with him in this alien airport. He relaxed and related the situation. As always, Yvonne was calm and understanding.

"This is as messed up as everything else in my life," Reggie complained.

"It's just some bad weather, baby. It's already clear here in Asheville, so I'm sure you'll be flying in the morning."

"Who the hell knows? Maybe I should just go back to Detroit and make them open the plant, huh?" Reggie joked. He wished he could do just that.

"Good idea. And while you're at it, ask them to put you on the GM board to be sure this doesn't happen again." Her sarcasm was playful and loving.

"Yeah, yeah. I know. I'm just ticked off as usual.

I love you, babe. I don't know why you put up with me."

"Because you are the love of my life."

"I hear that. Me too. So I'll, uh . . . I'll see you when I see you. I'll call you tomorrow when I know. Tell Donald I'll get there when I get there. He doesn't need to wait at the airport . . . waste his time. I'll call when we land."

"He'll be there, Reg. Not to worry."

"Okay. So Merry Christmas. Kiss the kids for me. Tell them Grandpa loves them. You too, baby."

"Merry Christmas. Travel safe." She hung up.

The calmness that Yvonne had invoked disappeared. Rage surged up in his craw. Against what? The weather? The airlines? GM? His age? Reggie began to breathe rapidly. His heart pounded. A cold sweat formed on his forehead. He was suddenly tired, immensely tired. There was a wavering weakness in his knees. *Oh, Lord, no,* he thought, *not a heart attack. Not now. Not here.*

As Reggie stood frozen with fear, the phone still in his hand, a dark-haired white woman suddenly appeared next to him, brushing off fresh snowflakes and smiling at him. She had brown, penetrating eyes that glowed with purpose. The look she gave him was unnerving. But it also took his mind away from what he suddenly realized was only a panic attack. He had had a few of them after he was laid off.

"Grounded?" Lisa Barone cheerfully asked.

"Say what?" Reggie said, startled by her directness.

"No plane, right? The snow?"

"Yeah. Grounded to the Ramada. . . . That's if they ever come back for us."

"You on the Blue Ridge to Asheville?"

"You our ride?" Reggie looked around for the Blue Ridge agent who had promised to return.

"Maybe."

"Maybe?"

"How many are you?" she asked.

"I think eight or nine. There's two kids. . . . Eight. Yeah, eight."

"I can do that," Lisa said. "So what's your name?"

"Reggie."

"I'm Lisa." She pulled off a wet leather glove and extended her hand. They shook.

"Where are the rest?"

"The gate."

"Okay, Reggie. Then let's go see if we can get this show on the road. You do want to get home for Christmas Eve, right?"

"Yeah. Sure. . . ." Reggie was confused. "You mean Christmas Day." The pleasant woman smiled warmly.

"Let's go get the others." As Reggie followed, Lisa made her way through the now deserted terminal with alacrity and purpose in her booted stride.

When Lisa and Reggie arrived at the Blue Ridge gate area, the passengers were sorting out their luggage that had been deposited behind the counter. Reggie went to find his suitcase, and Lisa strode right into the middle of the group and took charge.

"Who's for Asheville?" she asked in her cheery voice.

"We're flying?" a startled Andy asked. "They said the airport's closed."

"It is," Lisa answered. "But I'm ready to take you there anyway."

"How?" John Sullivan asked.

"I have a van."

"Just like that?" Marta asked suspiciously.

"Look. I was headed for Asheville when I heard that the airport was shut down. I've taken this flight myself, so I figured there might be a few folks stuck . . . and here you are."

"Why, child?" Amelia asked.

Lisa shrugged. Her smile had not left her face. "Just trying to be a good samaritan on Christmas Eve, I guess." There was a moment of silence as everyone looked at one another. Could this be true?

"What about the storm?" Ilena asked. "The roads must be a mess."

"Not really. I heard the snow's already stopped in North Carolina. They get to the roads fast in the mountains up there."

"She's right about it stopping," Reggie chimed in. "My wife said it's clear in Asheville."

"And you can take all of us?" John asked, stepping forward.

"No sweat," Lisa answered, facing him directly. "I've got a nice, roomy vehicle right outside the main entrance. It seats nine, and there's a rack on top for the luggage."

The passengers looked at one another again, silently seeking counsel and confirmation.

"It's Christmas Eve. Peace on Earth. Good will and all that . . ." Lisa paused. "Look. I'm goin' to Asheville. Are you folks in?" Lisa looked out the large window. The snow was lessening. "We can make it all right if we leave now."

"How long will it take, dear?" Amelia asked.

"I'd say seven, maybe eight hours. And that's drivin' careful."

"I can spell you," Reggie told her.

"Yes. Me too," Andy added. "I've got a chauffeur's license."

The group looked to one another, sensing a growing consensus that they would take a chance on the stranger. Finally Ilena spoke up.

"I don't know about you people," she said, "but I've got ten precious days home and I don't want to miss one second. I'm in, Lisa. Thank you. I drive a five-ton truck every day. I can spell you, too."

"What's it going to cost?" Marta asked, skeptically.

"I figure ten per person. Five for the kids. That'll cover the gas and my chains."

"Sounds fair," John announced. "I'm in."

"Me too," Reggie added.

Amelia smiled benignly at the group. "I think we all are, Lisa. It'll be a nice ride, I'm sure."

Ilena looked at her watch. "And we'll be home in time for Christmas Eve."

"You got that right, soldier."

"It's Ilena. Ilena Burton." The two women shook hands.

"Okay, then!" Lisa said. "Let's grab the bags and do it."

CHAPTER 11

THE GETAWAY

Ever the plucky adventurer, Amelia popped up the handle on her suitcase and was the first to wheel along behind Lisa. Reggie followed with two large green Pierre Cardin canvas travel bags. They were part of a set he had purchased at Costco last week. Andy, with two well-worn suitcases, sans wheels, walked side by side with Ilena. She carried a large, fully packed duffel bag slung over her shoulder. John, whose one compact Gucci two-suiter was on wheels, helped Marta with her luggage. They took up the rear. The kids moved along in front of them, both carrying their essentials such as their Game Boys, a few books, sweaters, jackets, and extra sneakers in Nickelodeon backpacks.

There was momentary shock as the group stepped from the warmth of the nearly closed terminal into the blowing snow and chill wind. Amelia clutched at her collar, reflecting on the warmth she had left behind in Florida. Marta gathered the kids and buttoned their coats. She reached into their backpacks and took out woolen cuffed hats with World Wildlife Fund logos on them. Ronny protested, but a stern look from Mom ended it quickly.

"I can imagine my kids would do the same," John remarked. There was a touch of melancholy in his voice.

"How long have you been away?" Marta asked.

"Five weeks."

"So you missed Thanksgiving?"

"Yes. Business . . ."

"Well, that's too bad," she said as they continued to walk after the others. "They grow up fast." John did not respond, other than to nod his agreement and tighten his lips.

When he reached the edge of the outside overhang, Reggie looked up at the gray clouds and snow and wondered if he had made the right choice. What if they got into an accident? Or maybe the roads wouldn't be plowed and they'd get stranded. He argued with himself until that voice within, the one that sounded like Yvonne, told him to stop being such a pessimist.

Lisa led the way to the end of the pickup-only parking area. A lone, refurbished vintage-red Volkswagen microbus, covered with snow and looking like a large, rectangular strawberry shortcake, was the only vehicle in the lot. Though decades old, it had been restored and repainted to almost factory condition—a "cream puff." The sight of the vehicle's age gave a few of the group pause, but its immaculate condition was reassuring to the others. Lisa stood before it with open arms and obvious pride.

"Here we are," she announced. "Your magic-carpet ride to Asheville."

"That is one classic VW," Andy said.

Reggie put down his suitcases and ran his hand along the exposed rear-door panel and onto the small rear fender. "I am impressed," he announced. "I haven't seen one of these in twenty years. And someone did a hell of a job restoring this baby. You do that, Lisa?"

"No," she admitted. "A friend . . . well, it's a long story. It originally belonged to my mom and—" A gust of wind interrupted her "Later. We'd better get loaded up and out of here." Lisa opened the rear door and showed Marta the back two seats. "The kids could be comfortable back here," she suggested. She helped Marta get them settled, then took a long-handled brush and cleaned the accumulated snow from the van.

At the same time, Ilena took Amelia's suitcase from her and helped her into the front seat of the van. "I'll take care of this," she said. "Make yourself comfortable, Mrs. McIntosh."

"Thank you, dear. And it's Amelia. Please."

"Yes, ma'am. Amelia." Ilena smiled and closed the door. She then joined the men, who were figuring out the luggage situation. Andy was up on the roof rack while Reggie and John passed the luggage up to him.

"We'll need a rope or something," Ilena called out. "And a canvas cover would be helpful, too."

"Flying in," Lisa's voice called out from the front of the van. She had the storage trunk open. In a moment, she appeared with a hank of new, half-inch nylon sash cord and a well-worn tarpaulin.

Five minutes later, when the last of the luggage had been neatly fitted onto the roof rack, John and Reggie began the process of tying it down with the sash cord. John passed an end up to Andy, who wrapped it around the rack and a section of luggage and then threw it down to Reggie, who slipped it under the rack and threw it back up to Andy. So it went until the luggage was secure and the three men were covered with fresh snow. But now the flakes were small and lighter. Standing on either side of the front of the VW, Lisa and Ilena guided one end of the tarpaulin up to Andy. As he pulled it over the luggage, John and Reggie, who were taller than the two women, guided it to the rear of the microbus. After that, they used the remainder of the sash cord to secure the tarpaulin to the rack, and they were ready to go.

As Andy jumped down from the roof and brushed snow from his black leather jacket, Lisa was cleaning off the van's rear window.

"It's letting up," she told him.

"That's good." He watched John and Reggie get into the van. "So where'd you pick up this hippie wagon?" Andy asked. His breath condensed in the midday, snowy air. From the tone of the word "hippie," Lisa was unsure whether Andy's comment was a question or a taunt.

"It belonged to my mom," she said. "I guess you could call her a hippie. Long before she married my dad, she once drove it all the way to San Francisco. A place called Haight-Ashbury. You ever hear of it?" Andy's brow furrowed in a scowl.

"The flower children? Yeah. I heard about it," he said softly. "The 'sixties.' Make love, not war," came out of his mouth with biting sarcasm. Andy paused. He saw that Lisa was no longer smiling. Now she was frowning. "I was in Vietnam then," he told her.

"Oh," was all she said. "I'm sorry if I—"

"No. No. No," he interrupted. "That was long ago, and those kids were right. Your mom was right." His thoughts went to his friend George, lying semiconscious in a bed in Asheville, waiting for him. No doubt facing his end in the shell of an infirm body and the whirling dreams of a mind forever altered by combat.

Andy and Lisa's conversation was not lost on Ilena, who was making a final check of the tarpaulin.

"Turbulent times back then," Andy said. His tone was apologetic. "I meant no disrespect."

"That's okay," Lisa said.

"In a way it reminds me of what's happening today," he went on. "But nobody's in the streets about the war. No draft, so it's just the boys . . ." Andy stopped as Ilena came around to join them. "The soldiers," he continued, correcting himself, "over there who know the real deal."

"It's a different America, sir," Ilena told him.

"Maybe," he responded, staring at her desert fatigues, field jacket, and tan combat boots. "Certainly a different color," he joked, pointing to her uniform.

"I'd say so, sir."

"Hey. Please. No 'sir' business. There ain't no bars on my shoulder. Never was. Corporal's all I ever wanted. Made buck sergeant, once, for about a week, before I got busted back. All I wanted was to come home in one piece."

Ilena nodded, knowing, soldier to soldier, what Andy meant.

"So? Are we good to go?" Lisa asked Ilena.

"Tight as a drum."

"Okay!" Lisa said exuberantly. When Ilena and Andy were in the truck, she slipped in behind the wheel and started the motor. It kicked over immediately and purred.

As they drove away, a large Ramada Inn van pulled up into the space the Volkswagen had just vacated. A small man dressed in an Eddie Bauer jacket with the Blue Ridge logo on the back got out of the van. He moved toward the terminal officiously, carrying a sheet of paper in his hand listing the Asheville passengers he was to pick up and escort to the Ramada. He entered the terminal, a man on a mission, determined to be home in time to trim the tree.

Just as the Volkswagen left the airport and drove onto the plowed highway, the snow stopped. Lisa let out a loud whistle, startling her passengers, then shouted, "She leaped to her van, to her ride gave a whistle, and away they all went like the down of a thistle! Christmas, here we come." She gunned the motor, and everyone smiled.

Then, until they were well clear of Atlanta, heading north on Interstate 575, the group tried to put together the entire "'Twas the Night Before Christmas" poem. And they did.

CHAPTER 12

NANTAHALA

It was nearly two o'clock. They were making good time, already on Route 76 in the Chattahoochee National Forest. The North Carolina border wasn't too far ahead. The roads were not heavily trafficked. Due to the freak storm, and because it was Christmas Eve day, many people just stayed home.

The conversation in the van had been minimal. Amelia was inquisitive, but the others didn't volunteer much about themselves. Ilena, who sat with the children in the backseat, talked a bit about her buddies in Iraq, but played down how dangerous it was when asked. Andy and Reggie, the two veterans in the van, understood her reluctance. No one pressed her. Besides, it was hard to hear her at times because of the musical and ping-cling noises the Game Boys made. Finally, Reggie asked Marta if they could stop playing with the toys for a while. She told the kids to use their earphones. Reluctantly, they complied but not before they threw a scowl at Reggie. He stared back at them, stone-faced, and they looked away. Reggie had been up since four that morning, and he nodded off from time to time.

Once, while Reggie was awake, Amelia asked him about his visit to Asheville. He talked a bit about leaving Michigan for North Carolina, but only in terms of being with his grandchildren for the holidays. He said nothing about being laid off at GM or that this was a move, not a visit, and that he was going to work for his son.

Andy spelled Lisa behind the wheel. She sat between him and Amelia in the wide front seat. When Amelia queried him about this trip, Andy talked about his Vietnam buddy George and how he hoped to get to Asheville in time. His concern for George was so obvious that no one asked him anything else.

Reggie, Marta, and John occupied the seat behind. John, who sat in the middle, studied several business reports that he had on his laptop. No one asked what they were or what his business was. At one point, Reggie noticed the Rolex Oyster on John's wrist and the fact that he was wearing a very expensive Armani suit. He thought John a caricature of "the man," and went back to sleep.

Marta kept to herself, staring out the window. She rolled the ugly scenes with her husband over and over in her mind. Her anger had given way to depression and fear. The uncertainty of the future weighed heavily on her soul. She checked on the children from time to time. Ronny and Nancy were totally immersed in and distracted with their now silent Game Boys.

As they drove through the early afternoon, the gray storm clouds gave way to blue skies and winter sunshine. The landscape in the Chattahoochee National Forest was a true winter wonderland. The trees, many of them conifers, were loaded with brilliant snow. The pristine meadows were framed with snowbanks made by the plows. With the Blue Ridge Mountains as a backdrop, the van moved through the forest as if in a Currier and Ives lithograph.

By two-fifteen everyone's stomach was grumbling. They were making good time.

"The North Carolina border's about fifteen miles ahead," Lisa announced. "I know a real nice café that's still open this time of year in the town of Blue Ridge. It's just ahead. How about some lunch?" Everyone agreed it was a good idea. When the kids heard the word "lunch" they stopped playing and sat up in their seats.

Blue Ridge was basically a summer resort and tourist town. It had once been an elite health resort because of its pure mineral waters. Tourists would ride the train to get there, then have dinner at the Blue Ridge Hotel and walk to the mineral springs afterwards. Tourists still rode the train and enjoyed antique and specialty shops, galleries, restaurants, and the mountain atmosphere of Blue Ridge. It was also central to the camping and fishing enthusiasts who took advantage of the park's developed recreation areas, campsites, picnic sites, beaches, trails, lakes, and streams. Many of the town's permanent residents worked in the Chattahoochee National Forest, or on construction. There was a great deal of development as the area prepared for the highly anticipated influx of retiring "boomers."

Lisa directed Andy through town onto Main Street and the Serenity Garden Café. Lunch service was just over, but nine customers could not be denied at this slow time of year. They were seated at a round table next to a window that looked out onto Main Street. Christmas decorations were displayed all over town, making the atmosphere festive and welcoming.

"This is lovely," Amelia commented when they were all settled and studying the menu. "My husband and I stopped here many times. Not this restaurant, but others in Blue Ridge. It's a very nice town." She smiled at the waitress who stood by patiently with pad and pencil in hand.

"Thank you, ma'am. Are we ready to order?" They were, and everyone announced their choice politely as she went around the table. Traditional southern Appalachian foods were the Serenity Garden Café's specialty. The favorite was local mountain trout—fried, broiled, pecan-crusted, smoked . . . all were on the menu. There were also lots of apple dishes—apple bread, apple butter, fried apple pies, apple cider . . . In spite of the weather outside, the kids zeroed in on homemade Georgia ice cream. Then there was the standard fare—barbequed ribs, country ham, fried chicken, mashed potatoes and gravy . . . all sensational!

As they ate, the conversation centered around the town, the area, the park, and what time they might get to Asheville.

"We've got a little more than a hundred miles to go," Lisa announced. "I have made it in two hours, but that was without snow." She checked her wristwatch. It was 2:25 P.M. "If we're on our way by three-thirty, I'd say we'll roll into Asheville at six-thirty . . . seven at the latest." Everyone was pleased.

"As long as we're sitting around," Amelia suggested, "why don't we pay Lisa now?" She took out her purse and handed her a ten-dollar bill. All the others followed suit.

When the check arrived, John signaled to the waitress.

"I'll take that," he said.

"Oh, no," Reggie objected. "I can pay for myself." Andy and Ilena agreed.

"The treat is mine," John told them as he handed the waitress his Platinum American Express card. "My celebration."

"Celebration of what?" Amelia asked.

"Of getting home for Christmas after a long trip."

"We're all doing that, sir," Ilena said.

"Yes. Of course," John answered. "But I just signed a huge contract in Europe, and, well, let's call this a business expense. Or if you wish, the Christmas office party that I missed." No one objected after that.

A half hour later, they drove past a sign reading YOU ARE NOW LEAVING GEORGIA THE PEACH STATE— Y'ALL COME SEE US AGAIN, HEAH? On the radio, country music played softly. Marta, Ronny, and Nancy had dozed off.

"There goes Georgia," Andy said.

"And here comes North Carolina," Lisa added. She was driving again as they passed another road sign. This one read WELCOME TO NORTH CAROLINA— THE TARHEEL STATE. DRIVE SAFELY.

Amelia saw the sign and laughed.

"What's funny, Ms. McIntosh?" asked Andy.

"Tarheel. And it's Amelia, remember?" She turned

to the people behind her in the van. "Do you know why it's called the Tarheel State?"

"Can't say that I do," John said politely, looking up from his laptop.

"I'm from Michigan," Reggie said, politely feigning interest as if being a geographic stranger shielded him from answering.

"No, ma'am," said Ilena. Amelia smiled, warming to her prior role in life as a teacher.

"The Civil War. There was a big battle near here. Soldiers from all over the Confederacy—Georgia, The Carolinas, Alabama, Mississippi . . . even some from Virginia."

"What was the battle?" Ilena asked.

"I can't recall its name right now," Amelia said sheepishly. "A senior moment. Anyway," she continued, "a column of rebel soldiers retreated, leaving a regiment of North Carolinians to fight the Yankees alone. Later, the North Carolinians met up with those fleeing troops and told them, 'Next battle we'll put tar on your heels to make y'all stick and fight.' When General Robert E. Lee heard the story he said, 'God bless the Tarheel boys.' That stuck, too."

"How'd you know that?" Ilena asked.

"I was a college professor. Art history. My husband, Joseph, God rest his soul, taught chemistry. We were at Morehouse College. We retired eight years ago. He passed on last year."

"I'm sorry," Andy and Marta said simultaneously. She and the kids were awake. The others muttered the same.

"Thank you, dears."

"Morehouse is a black college," Reggie said with a tone that seemed to repudiate Amelia's claim.

"And a darn good one, Reggie," she answered. "Joseph was African-American. They have several white teachers there, too." Reggie grunted and looked out the window.

"So, uh, Amelia, how'd you come to live in Asheville?" Ilena asked in a loud voice from the rear of the van. The kids were back to their Game Boys and the sound was on. Before anyone could say anything, Marta turned and said, "Earphones." The kids put them on.

"We had a summer place there, dear. Joseph did research, and I wrote. Asheville is beautiful. The mountains, the forests . . . We just loved it. I still do, but . . . well, it's kind of lonely now."

Several moments passed with no one speaking. John checked his cell phone. He glanced out of the window at the passing scenery, searching for a cell phone tower.

"My cell phone battery is low."

"There's no signal once we get up into the mountains, anyway," Lisa told them all. "One place the future hasn't overrun. At least not yet." Ilena checked her cell phone.

"Well, mine's okay for now. Anyone want to use it to make a call?" No one answered. She snapped it shut and put it back in her fatigue jacket. "How about I drive a while?" Ilena asked.

"Sure," Lisa responded. "That'd be nice. I'm a little logy after that meal."

"A wonderful meal," Amelia added.

"Glad you liked it, Amelia. Look, the turnoff for the Great Smoky Mountain Parkway is just up ahead. The snow in the mountains is gonna be deeper than down here," Lisa announced to every-one. "I learned that lesson the hard way once.

That's why I bought the chains. When I pull over, let's put 'em on."

The winter solstice had been only a few days ago. It was close to four o'clock, and a brilliant orange sun had descended halfway behind the forested surrounding hills. It cast long, dark shadows across the snowy fields. Lisa pulled to the side of the road. The tires made a crunching sound against the packed snow and ice. The van stopped. Lisa, Andy, and John got out. Lisa opened the front storage compartment and took out the set of chains.

Reggie got out of the van. He saw the others busy with the chains. Another pair of hands was not needed. Not needed. Unwanted. The words echoed silently in his mind. A feeling of profound melancholy, the kind that reaches down and wraps its hand around one's heart, caused a palpable ache in his chest. He felt the sudden need to seek distance from the others. With the sounds of the chains being laid out on the frosty roadside, Reggie stepped across the blacktop road, now dull white from plow scrapes and salt, and into the black shadow of the woods. That part of his face that the sunlight touched with its orange hue revealed how painfully his uncertain future weighed upon him. He was discarded. Useless. A man with less time to live than he had lived. And now he had run out of choices. He was heading for a future he had not planned. Reggie breathed in the cold mountain air. His mind floated back to the special winter training he had received at Camp Drum in upper New York State with the Tenth Mountain Division. He breathed again and found solace in the chill air. He had overcome adversity in that harsh environment, and later in Vietnam. He could overcome this, too.

"Hey, Reggie," he heard Andy call out from the nearby road. "We're ready to go." He heard a van door slam shut. *Time to join the others and get on to Asheville,* Reggie thought. He took one last look around the forest. Camp Drum was nearly forty years ago. *Tempus fugit—time passes.* He hurried back to find his future.

The chains made a clattering, high-pitched sound on the neatly plowed road as they ascended steeply into the Great Smoky Mountains. Darkness crept inexorably in around them. The snow pack grew thicker, though the road was still well plowed. The chains provided traction, but their progress was now much slower. A small road sign announced they had reached the Nantahala National Forest.

CHAPTER 13

AVALANCHE

The Great Smoky Mountain Parkway became increasingly narrow and winding. The road rose up into the mountains. Ilena, now driving, saw beams from headlights reflecting off the tall, snow-coated pines from the hilltop ahead. The wind was stronger up here, causing a mist of snow to swirl from the trees onto the road. She eased off the accelerator and shifted down to second gear to gain more traction and control. She squinted at the glare of a pair of oncoming high beams as they came over the crest of the hill. It was a car, slipping and fishtailing down the slope toward them. Ilena's fingers clenched the steering wheel as she attempted to gauge the oncoming car's path and speed.

"Hang on, everybody!" she shouted.

"Dim those lights, you moron," Andy yelled in anger toward the unseen driver as he shielded his eyes.

"Can you see, Ilena?" Amelia asked.

John leaned forward. Reggie sat up.

Marta glanced back at Lisa and the kids, who were in the seat behind her. Everyone was alert to the danger.

"Yeah," Ilena said quietly. "I'm okay."

"He's out of control," Andy cried. "Give him room." Ilena made her calculations and reached a decision. Her instincts, honed on the highway of death, the five-mile Matar Sadam Al Duwali Road to the Baghdad airport, kicked in. It was the most dangerous highway in Iraq—a white-knuckle ride, coming or going. To reach Baghdad or leave it, you had to survive the airport road first. How many times had she seen an IUD explode? How many times had the convoy leader shouted on the radio, *"Emshee! Emshee!"* Arabic for "Go! Go!"?

Ilena eased the van to the right, a narrow shoulder, and slowed cautiously to a stop. The oncoming car, obviously without chains, weaved back and forth between the middle and both shoulders of the road. The driver was clearly inexperienced on icy road surfaces. It came down the hill on a path that might put it dangerously close to the van. Ilena remained focused, and when the car was just about twenty yards away, she saw it slide toward their side of the road. She had anticipated this and gunned the engine. The van's wheels whirred momentarily, then the chains caught. The microbus lurched forward onto the road to the right of the oncoming car. Those on the left side, Ilena, Marta, and Lisa, saw the occupants—a terrified woman with two children strapped into car seats behind her.

Everyone in the van tensed as the car shot by, missing them by three or four yards. Ilena's cool head and skills had put them beyond harm's way.

The out-of-control car swerved back to the center of the road.

"Good move," John said, applauding.

"Fine driving, soldier," Andy added.

"Yes. That was quite smart, dear," Amelia said. Ilena looked in the rearview mirror at the diminishing image of the car.

"I hope she makes it down the hill." Reggie, seated next to the window, shifted forward in his seat. "It was a woman with two kids. A fool's errand."

"She shouldn't be driving on a night like this," Andy said. "What could be so important to risk your life for?"

"Maybe she was in trouble," Marta suggested.

"Or a sick kid," John chimed in.

"She could have killed us all," Marta said, looking at her kids. "What are we doing here?"

"Getting home for Christmas Eve, dear," Amelia answered. "And safely, I might add, with good drivers."

"That's right, Senora Amelia. Ilena had it covered," Andy affirmed. "Let's hope God is that other woman's copilot tonight." He made the sign of the cross and then he kissed his index finger. "I drive a taxi part-time in the city. You learn defensive driving pronto, or you're back-page news in the *Post*."

"You said the city. What city?" Lisa asked.

"There's only one city that calls itself 'The City' in the U.S.A., *chica*. And that's the *Grande* Apple— *Nueva* York." Andy spread his arms with a flourish that brought a smile to everyone's lips. Even Reggie allowed himself a slight grin.

* * *

The road was rising rapidly up into the Great Smoky Mountains. The sun was behind them, and it would soon be totally dark. A pleasant quiet settled in the van. Then Ronny and Nancy, now calmed down after the encounter with the out-of-control car, went back to their Game Boys. The sound volume was up to an annoying level—ping-ping, clack-clack, pop-pop, and musical glisses.

"Hey, lady? How about you tell them to cut out that racket?" Reggie complained.

"They're just kids playing," Marta said defensively, although she felt put upon by the noise as well.

"Well tell 'em to play quiet. It's givin' me a headache again."

"Put on your earphones, kids."

"Aw, Mom," Ronny complained. "It's more fun with the sound out loud."

"Just do it!" Marta commanded with emphatic finality.

"He's a grouch," Nancy muttered.

Reggie turned around in his seat and glared at her. "Say what, child?"

Marta saw Reggie was upset and on edge. Everyone was, after the close call they had just experienced. "You apologize, young lady," she told her daughter.

"I'm sorry," Nancy said softly, lowering her head.

Reggie regained his composure. "Apology accepted. It's just I'd appreciate it if you kept the noise down."

Ronny and Nancy put on their earphones, but Reggie could still faintly hear sounds of the games. He leaned forward. "Let me spell you a while," he told Ilena.

"Be my guest," she answered. "Next place I can, I'll pull over."

The last glow of daylight revealed a flat section of shoulder ahead. Ilena pulled the van off the road and stopped. Reggie and Ilena got out their respective doors. The sudden contrast of leaving the VW's warm interior and plunging into the late-afternoon winter air sent chills down both their spines. As they passed one another at the van's rear, Ilena stopped to say, "It tends to pull to the left a little."

"Okay. How're the chains?"

"Excellent. It's only snowpack on the road. But I felt a little ice from time to time, so take care."

"I always do, uh . . . Miss?"

"Burton. Ilena Burton." She extended her gloved hand.

"I'm Reggie Howard. That was smart driving back there."

"Thanks." They both heard the van's side door slide open as John got out. "Looks like we're taking a break," Ilena said.

"Anyone want to stretch?" John asked.

"Mommy," Ronny announced from the rear seat. "I have to go." Marta got out. Ronny followed.

"Could you take my son?" she asked John.

"Sure."

Marta looked at Nancy. "How about you, Nancy?"

"I'm fine," Nancy said, slightly embarrassed. She glanced at the foreboding woods and opted for the comfort and warmth of the van.

"You're sure?" her mother questioned.

"I said fine!" the preteen answered with an incredulous tone. Was her mother trying to embarrass her?

Everyone except Nancy and Amelia got out. They stretched and breathed in the fresh air. Marta studied the woods and frowned.

"Maybe we could find a restroom nearby," she said, looking directly at Lisa.

"I'm afraid all the sites and camping areas are closed for the winter," Lisa told her.

"There's nothing to be afraid of," John announced as he took Ronny's hand. "Well . . . maybe just a wolf or bear. . . ." That stopped Ronny in his tracks.

"Wolves and bears?" he asked, looking at the darkening woods across the road.

"That's just great," Marta said.

"I'm only kidding, son," John said quickly. "Let's do it." They continued across the road.

"It's a man thing, miss," Andy said to Marta. "You know . . . joking about fear."

"I don't need 'man things' in my life . . . or in my children's," Marta retorted bitterly.

"Sorry," Andy said with a shrug and a sheepish grin. "Forgive me."

Marta saw he was sincere.

"No. It's okay. I didn't mean anything." She was embarrassed at having been so curt. "We just . . . Their father and I . . . we're separated, and the kids . . . I apologize."

Andy moved closer to her and shook her gloved hand. "I'm Anselmo Casiano. Andy. No apology required. I understand. I think we're all a little, uh, unnerved today, anyway."

*   *   *

John held Ronny's hand as they walked into the woods on the far side of the road. Ronny hesitated, pausing at the forest's edge, uncertain of what he could not see. A large clump of snow fell from the branches nearby. Ronny jumped and trembled.

"What was that?" he asked nervously, pulling John's hand away from the woods.

"Nothing, son. Just some falling snow."

"You sure?" asked Ronny, grasping John's hand tighter.

"I'm sure. Let's do it." They entered the woods.

A few moments later, the people outside the microbus heard a strange howling sound from the forest across the road. It was followed by what was obviously Ronny imitating John's howl. That was followed by robust laughter from both John and Ronny that echoed down the slope.

"Like I said," Andy told Marta. "It's a man thing."

"I guess boys will be boys," Ilena said.

Everyone laughed except Marta, who just grimaced.

"I still don't think that's funny!" Marta insisted as John and her son emerged from the woods, arm in arm, sharing their little joke.

Everyone got back into the van as Reggie took the wheel. After they were seated and belted in, Reggie adjusted the mirrors and seat and pulled out onto the snow-packed road. It was close to five P.M. and nearly dark.

As they continued on, they saw no other traffic. It was quiet in the van. Other than Reggie shifting gears from time to time, the crunch of the tires on snow was the only other sound as they drove through the forest. Blowing snow turned to water on the warm windshield. When Reggie turned on the wipers, some of it crystallized into ice. The wiper blades scraped against the glass with a staccato beat. Reggie increased the defrost blower to warm the blades.

Reggie drove slowly and carefully. He felt the dropping temperature radiate from the window next to him. The darkness, snowpack, wind, and altitude were causing the thermometer to dip below zero. He turned the heater fan to its maximum setting. Amelia was asleep next to Andy, with her head on his shoulder. Andy, who was now sitting next to Reggie, had a map open on his lap. He held a flashlight to read it. The yellow beam emanating from a dying battery jostled up and down as the van moved onward and upward along the Great Smoky Mountain Parkway.

Marta and John napped in the middle seat. Lisa, still awake, sat between them. Ilena was now in the back with the kids. Their Game Boys lay on their laps as their eyelids had become heavy, eventually closing for a much needed nap.

Reggie glanced down at the scratched face of the clock on the dash of the van. Two strips of gray duct tape held it in place. That's odd, thought Reggie, work out all the dents and dings in this old VW, paint it, but not fix the clock. Lisa noticed him checking the clock.

"That's not the original clock," she said. He nodded. "Just a few more hours and we're there," she added quietly, not wishing to wake her sleeping companions. Reggie glanced over his shoulder and eyed Lisa.

"That's what you said," Reggie admitted. He liked Lisa. There was a special quality she had.

Softness, and the kindness that comes with experiencing deep pain.

Andy, who was intently studying the map, looked up as the air-cooled engine in the VW's rear coughed once.

"If the road is clear," he said. "Otherwise we might have to detour."

"Detour to where?" Reggie asked. Off to his left he noticed a narrow country road leading up into the forest. What caught his eye was some kind of statue or marker or stone pillar. He could not tell exactly what it was in the dim beam from the headlights. It was covered with snow. Across from the object was a road sign.

"There's Comfort Mountain . . . somethin'," he said.

"What a beautiful name," Lisa remarked.

Ilena overheard the conversation and looked out her window. She studied the snowy landscape. How peaceful it looked. Aware of traveling through it without fear of ambush, she suddenly was overcome by a ponderous sense of fatigue, a release of tension from war and death.

"You see it on that map?" Reggie asked.

Andy leaned closer to the map and brought the flashlight down. He ran his finger along the green ribbon that was the Great Smoky Mountain Parkway.

"Yeah. Here it is. It's called Comfort Mountain Road. We're closer than I thought. I'd say another—"

A deep rumbling sound interrupted him in midsentence. It got everyone's attention. Those who were asleep or resting, sat up alert, except for the

children. The sound grew louder and louder as if
an immense invisible beast were charging down
the road ahead, reaching out for them.

"Stop the van!" Lisa commanded.

"What is it?" Reggie asked.

"Just pull over. Now!" she insisted. Reggie's re-
flexes obeyed. He found a safe place and pulled
over. The moon, nearly full, had by now appeared
above the treetops. The microbus came to full
stop, but Reggie kept the engine running.

"Shut off the engine," Lisa said. "I want to listen."

"What's up with you?" Reggie asked. He turned
off the engine. The rumbling continued.

"John, can you open your window?" Lisa asked.
He did. She leaned across his lap and poked her
head outside.

All were now erect in their seats. Hearts pounded
in tune with the rumbling—a resonance of shared
primordial fear. Something was wrong—something
to fear.

The rumbling grew louder and more threatening. It was the sound of a thousand thundering
hooves, a sky filled with colliding thunderheads.
The earth seemed to tremble. The van shook. The
windows rattled within the door frames. A cloud of
fine white powder descended on them, blocking
the moon and covering the van. Reggie turned on
the engine. Ronny and Nancy were now up and
silent. Their fear joined the others.

"Is it snowing again, Mommy?" Nancy asked.

"Avalanche," Lisa announced somberly. "Not
too far ahead." Marta looked at her kids.

"An avalanche? Oh my God!"

"Easy," John said, taking her hand. "Easy. What
do you think, Lisa?" She leaned back into the van.

"I think it's up ahead. We just wait. Nothing we can do except pray we're not in the wrong place."

"Hell," Reggie said, turning the windshield wipers on high. "I'm gonna turn around and get out of here."

"No. There's a white-out. You won't be able to tell where the road is. Just wait," Lisa said. "We're better off here because . . ." The rumbling suddenly stopped. An eerie silence replaced it. Nothing was moving. Not even the wind in the trees. The white powder settled. The moon broke through it.

"Sounds like it's over," Andy said hopefully.

Lisa signaled for John to open the door. They both got out. Reggie got out, too. They were black shapes emerging from the snow-dusted van into a world of white. Every inch of forest, mountain, and road, every tree, every limb was covered in a fine, white powder. Unconsciously, the three stepped closer together.

"You ever see anything like this?" John asked.

"Once," Lisa said. "No sky, no earth, no separation."

"Like that painting I saw once in the Museum of Modern Art. White on white," John commented. Reggie reached out and touched the van, wiping away the fine powder, as if to reassure himself that something other than white existed.

"The avalanche kicked all this snow into the air," he said. A still breeze began to blow. Snow swirled. "The wind will clear it away."

Slowly, the others stepped from the van, drawn by the sight. Fed by the moonlight, everything around them was cast in a brilliant silvery hue. The powder glistened as it blew around them. No one spoke. Each responded to the phenomenon on a primal level. At that moment, it was nature in charge, and they were simply part of it.

"Beautiful, isn't it?" Lisa said.

"Lovely," Amelia replied, brushing some of the powder from her coat.

"Is it over?" Andy asked.

"Yes."

"What if there's another one?" Marta worried. No one answered her. She pulled the kids close to her.

A line of pale white clouds was now visible above the mountains. The moon grew brighter.

"It's over," Lisa said. "Let's see what's ahead of us. Take it real slow, Reggie."

"You got that right," he answered as they all climbed back into their seats and shut the doors.

"Isn't this exciting?" Amelia asked. "I've never been through an avalanche before."

"Yeah," Reggie remarked. "Any night you almost get killed is exciting." He slowly pulled back onto the road and drove forward, up the hill. "Any time the elephant don't come out and step on you," he muttered softly to himself.

Andy's eyebrows arched. "The elephant, huh?" he said, leaning over to Reggie. A private moment. "You were there?"

"Yeah."

"When?"

"Seventy. The 199th Light Infantry Brigade."

"I was there in sixty-eight. 82nd Airborne." Each nodded in the darkness; neither saw the other's acknowledgment.

*   *   *

After several minutes of excruciatingly slow progress up the steep hill, Reggie stopped the van. There, in the glow of the headlights and the full moon, was a mountain of snow blocking the road. It rose up on both sides like a giant alabaster dam.

"Oh, man," Reggie said aloud. He hunched over the steering wheel and slowly shook his head from side to side. They would have to find another way to Asheville.

CHAPTER 14

COMFORT MOUNTAIN ROAD

It was warm in the van. The commingled scents of gasoline fumes and people under stress was strong, but somehow being together was comforting. They had fuel and each other. The adversity of the storm, their cancelled flight, the decision to go with Lisa, their close proximity in the VW, the near collision with the out-of-control car, and now the avalanche blocking their passage to Asheville had transformed them from a group of strangers to traveling companions with a common purpose.

"So? Anyone got a shovel?" Andy asked, feigning humor to ease the fear in the van. No one laughed. Reggie leaned back against the driver's seat.

"Man, it's like something doesn't want us to get home for Christmas," he said, surprised that he had referred to Asheville as home. "We sure ain't drivin' through that mess." John checked his cell phone.

"There's no signal here."

"Then I guess we've got to go back," Lisa suggested.

"Maybe we should wait for someone to come," Amelia offered. "You know, like the police."

"We're the only fools out here," Marta grumbled. "I knew this was a bad idea." Andy had the flashlight on and was studying the map.

"Well, we can't just sit here," Ilena said.

"If there was one avalanche, maybe there will be another," Marta said. "We've got to get away from here." There was slight panic in her voice.

"What if it comes on top of us?" Nancy asked, fearfully.

"It won't, Nancy," Lisa said. "Everything that was going to come down the mountain already did."

"Comfort Mountain Road," Andy said aloud.

"What about it?" Reggie asked.

"It's that road we passed before," Ilena said from the rear seat. "I saw some kind of gate or entrance there. Maybe there's a way around this."

"Or a house to make a call from," John added.

"And maybe it's blocked, too," Reggie said. His tone was argumentative. "I say we go back down Seventy-Four and around through Tennessee."

"They had more snow off to the west," Lisa told him. "The odds are those roads are worse." A long moment of silence followed. Only the sound of the wind and the blowing snow brushing the top of the van was heard.

"Well, if we stay here, we'll run out of gas and freeze," Reggie announced. He gestured toward the map in Andy's lap. "Let me see that." Andy handed him the map and flashlight. He pointed out Comfort Mountain Road. "It doesn't show where the road goes," Reggie said. "What makes you think that it goes around this mess?"

"Maybe it does," Andy answered. "We could try." Another moment of silence and worry filled the van.

"Okay," Lisa began. "So we can't stay here. I say we have a look. I mean, why would they build a road unless there were houses and it connected to another road? If we see it doesn't, then we can backtrack and try another route, or find a motel, or something. It's not even seven o'clock. We can still make Asheville tonight."

"She's right," John said quickly.

"I say it's worth trying," Amelia added. Ilena and Andy agreed.

"I vote for going back immediately and finding a main road around," Marta announced. They all looked at Reggie. Somehow being in the driver's seat gave him more authority.

"What do you think, Reggie?" Andy asked.

"Well, that road's on the way back down the mountain anyway, so let's give it a shot. Just a mile or so. If there's nothing, we turn around and head back."

"Sounds like a plan," Andy said, answering for everyone except Marta, who said, "A bad plan," folding her arms defiantly.

"Look at this as an adventure," Amelia told Marta.

"Oh, good Lord." Marta sighed. "How empty your life must be to see adventure in this mess." Amelia turned away, openly hurt by Marta's comment.

"She didn't mean that, Amelia," Andy said, glaring at Marta, who was immediately sorry for her outburst.

"What's wrong, Mommy?" Nancy asked.

"Nothing," Marta said contritely.

"Then why are you fighting?"

"We're not fighting." Marta turned to Amelia. "I'm sorry. I'm just . . . you know."

"That's okay, dear." Amelia smiled kindly.

"Don't you worry, Marta," Andy added. "We're going to be all right."

"Says you," Reggie told him.

"Why don't you give it a rest, Reggie?" John piped up.

"Why don't you go back to sleep, pal," Reggie answered.

Lisa leaned forward between John and Reggie. "If you guys can't control the testosterone, I'll take the wheel," she scolded them. Another tense, and perhaps embarrassing, moment of silence followed.

"What's tes . . . uh, trone, Mommy?" Ronny asked. Smiles broke out on everyone's faces. The innocent question from a child's lips had cleared the charged atmosphere.

"It's, um . . ." Marta groped for an answer.

"It's why men grow bigger than women," Lisa offered.

"But not always smarter," Ilena added. That remark made everyone laugh and completely broke the ice.

"Okay, then," Andy said firmly. "Comfort Mountain Road, it is. And like Reggie says, if there's nothing after a few miles, we turn around and backtrack." He turned and looked at everyone in turn—eyeball to eyeball. "Okay?" Andy's words were more of a statement than a question.

Annoyed and tired, Reggie took his hands off the steering wheel. "Enough with the 'okay' already.

Let's do it." Taking the steering wheel again, he backed up the van, made a cautious K-turn, and then drove slowly back down toward Comfort Mountain Road. The world outside was silver-white now, illuminated by moonlight. It was bright enough that they didn't really need headlights. Their yellow beams reflected off uncountable snow crystals, mixing moonlight and lamplight into dancing points of gold and silver.

"It looks like Christmas," Ronny remarked. Everyone knew what he meant.

They reached the turnoff to Comfort Mountain Road in less than ten minutes. As they made a right turn into the road, they passed the snow-covered structure a few of them had seen earlier. It was larger than Reggie recalled and now, in the moonlight it looked more like a monument or statue than anything else.

"What's that?" Andy asked Amelia, who was seated on the right side of the front seat.

"I can't see exactly," she answered. "Some kind of marker or entrance." Lisa, who was on that side in the second seat, and Ilena, who was on the right in the backseat, also scoped the object. As they passed, a gust of wind blew some of the snow from it. There appeared to be an arm, or hand. And it seemed to move as though it had shaken the snow from itself. When they had passed it, Lisa glanced at Ilena and raised her eyebrows. Ilena just shrugged and smiled.

"A plow was here," Reggie remarked as the road began to climb up the mountain. Thick woods, consisting mostly of deciduous trees, now bare, lined their way.

"That's a good sign," Andy commented as the

Great Smoky Mountain Parkway faded from sight behind them. Ronny turned and looked back at the pillar. He cocked his head and peered into the night.

"Did you hear that?" he asked his sister.

"No. What?"

"A dog bark."

"Maybe it was my game," she said, lifting her Game Boy. "I just reached the fourth level." She focused her attention back on playing. Ronny kept on looking out the rear window until the Parkway passed out of sight. At that moment he thought he saw someone, or something, crossing the road into the woods. He rubbed his eyes and looked harder. But whatever he saw, or thought he saw, was gone.

Reggie guided the van carefully and slowly, higher and higher up Comfort Mountain Road. About a half-mile up the road the plow had stopped and turned around. There were no driveways or houses in sight, no tire tracks coming down the mountain. *Not good,* Reggie thought to himself as he shifted down into third gear. The chains were working well. Those seated next to the windows peered out for an indication of another road, a house, or any sign of life.

CHAPTER 15

A VISION OF SHELTER

The mountain rose steeply ahead, and progress slowed on the unplowed road. Reggie glanced at the odometer, then stopped the van.

"That's a mile," he said, staring through the windshield. Ahead, the road was illuminated by the van's headlights for about ten yards. Beyond, only a dim sliver of forest-lined road was visible. "Far as I can see, we're in the middle of nowhere. The road's gettin' steeper. I say we turn back."

"We said we'd try a mile or two," Andy said, stressing the number two. "If we find a house, maybe they can tell us how to get around the avalanche."

"I don't know, Andy. Maybe Reggie's right," John said unconvincingly.

"I say we keep going," Ilena remarked.

"How about a vote?" Amelia suggested. There was a mischievous smile on her lips.

"This isn't a joking matter, Amelia," Marta told her sternly. "There are children in this car. My children."

"I know, dear," Amelia answered. "I was just trying to keep things light."

"And I want things to be safe," Marta replied.

As the others were discussing what to do, Ilena,
still in the rear seat, peered out of her window. She
then cranked it open.

"Hey!" Marta exclaimed. "I said there are children here. It's freezing outside."

"Just a sec," Ilena said, holding up her hand. "I
think I see something. Let me out, John." John slid
open the side door and got out. Ilena pushed the
back of his seat forward and followed him. The icy
air filled the van, causing Amelia and Marta to
shudder.

"Close that," Marta ordered. John reached in
for his coat before sliding the door closed.

"What's up?" he asked Ilena.

"I'm not sure." She pointed across the road toward the woods. "I saw . . . it looked like a house.
Maybe just shadows. The moon. I've got boots on.
Let me have a look. Like Andy said, maybe we can
get directions."

"Or make a phone call. It's getting late."

As Ilena started to trudge through the virgin
snow to cross the road, Andy, who also had boots
on, got out and followed her. John, who was wearing wing-tips, got back into the van.

"What's going on?" Reggie asked him.

"Ilena said she saw a house or something."

"Ain't nothin' here but trees and snow," Reggie
muttered aloud. "Waste of time."

"Well, maybe there's something. We can get directions or make a call . . ."

"The only direction I want is back down this
godforsaken mountain."

* * *

Ilena reached the edge of the road and stared into the woods. Andy came up next to her. She squinted and turned her head sideways.

"Using the rods?" Andy remarked, remembering how in AIT, Advanced Infantry Training, they were taught to do that at night. It allowed light to better reach the retina's rods that were on the circumference of the rear of the eye and more sensitive to light.

"Yes," Ilena confirmed. Then she pointed. "There! To the left, past that large pine. Isn't that a cabin?" Andy followed the direction of her finger but saw nothing.

"I don't see it," he told her. She got down on her knees for a better angle. The moon went behind a cloud.

"Darn it. Now I can't see it," she said. "But it sure looked like a cabin. Moon's gone, and the wind's blowing the snow around again. Hard to see." They heard a door slam as Reggie got out of the van and crossed the road to join them.

"What's going on?" he asked.

"I saw something. Maybe a cabin," Ilena answered, standing up and brushing the snow from her desert camouflage fatigue jacket. The incongruity of that action in the snowy setting was not lost on the two men.

"You see it?" Reggie asked Andy.

"Can't say that I did."

"It's the moon, blowing snow, the trees. . . . It'll play tricks on you. Make you see what you want to see."

"Maybe we should check it out, bro," Andy told Reggie. *Bro?* Reggie thought. He instinctively reacted negatively until his memories caught up to him. Long ago . . . Vietnam. A sign of camaraderie. Andy noticed the look on Reggie's face.

"Old habit . . . You know?" Andy said. "Haven't used it much since . . ."

"Yeah, bro." Reggie nodded. He slapped Andy gently on the shoulder. "Me neither." Andy smiled and put his fist forward. Reggie made a fist and touched Andy's. The Dap—an unwritten ritual of brothers in war, now resurrected by these two combat veterans in a time of stress.

"I'm going in there to have a look," Ilena told them.

"What's up?" John yelled from his window. "We're burning gas here." Andy went back to the van while Ilena and Reggie moved closer to the woods.

"There may be a cabin down there, folks. We're gonna' have a look. Lisa? You have that flashlight?"

"The glove compartment," she told him. Andy opened the front door. Amelia had already taken the flashlight out. She handed it to him, saying, "Be careful."

Andy joined Reggie and Ilena at the forest's edge. "I've got the flashlight."

"Okay, troop," Andy said. "Let's do it."

"You guys are nuts. I'm going back to the van," Reggie told them as he pulled up the collar on his down jacket. "Make it fast. We've gotta find another road to Asheville."

Ilena turned on the flashlight, shining its narrow beam ahead. She led. Andy followed into the snowy woods.

"Hey, bro," Reggie shouted after them. "While

you two play Daniel Boone, I'm turnin' us around. I want to see my grandkids tonight."

Reggie got back in the van, started the engine, and pulled forward. He then turned as far left as he dared.

"Is there anything out there?" Lisa asked.

"Yeah. Blowin' snow, shadows, and two crazy people."

"But we have to wait for them," Amelia chided.

"You think I'm gonna leave them?" Reggie asked.

"Then where are you going?"

"Just saving us some time and turning around. They won't find anything. It's time to get off this road to nowhere." Reggie carefully started to back up. He saw that he would have to make a double K-turn on the narrow, snow-covered road.

The moon came out from behind a large cloud as Ilena and Andy made their way cautiously through the knee-deep snow. Its silver light filtered through the tall pines, illuminating the spaces between the trees and brush. The going was difficult. From time to time, their boots got caught in roots or branches hidden beneath the deep snow. Ilena was in great physical shape. Andy, who was over sixty, kept up, but it was a strain. At that moment he was thankful he exercised regularly and jogged five miles twice a week.

The woods had a pristine, almost primeval feeling. Both Ilena and Andy had the sense that they might have been the first humans to ever pass this way. It might have been colonial times and they were trappers in search of valuable beaver pelts. Ilena imagined savage Algonquin or her own ancestors, the friendlier Cherokee, lurking beyond the flashlight's edge. The gusting wind had stopped for the moment, no longer whistling through the treetops. Neither spoke. An owl hooted.

"What's that?" Andy, the city dweller, asked.

"An owl on the hunt," Ilena answered, remembering what her grandfather, a Cherokee tribal leader, had taught her. As she trudged along, she reminisced about the anger the old man felt toward white men for driving his people far to the west. The Trail of Tears it was called. They took the land promised to the Cherokee. Broken treaties. Many died. The federal government did nothing. And then she recalled why Comfort Mountain had sounded familiar to her. Her grandfather told her that once there was an orphanage for Cherokee children on Comfort Mountain. "There was no comfort for our people there," he had told her.

Her reverie was interrupted by something moving to her left. Instinct told her not to turn toward it too quickly. She heard Andy breathing heavily behind her as he pulled himself over a large, fallen, snow-covered tree trunk. She slowed to allow him to catch up, and while she did, her eyes lifted slowly to the left where she caught a fleeting glimpse of what appeared to be two animals. Dogs? Or wolves? Wolves? She had heard somewhere that they had reintroduced red wolves into North Carolina, but that was in the eastern part of the state. Was it possible they had come this far west already?

"Hey!" Andy exclaimed, excited. "What's that?" He was pointing off to the left through a copse of tall pines. Ilena turned the light in that direction.

The shape she had seen from the road took form. It was a structure. An old log cabin. It was dark. No sign of any inhabitants.

"Yes!" she cried. "A cabin!"

"Yeah. I see it," Andy said as he came up next to her. "You were right. Let's go." Spurred on by the vision of shelter, they both moved quickly through the snow into a small clearing beyond the pines.

It was, in fact, a log cabin—something out of history. It was square, with two porches, front and back, and two chimneys.

Up on the road, Reggie was making his third attempt to turn the van around. He was having difficulty sensing the edge of the road, because the forest came right up to it, and there appeared to be a deep ditch along both sides. He was getting frustrated.

Ilena shined the flashlight along the front of the cabin. The logs were roughly hewn, the spaces between packed with dried mud and straw. The roof was made of hand-cut cedar shakes. The two field-stone chimneys on either end of the roof thrust up toward the open, starry sky. Someone had cut a lot of trees to make this cabin and clearing. Someone who knew what he was doing. Two rippled-glass windows in front were dark, eerily reflecting moonlight.

"Hello," Ilena called out.

"Anybody home?" Andy added. Their greeting was met by total silence.

"You think anyone lives here?" Ilena asked as

she aimed the flashlight at a stack of logs piled on one side of the front porch. An old ax, reflecting the flashlight's beam, was buried in one of the logs. Andy and Ilena stepped closer to the front door of the cabin.

"Hello! Hello!" they both shouted. No one stirred inside. No one answered. Ilena cautiously stepped up onto the porch. Andy followed. The timber boards beneath their feet creaked.

"Hello," Andy called out again as he knocked on the door. It was made of the same planking as the porch. His knock caused the windowpanes to rattle. He stepped to the side of the door and gently pushed Ilena back behind him. Who knows what kind of reception they might get? A shotgun? After all, they were in what might have once been described as hillbilly country. The wind began to gust again. Ilena shined the light past the porch around the edge of the cabin.

"There!" she exclaimed. "It looks like tracks." Ilena pointed out trails in the snow leading from the woods to the cabin, and then away.

"People? Or dogs, you think?" Andy asked.

"Or maybe wolves," Ilena said. "I, uh—" Just as she was about to tell him what she had seen in the woods they heard the frantic spinning of the van's tires and chains in the distance, and then a loud crash that echoed and rattled through the pines.

"That wasn't good," Ilena said.

"We'd better head back now," Andy told her.

CHAPTER 16

GROUNDED

The van slid backward off the road and down a steep embankment. The tires and chains spun wildly as Reggie tried to stop the slide and get back up on the road, but it was impossible. The van kept sliding into the snow-filled ditch alongside the road, gathering speed. It then bumped up against the trunk of a huge Norway spruce and settled in the heavy snow. Reggie shifted into low gear and gunned the motor. The wheels and chains spun, digging deeper into snow and mud beneath. The van was stuck up to the middle of the tires.

Andy and Ilena arrived breathless from running through the snowy forest.

"Stop gunning it," Andy shouted, immediately assessing the situation. "You're only making it worse." Reggie, frustrated, angry, and ashamed, took his foot off the gas pedal and gripping the wheel, stared straight ahead. Lisa got out of the van and opened the front door to help Amelia. John remained inside trying to calm Marta, who was panicked.

"Are you out of your mind?!" she screamed at Reggie. "You could have crushed my children!"

"They're okay," John told her. "Let's get you all out of there."

Ilena rushed to help John while Andy tried to open the rear hatch of the microbus. But it was jammed against the tree and badly dented. Fortunately, the window had not shattered. He could see Nancy and Ronny inside. They were pale and frightened, more from their mother's screaming than from the accident. They were not hurt. Andy shook his head, realizing that they were now marooned. There was no way to get the van out onto the road. Picturing the map, he estimated they were at least fifteen miles from the nearest service station. Their cell phones were useless in these mountains. Their only hope was that there might be a phone or radio in the cabin. Thinking better of alarming the others, he turned his attention to getting everyone out of the van safely.

"The kids are stuck in there," Ilena announced as she backed out of the side door. "Marta won't come out without them."

Reggie left the motor running and the lights on and got out on the driver's side. He opened the door next to Marta. "I'm sorry," he said. "But you've got to calm down and help us get the kids out." He took Marta's arm and gently but firmly pulled her out of the van.

"It's your fault," she said, calming a little. "No one asked you to turn around."

"I said I'm sorry," Reggie told her. "Chewing me out isn't gonna get anything done." Inside the van, John was able to pull away the rear seat. He lifted Ronny and passed him out the other side door to

Ilena. Then he helped Nancy get over the seat and passed her to Andy.

Meanwhile, Lisa had helped Amelia up onto the road. The two women watched as John and Reggie carried the children up the embankment.

"Let's all get up on the road," Andy suggested. "Leave the motor running and the light on. We've got something to tell you all." He and Ilena then slipped their arms under Marta's and guided her up to the road.

The wind was gusting again, swirling snow crystals around the huddled group, coating their clothing, hair, and faces until they looked like they had walked through a bath of confectionary sugar. It was well below freezing. The moon was out again. Its light outlined the forest and mountains around them against a cloudless, starry winter sky.

Before Andy and Ilena spoke, the mood on the road was somber. Like an infectious disease carried by a single host, panic had spread through the group. Nervous glances were cast at the towering, snow-covered mountains surrounding them; the bitter cold and the disabled van were all very disturbing and disheartening. What had started out as a happy surprise, a way home for Christmas Eve, had turned into what appeared to be a serious blunder. The recriminatory looks that Marta and John threw toward Reggie stoked anger and fear. They were isolated in the middle of nowhere with neither food nor water.

Nancy and Ronny huddled in the midst of the group while Andy and Ilena described the cabin as a place they could find shelter and warmth. A palpable wave of relief surged through the shivering circle.

"Thank God," Marta said aloud, summing up how they all felt at that moment. "I'm sorry, Ilena. I was . . . . I mean, what I said before about you seeing something in the woods. I feel like a fool. Now we're all going to be okay, right?"

Andy glanced at Ilena and Reggie. An unspoken thought passed between the three of them. They knew it was they who would take responsibility for bringing the others through this night safely. The best of what Andy and Reggie had learned about themselves those many years ago in Vietnam was part of a long line that now led to Ilena and what she had recently learned about herself. The commitment to helping others survive was a reflex that once learned and practiced under fire never left.

"The cabin's through there," Andy said, pointing where he and Ilena had emerged from the woods. "Like we said, no one was home. We didn't get a chance to look inside, but there's no telephone or electric line."

"There could be propane around back. Maybe a generator," Ilena added.

"Maybe he's got a radio or something," Reggie suggested. All three took a positive tone.

"Right," Andy confirmed. "But, if worse comes to worse, and we can't get a wrecker up here tonight, we'll have a place to be warm and dry and figure things out by morning."

"We'd best get moving before someone gets hypothermia," Ilena suggested. "It's going to be one very cold night."

CHAPTER 17

DARK AND DEEP AND COLD

Reggie looked at the van, sizing up how much luggage there was tied on top. "Let's get everyone down to the cabin first. Then a few of us can come back for the luggage," he suggested. "I'll shut off the engine." He didn't wait for approval, but slid down the embankment and went to the van. He turned off the lights and motor. Ilena clicked on the flashlight so he could see his way back to the road, where they all waited. Once their eyes adjusted to the night, and the moonlight, it was bright enough to see fairly well.

Andy led the way. Lisa, with Amelia holding on to her arm, followed him. John was next. He carried Ronny with the boy's legs astride his shoulders. Marta walked alone behind them. Reggie carried Nancy on his shoulders, much to the girl's chagrin. She had initially objected, but relented when she saw how deep the snow was in the woods. Ilena took up the rear position so as to observe everyone and help anyone who might fall behind. She was also keenly aware that she had seen something before—shadows or animals? Maybe wolves? She wasn't sure. Her instincts, sharpened by her military training and service under fire, kept her sharp and on guard just as though she were on a dangerous patrol.

Andy guided the group through the footsteps Ilena and he had made earlier when they heard the car crash and ran to the road. It was a direction toward the cabin, but not much of a path. However, it made the going a bit easier than if they had had to trek through totally virgin snow.

The yellow glow from the flashlight was overwhelmed by the silver moonlight that filtered through the tall trees and reflected off the snow. It served more as a beacon for the travelers than as illumination of their path.

There was no wind down on the forest floor, just a murmur of it high above in the treetops. The only other sound was the crunching of shoes and boots on snow, and some heavy breathing as they trudged along. It was, from the moment they entered the woods, tough going. In some places the snow was more than two feet deep. It covered fallen tree trunks and thick brush. Marta was thankful that there were strong men to carry her children. Ahead, somewhere in the dark unknown, was the promise of shelter and a warm fire.

As they passed through an opening in the trees, the moonlight was stronger. Lisa felt Amelia squeeze her hand. The older woman smiled at her new friend, grateful for her strong arm. But she was feeling the cold and a slight fluttering in her chest from the exertion of walking. Lisa sensed they were moving too fast for Amelia.

"Could you slow it down a bit, Andy?" she asked. Andy stopped and looked back. Lisa tilted her head slightly toward Amelia, indicating the older woman was tiring. Andy understood. He nodded and continued on at a slower pace.

From his vantage point on John's shoulders, Ronny had a good view ahead and around the small column. The forest was thick here. The moon cast long, dark shadows that fed the boy's imagination. He tightened his grip on John's neck and fought to control his fear. John, who aside from Ronny, carried Marta's heavy purse slung over his shoulder, felt ice crystals forcing their way between his wet socks and wing-tip shoes. The ice caused his toes to tingle. The bottoms of his feet were numb. Christmas Eve. Comfort Mountain would not be a comfort, he thought, if frostbite invaded his feet. Like Ronny, he peered ahead, hoping for a sight of the cabin.

Ilena scanned the woods behind her and again thought she saw something move in the shadows. She turned back and looked ahead, carefully counting her steps; one, two, three, four—then spin and look. Yes! There was something back there. Two or three distinct forms that had crouched low to the ground when she turned. Wolves? Perhaps coyotes or wild dogs. *No reason to alarm anyone,* she thought to herself. Her eyes scanned the path being made by the five adults ahead of her as she sought a fallen tree limb she might use to drive the animals away should they be hungry and bold enough to attack. The idea of seeking a weapon caused her thoughts to flash back to Iraq and her company and comrades, who, at the moment, were in a far different climate both physically and mentally. She felt a pang of guilt, and at the same time relief, that she was cold, alert, and in control; not hot, tired, and the target of an unseen, unknown enemy. She wished she had her M16 with her, or the nine-millimeter she strapped to her thigh.

As Andy led onward, he tried to remember how far away the cabin was from the road. Ilena and he had run to the road when they heard the truck, fearful that something terrible had happened. They had been walking about ten minutes now. It seemed too far, but they were walking slowly. His army training, though it had taken place long ago, had kicked in, and he had made note of a few markers as they ran—a fallen tree, a pile of brush, three cedars close together. It was as though they were on patrol. Ilena must have done that, too, but she was too far back to ask. He wondered if Reggie was also marking terrain.

The relief that Marta had felt on the road was now gone. The woods, deep snow, frigid tempera-ture, and silent strangers caused a welling up of nearly incapacitating fear. What if it snowed more and they were trapped in the cabin without food? How could they get help? They might be missed, but no one had given the license plate of the van or Lisa's name when they'd called home from the airport. What if the people who lived in the cabin were inhospitable, or worse? There were stories of mountain men, hermits, and moonshiners who detested strangers. What might they do to her chil-dren? Her ramblings were disturbing. *Maybe I'm be-ginning to freeze,* she thought. Her Uggs, worn thin, purchased more for style than protection, were in-adequate. Her feet were nearly numb. Her hands were ice-cold in her thin leather gloves. She glanced back at her children. At least they were in strong, caring hands. Ronny rode on John's shoulders as though he were on a camel. And Reggie was a big man. He would take care of Nancy. *What a mess,* she thought, almost blurting the words out in fear and frustration. *What the hell am I doing here?* And then, out of the silence, Ronny spoke the classic child's question that everyone heard.

"Are we there yet?" It brought a smile to Reggie's half-frozen lips. Ice had formed on that part of his moustache and beard around his mouth.

"Almost," Andy shouted back. He stopped and looked back at Ilena, spreading his arms questioningly. "At least I think so." She waved and nodded in the affirmative. He then zeroed in on Amelia and Marta and knew they had to get to shelter soon. The two women were not physically prepared for this situation. He also noted that John was limping slightly, favoring his right leg. Andy had on winter boots, as did Reggie, Lisa, and Ilena. But John, Amelia, Marta, and the children were not dressed, or in shape, for an arduous winter hike. Perspiration would dampen their undergarments first, then their clothes, pasting them to their backs and armpits. A few were already shivering and must also feel tingling and pain in their toes and fingers. He felt he had taken on responsibility for the group, and he was now worried about frostbite, or worse.

"May we stop a moment?" Amelia asked. Andy turned to see that Amelia's cheeks were flushed and she was breathing rapidly. "I'm not used to all, all this, uh, hiking. And I think Lisa needs a rest, too. She's been half carrying me."

"Of course," Andy said. He held up his hand. "Let's take a short break, everyone." John lifted Ronny from his shoulders, grateful for the rest. Reggie did the same with Nancy, although he could have gone on longer without stopping.

"A little rest sounds good," Marta said. "A fire would be better."

"Soon," Andy promised. Marta spied a fallen tree and sat down on the snow-covered trunk. Ronny and Nancy joined her. She wrapped her arms around them, gathering them tightly against her coat. For a long moment, everyone was quiet, absorbed in their private thoughts about their situation. Andy came back to the group, holding the flashlight.

"How's everyone doing on our little hike?" he asked, trying to strike a cheerful note.

"My feet are numb," Marta complained, "and the children are shivering."

"It isn't far," Andy assured her. He noticed that Ilena had picked up a sturdy birch limb and was staring out into the woods behind them. Her vigilance was also noted by Reggie. The two men exchanged a quick glance. Ilena noticed them and gestured that it was time to get moving. "Everyone ready to go?" Andy's question was more of a command.

John, Ilena, and Lisa said "yes" in unison.

Marta released the children. Reggie lifted Nancy onto his shoulders again, and John took Ronny on his. Some feeling had returned to his toes, but he said nothing about them. Andy moved to the front of the column. His flashlight danced across the snow before them.

"Okay, then," Andy called out. "Let's move. It's not too far now." He tried to give his voice as much authority as he could muster, and sensing they had to get to shelter soon, Andy's pace was quicker than before. Everyone followed without complaint. He crested a low rise with some difficulty and then slowed to allow the others time to transit the slope. He clutched the trunk of a young cedar. Its burden of snow fell on him while he caught his breath. As he brushed it away from his face he saw the cabin ahead.

"There," he shouted over his shoulder. "There it is!" The others arrived and clustered behind him, staring down at the dark shape in the clearing, forcing their eyes to focus and confirm that this structure was indeed real. Andy shone the flashlight toward the old cabin. The beam fluttered on it as his hands shook from the cold. "There it is. Shelter!"

CHAPTER 18

A QUESTION OF SURVIVAL

Andy led the way down to the cabin. Propelled by reserves of strength they could not imagine they had, everyone moved quickly at the prospect of getting out of the cold. Adrenaline worked its wonders. They approached, still in a column, down the hill and into the clearing with frozen cheeks, numb faces, leaden feet, and unfeeling toes.

The path that Andy and Ilena had made earlier was wider here and more defined. John lifted Ronny from his shoulders again and set him down, as much to stretch the boy's legs as to allow John to help support Marta, who was nearly exhausted. Reggie saw what John did and put Nancy down, too. She started ahead to join John and help her mother, but paused and smiled a "Thank you" to Reggie. *That girl has spunk,* Reggie thought, as she trotted away.

Once they were all in the clearing, Ilena checked behind, scanning the woods. The animals were not apparent. She caught up to Reggie. He put his arm on her shoulder.

"Never should have doubted you, trooper," he told her.

"Doubted me?"

"The cabin."

She smiled. "A lucky guess. I was just looking in the right direction at the right time."

"Whatever," he said. "Don't matter. There it is."

Ilena smiled at him again and walked ahead. Ronny and Nancy were with their mother, who had her arm entwined with John's.

"Everyone okay?" Ilena asked.

"Yes," John said, speaking for all. Ilena moved on to Amelia and Lisa.

"Thank you for helping an old lady, dear," Amelia was telling Lisa as Ilena arrived. "You know, there was a time when my husband and I would hike these mountains—rain, shine, or snow."

"Well, as far as I'm concerned, you can still do it, Amelia," Lisa told the older woman. Amelia smiled and nodded, then took Lisa's hand, patted it, and drew it to her breast. Ilena was touched and almost teary. She moved past them and caught up with Andy, who was about thirty yards from the cabin.

"Well done, Andy," she told him. "You homed in like an airborne pathfinder."

"Yeah, well, like I told you, I trained with the Tenth Mountain Division."

"I suggest we check this place out before we all go barging in," Ilena said. "Maybe someone came home while we were gone." Andy nodded and raised his hand to the others.

"Hang on a minute," he shouted to them. They all stopped, clustered together fifteen yards away in the clearing. There was no wind in the clearing, and with shelter in sight, no one was concentrating on the cold anymore. "Okay. Let's do it," Andy told Ilena.

They both walked quickly to the cabin and climbed onto the porch. It creaked loudly into the silent night. The cabin was still dark and silent. Ilena now noticed that the small windows were old, rippled glass. Andy knocked. No answer.

"Anyone home?" he called out. No response. He tried the door. It was not locked, but he didn't open it. "How about you go around back while I go in here?" he suggested.

"Sounds like a plan," Ilena said. She walked down to the end of the porch, stepped off, turned left, and disappeared from view. Andy opened the door slowly and went inside.

The group listened to the sound of Andy's boots crossing a wooden floor. They heard a door open from behind the cabin. Ilena was inside, too.

"That you, Ilena?" They heard Andy ask, but there was no audible answer, just silence, and more creaking sounds. The yellow beam of the flashlight flickered through the rippled-glass windows. Finally Andy emerged at the cabin door with an old kerosene lantern in hand.

"Nobody's home," he called out. "There are some old lamps. Anyone have a match?"

"I do," Reggie called out. He fished a vintage Zippo out of his pants pocket as he walked to the porch. The rest of the group followed. Andy held the lamp while Reggie lit the wick. The rest of the group filed past and into the cabin, where Ilena stood with the flashlight.

"There's no wood inside," Andy told Reggie.

"Ilena found some split wood out back, but it's wet."

"We've got to get a fire going. The women and kids—"

"Yeah. I know. There's some old wooden furniture in there. We can break it up and maybe dry out some of the splits."

It was cold inside the dark cabin. Andy brought the lamp in and set it down on a rough-hewn table near the fireplace. Ilena put two more empty kerosene lamps on it.

"There's an outhouse in back," she said, "and what looks like a smokehouse. Before we start breaking up the furniture, maybe there's something dry we can burn out there."

"I'll go with you," Reggie volunteered. They took the flashlight and left.

CHAPTER 19

THE CABIN

Lisa's eyes darted around the cabin. She spotted an old white blanket with a broad red stripe down its center, thrown over the back of a wooden chair. She took it and wrapped it around Amelia, who was shivering.

"Oh, thank you, dear heart," Amelia said as she collapsed into a rocker near the empty fireplace. Marta pulled a low wooden bench from against the wall and sat Ronny and Nancy down. She began to remove their wet shoes and socks. Both children shivered reflexively. John, who had begun to explore the room, spied another old, worn blanket and gave it to Marta to wrap around the kids' feet.

"If we rub their feet, it'll get the circulation going," he told Marta. "You kids huddle together to get warm." Nancy put her arm around her brother.

"Mom," Ronny complained.

"Ronny! This is serious. Do what the man said."

"All right," he said reluctantly.

"I don't like it any better than you do," Nancy

told her brother. But the love and concern in her voice was obvious. John winked at her, and Nancy smiled back.

"I'm going to take the lamp for a minute," Andy said. "There's a small room in back. I want to check it out." He moved away, leaving the rest of the group in semidarkness. Moonlight filtered through the small windows.

"If we burn the furniture, how long can that last?" Marta asked. "And what about food?" She was now shivering herself, and her tone of voice frightened the children.

"Are we going to die, Mommy?" Ronny asked.

"Of course not, child," Amelia answered before Marta could. "We're going to be just fine."

On the way to check the outhouse and smokehouse, Ilena and Reggie double-checked the pile of splits on the back porch. They were, as Ilena had originally reported, very wet. But they did discover a large ax and a smaller one behind the pile.

The outhouse offered nothing to burn except itself. The wood inside was dry. It was obvious that it had not been used in a very long time. They felt better about the dry-wood situation.

"I think we might have use for this place," Ilena suggested, "so before we chop it up let's examine all our options." Reggie agreed, and they moved on to the smokehouse.

The back room of the cabin was much smaller than the main room. There was a fieldstone fireplace, smaller than the one in the main room, but quite ample. It had an iron spit setup. Andy surmised it was used for cooking because it was close to the kitchen and the rear porch. The best part of the fireplace was a canvas set off to the right side. It was brown, like the log walls, and in the yellow light of the kerosene lamp, Andy almost missed it. He went to it and pulled it aside. Underneath was a stack of dry splits that was more than enough to get a good fire going.

The bed was simple, with no headboard—just two large duck-down pillows leaning against the wall. A threadbare quilt covered the bed. Andy peeled back the quilt and saw there was a coarse white sheet covering a thin horsehair mattress. There were no bureaus or chests. A nightstand stood next to the right side of the bed. A small window was above it. No clothing hung from four wooden pegs behind the bedroom door. It felt as though no one had slept here for a long time, and that made him uneasy.

They had been outside the cabin for about ten minutes, and as they trudged from the outhouse to the smokehouse, Ilena and Reggie were acutely aware that the temperature had dropped considerably.

"We've got to organize things," Reggie said aloud, but as though he was talking to himself.

"For sure," Ilena responded. "I was thinking the same thing. We're going to be here for the night. We know we can get some heat going and melt snow for water. But food is the problem."

"Uh huh," Reggie grunted, nodding his agreement.

When they entered the smokehouse, they felt as though they had discovered a treasure trove. Several long strips of meat jerky were hung over the smoke pit. Reggie touched and smelled them.

"They're good," he said, smiling. Ilena was at the far side of the diminutive shed on her knees.

"Bring the flashlight over here," she said. Reggie turned the now fading beam toward her as he walked. He saw her lift open a small door in the floor of the smokehouse.

"What have you got?"

"Something good, I hope. Shine that light in here." Reggie aimed the beam down. The open door revealed a small root cellar. Inside were a basket of carrots and beets and a sack of potatoes.

"It's not your complete Christmas Eve dinner," Ilena said, "but it sure looks like we have some of the fixings."

Andy returned to the main room with three logs under his arm. He set the lantern down on the table. For the first time he took notice that all the furniture was simple, practical, and handmade.

"I found some dry wood," he said as he placed the splits next to the fireplace. "Now we need kindling or paper. There wasn't any back there."

"I'll check out the rest of this room," John offered as he picked up the lantern.

The children had stopped shivering. Marta had not. Amelia was still in the rocker and cold. Lisa hovered nearby, concerned about the older woman having hypothermia.

"Andy? Maybe we should start to bring the luggage down from the van," she suggested. He was kneeling in front of the fireplace, poking into it with a log.

"As soon as Reggie and Ilena get back," he told her. "But right now we need a fire."

John, who had removed his wet shoes and socks,

made his way across the room to what appeared to be a kitchen area. He was still very cold. His wet suit pants clung to his legs. The planked floor was rough. He proceeded cautiously to avoid getting splinters in his feet.

The kitchen was tucked into a corner of the room. It had an oak-plank table, perhaps five feet long, with six simple three-legged pine stools around it. A cast-iron sink was set into a wooden counter. There was no sign of a pump or faucets. If they wanted water it would have to be drawn from the stream they had heard flowing behind the cabin. John held the lamp higher and moved farther into the kitchen area. There was a cast iron, wood-burning stove with two large openings on top for pots and a narrow side oven for baking. Two cabinets set against the wall drew his attention. He opened them to find they contained an eclectic collection of plates, cups, saucers, utensils, and pots.

"I could use that lantern, John," Andy called from across the room. "I don't know how long the kerosene will last, and I can use it to start the fire."

"Okay," John said. But just as he turned to go back to the fireplace he noticed a brass handle and a narrow door next to the farthest cabinet. "Just a sec," he told Andy. Holding the lantern high, John opened the door and poked the lantern inside. The yellow light from the flickering wick revealed a small pantry. In it was a sack of flour, a smaller one of salt, three mason jars filled with blackberry preserves, a large jar of lard, a tin of coffee, and one filled to the brim with tea. Behind the tins was a bag of sugar. He went into the pantry.

In the far corner the lamplight revealed a package of dry kindling wrapped up with hemp. Next to it were several splits of wood. They were cut in half; probably meant for the stove. And next to that was a small barrel with the magic word *Kerosene* painted on its side. John felt as though he had won the lottery. As he was about to announce his wonderful find, he heard the rear door of the cabin fly open. Reggie and Ilena were back.

"Hey, everyone!" Ilena's excited voice cried out. "We've got wood and food!"

"Me too," was all John could think to say. "Me too!"

CHAPTER 20

SETTLING IN

The fire warmed their bodies and spirits. Three more kerosene lamps had been lit; their glow joined the yellow firelight to illuminate the cabin's main room. What had initially looked like a cold, dark, and perhaps dangerous night ahead, now took on a festive spirit. Everyone felt better. Amelia and Marta were warm and comfortable. They were in the kitchen sorting out the food and planning a meal.

The children's clothes had dried quickly. They were settled close to the fire with their Game Boys. John was also there, warming his feet while waiting for Lisa, Andy, and Reggie to bring the luggage down from the van. At first they thought John might have frostbite on two of his toes, but Ilena was able to get circulation going in them. They were slightly swollen but did not show any tissue changes. His socks and shoes were near the fire drying.

Andy, Reggie, and Lisa, who had all been dressed

for winter, were on their way back from the van with the luggage. Ilena had told them about the animals she thought she saw, but the trio did not see anything on their way to the van, or now, as they made their way back to the cabin with the luggage.

Ilena had found two wooden buckets on the rear porch that were perfect for hauling water up from the stream. She carefully made her way down a slope in the clearing behind the smokehouse and into the woods. The gurgling of the stream grew louder as the slope's angle grew steeper. The snow in that part of the woods was not too deep, and there appeared to be a deer path down to the stream. Then she saw it in the moonlight. It was only five or six feet wide and flowing nicely. Ice had formed along the banks. There was a clear spot in front of her where the ice had been kicked out. Deer, she guessed. She made her way to the bank and proceeded to fill the first bucket. The water was clear and cold. When the bucket was full, she set it down and took off her glove. Cupping her hand, she dipped it into the stream and tasted it. It was delicious. She took several more sips, realizing she was very thirsty. *So must everyone else be,* she thought and turned to get the other bucket. Her eyes were immediately drawn to the woods behind her where three red wolves were standing and staring at her. One was large, perhaps sixty pounds; the other two were smaller. Probably females. They did not seem to be threatening. So the story about reintroducing them to these mountains was true. *That was a good thing,* she thought. Ilena then recalled her grandfather's lesson about wolves. His voice, strong and clear, came back to her.

"The wolf is our brother. The white man fears him, as once he feared us. His answer to fear is to kill. As he killed so many of us, he killed the wolf, too. Never fear the wolf. Treat him with respect and share the forest. He hunts the deer and raccoon, not the people. Bow to him, Granddaughter; greet him softly, and he will let you pass."

Ilena bowed slowly to the wolves. They did not move. The large one, the male, tilted his head with curiosity, not aggression. She took the second bucket and filled it.

"Thank you for sharing your water," she told them softly. She picked up both buckets and walked back up the slope. The wolves held their ground but gave no sign of attack. As she passed within fifteen yards of them, she stopped and bowed again. "Merry Christmas, my sisters and brothers. Good hunting to you." Then she moved on, back toward the cabin. Off to her right, in a thicker part of the woods something else moved. It was larger, darker, and slower than a wolf. A bear? She quickened her pace up the hill toward the clearing, glancing once behind. She saw nothing but felt the stare of strong, benign eyes in the middle of her shoulder blades.

Lisa walked behind Reggie and Andy. They were carrying the heavier luggage—two pieces each and the children's knapsacks. She had Ilena's duffel and Amelia's suitcase.

"Uh, listen, man," Reggie finally said to Andy after a long silence. He had been forming the thought in his mind for some time. "I'm real sorry about the van. I lost the edge of the road. Thought the chains would hold, and then—"

"Forget it," Andy interrupted. "Ain't no thing."

"Ain't no thing?" Reggie laughed. "Ain't no thing. You spent some time with the brothers, huh?"

"Only reason I got back to the world," Andy told him. "Everybody was brothers."

Reggie set down a suitcase and reached out a clenched fist. "You got that right."

Andy did likewise. They tapped fists three times. The conversation, and what seemed a fraternity or Masonic secret handshake, caused Lisa, who had heard the conversation, to smile. They obviously shared an understanding blocked to her, but their smiles and sense of camaraderie as they took up their burdens and continued the trek toward the cabin was clear.

Several of the wet splits that had been out on the front porch were now drying near the fire. John had taken charge of them, turning them every ten minutes.

"I'm going to get a fire going in the bedroom," John announced. Reggie grabbed a few splits and some kindling to help him.

"Take some kerosene from the pantry to give it a boost," Ilena suggested. She had not mentioned the wolves, or the other "something" she had seen outside.

"I'll bring some more of those wet splits in," Andy offered. Ilena got up and joined him. "Listen, everyone," Andy said, getting their attention. "I know we haven't talked about this, but it's possible someone still lives here."

"Not for a long while," Ilena said. "My guess is

that this is a hunting cabin or a getaway for some city folks."

"Or an artist or writer," Amelia added. "A lot of them have places like this to find peace and quiet to do their work."

"Well, whatever," Andy continued, "I think we should treat it with respect and leave it as we found it."

"Of course," Lisa said. "Why would we do otherwise?"

"I don't mean we would," Andy answered. "But we are using a lot of what's here. I'm concerned that if someone is planning to come here, say next week, thinking he has supplies and fuel and . . . well, I think maybe after we get the van out and get back to civilization we should consider coming back with some stuff to leave here . . . to sort of replace what we took."

"That's a great idea," John said. Everyone agreed.

A little while later, as the children napped on the bed quilt that Marta had folded and laid down near the fire, Lisa, Amelia, and Marta made progress with dinner.

"I was a cook in a lumber camp once," Lisa said as she peeled potatoes over the sink. She bent down to stoke the fire in the stove.

"You were?" Amelia asked.

"Oh, yes. Well, assistant cook, anyway. Near Bryson City one summer. That's west of Asheville. Hardwood lumber for furniture."

"Yes, I know, dear," Amelia said. "We make some very fine furniture in Asheville." She looked around the cabin. "But everything here looks homemade, now, doesn't it?" The women looked around at the cabin's furnishings and agreed. It was all quite primitive. Definitely handmade. And old, very old. Without saying it, they all wondered about the people who had made it and where they might be.

It was a little after ten o'clock. The children slept. Andy and Ilena went outside to get more of the wet wood and try to split it. John and Reggie were in the bedroom getting a good fire going. And Marta and Lisa were preparing a modest dinner of potato, carrot, and beet soup while Amelia rolled some flour and lard into a batter for bread. They would have the blackberry preserves for dessert.

CHAPTER 21

DRAWN TOGETHER AND APART

The luggage was stacked along one wall of the cabin. Bags were open, and clothing more suitable to the circumstances had been extracted. Some of the clothing had gotten damp while on top of the van and in transit down to the cabin. Ilena had found a fishing pole in a corner of the front porch. She stripped some line from the reel and fashioned a clothesline near the fireplace in the bedroom, where John and Reggie had a nice fire going. The room had become toasty warm, and the damp clothing dried quickly. Andy noticed Amelia, Marta, and Lisa were busy in the kitchen.

"How goes it, ladies?" he asked.

"No one will go to bed hungry tonight," Amelia answered. "Just a little while longer."

"That's right," Lisa added with a grin. "It may not be the best Christmas Eve dinner you've ever had, but I guarantee it will be memorable."

John was wondering how it would be to spend the night with this group of strangers. There were three men, four women, and two kids. He felt awkward about bringing it up now. As if he were prescient, Andy spoke out again.

"We'll sort out the sleeping arrangements later," he said and went to the hearth and rubbed his hands. "Man, that fire sure feels good."

"Yeah," Reggie agreed. He walked stiffly across the room and put on his jacket. "We've got two fires going now. It's freezing out there. I'm gonna make sure we got enough wood to get us through the night." He opened the door and stepped out onto the porch. After sitting before the fire with the heat baking his back, he found the cold night air invigorating. Like a teenager sneaking away from his parents to have a forbidden cigarette, Reggie looked around and then slowly reached into his pocket and retrieved an unopened pack he'd purchased at the airport. With his Zippo in one hand, and the cigarettes in the other, he contemplated lighting up. He felt as if Yvonne were watching. That old line he'd heard in church about God seeing all things applied to her. Even if she wasn't around, there were some things, mostly when he strayed from the straight and narrow, that she always knew.

"Yeah, yeah," he muttered, gazing up at the moon and picturing Yvonne. "I know. Five years since I had one." He hesitated, putting together the rationale in his mind, then giving it voice. "Well, it used to be one long, deep drag; watch the smoke rise, and somehow all the pieces of the puzzle come together." He opened the cellophane wrapper, flipped open the box, ripped back the aluminum-foil cover, and felt the cigarette filters beneath his thumb. "I'm a grown man," he rea-

soned to the moon, to her. "A few puffs can't hurt.
I've got to figure out how to make this move to a
new life work. Couple of drags, little communion
with Brother Moon, and maybe I'll make peace
with working for my son." Reggie heard the cabin
door open. It was Andy walking out to join him.

"Need any help?"

"I can handle it. Just takin' a break." Reggie gestured with the pack of cigarettes. "Smoke?"

"Yeah. Lousy habit. I must have quit five or six
times."

"Me too. It's just, uh . . . well, not likely you're
ever going to meet my wife, but, uh, you never saw
this? Okay?"

"Sure. Our little secret. You quit for good, huh?"

"Five years," Reggie said, offering the pack of
cigarettes and Zippo to Andy.

"Five years is good."

"I got past the day-to-day stuff, you know, coffee,
beer, social situations. But well, things are going
on in my life and . . ."

"That's cool," Andy said as he flipped open the
Zippo and lit up. "You don't have to justify anything to me." He took a deep drag.

"Yeah, well, Yvonne, that's my wife, she calls
them coffin nails. Sort of a crusader about it."

"My wife made me quit, too."

"Really?"

"Yeah. I obeyed. She was right. It can kill you."

"There's a lot of things can kill you, as we both
know," Reggie said as he took the cigarettes back.
He took one out and pounded its filter against the
box, packing the tobacco down.

"My wife died six months ago," Andy said softly.
"She never smoked."

"I'm sorry, man."

"We spent a lot of time planning what we were going to do in this time of life, you know?"

"I hear that. Stuff happens, huh?"

"That it does, *amigo*." Andy took another long drag on the cigarette. Reggie watched the orange ember at the end of the butt grow bright.

"Just don't be in a hurry to join her," Reggie said, looking down at the unlit cigarette in his own hand.

"I'm not in a hurry to go anywhere. It's like we were talking about before . . . getting back to The World," Andy said softly. He shrugged. "Like you couldn't wait to get back, and then back wasn't what you thought."

Reggie nodded. "Same old, same old. Just when you think you got it covered, got it all figured out, it changes." He slipped the unlit cigarette back into the pack. He offered it to Andy. "You want these?" Andy smiled and took them. He handed back the Zippo.

"Yvonne, is it? Your wife?"

"Yeah."

"It's like she sent me out here to take these from you."

Reggie cocked his head and looked at Andy. He smiled, for the first time all day. "I don't doubt it, bro. Not for a sec. Man, am I hungry. Let's chop some wood."

Amelia stood over the cast-iron sink. She rested a pewter water pitcher she had found in it.

"I'm ready." Lisa grabbed the one bucket that

still had water and poured some into the pitcher. A few drops fell on Amelia's hand.

"That's cold," she said.

"Ilena said the stream was lovely." Amelia rinsed out the pitcher, and Lisa filled it to the brim. The men had moved the table closer to the fireplace. Lisa carried the water over to the table. Amelia was right behind her with a wooden tray that held a mixture of cups and glasses.

"Here's a nice, cold drink," Lisa announced. Ronny and Nancy were first at the table. They each drank two glasses of water.

The front door opened. Reggie and Andy came in with arms full of newly cut splits. They stacked them near the fireplace. Ilena, who had been stoking the fire and keeping it going, helped spread the wet wood out to dry.

"That should get us through the night," Reggie said. He sat down on the dusty, rough-hewn plank floor and leaned back against the cabin wall. His muscles ached and twitched, unused to the sudden burst of labor splitting logs.

"Are you sure?" Marta asked. Her doubt and moodiness had returned. There was an edge to her voice. Reggie ignored her.

"Not to worry, Marta," Andy assured her. "We won't run out. There's a great big forest outside."

"They'll clear the road by morning," Lisa said, "and then we'll—"

"And then what? What do you know?" Marta said, interrupting with an even more accusatory tone of voice.

Her hostility changed the atmosphere in the room. It got everyone's attention.

"Well, I don't exactly, but—" Lisa began.

"None of us do," Reggie concluded. "But instead of doubting everything, you should be glad Ilena found this place. There's warmth, shelter, water, and food. We'll deal with what we have to do in the morning."

"We wouldn't have to deal with anything if she hadn't come along with her van," Marta said, pointing at Lisa, who had walked back to the kitchen with Amelia. "Some good samaritan she turned out to be."

"You didn't have to come!" Reggie said angrily, getting to his feet. Ronny and Nancy looked up at him, towering above them. They were frightened. Lisa came back out of the kitchen.

"I guess we should complain to our travel agent," Lisa joked. "Hey . . . that's me, huh?"

"That's not funny," Marta said, dismissing Lisa's attempt to defuse the situation. "And you didn't have to wreck the darn thing!" she said defiantly, pointing at Reggie.

"It was an accident, Marta," Andy interjected. He was not happy with the discord she was causing. They were a group of strangers thrown into a dangerous situation in close proximity. "Reggie was only trying to help. Didn't we put all that behind us back on the road?" he asked. Marta sulked and looked away. Amelia, who could see and hear everything from the kitchen, noticed anxiety on the children's faces. The arguments swirling around their mother were disturbing them.

"Well, everybody," Amelia announced as she came into the main room. "I guess we have no choice but to use the facilities, as poor as they might be. But we can refuse to pay at checkout time." She glanced over at the kids, who were confused about the conversation. "Meanwhile, these children look hungry, and dinner is almost ready. How about we stop this bickering and set the table?"

"There's no bathroom, either," Marta complained, ignoring Amelia.

"Good grief, lady," Reggie finally said. "What in the name of . . . What is wrong with you?" His tone of voice frightened the kids again.

"Easy does it," John said. He had hesitated getting into the middle of things, but now, as a parent seeing the kids' fear, he couldn't resist. He, too, didn't want things to spin out of control. They were all under one roof with a common need to survive. That was enough pressure. They were tired. Hungry. Strangers. Disappointed to miss Christmas Eve with their families. Although their lot had improved greatly from the time they left the van, nerves were still on edge. Tempers could erupt.

"I *am* easy," Reggie said. "I told you all I wasn't going to apologize for messing up anymore. She keeps bringing it up. And blaming Lisa. And now complaining there is no toilet. What's next? Complaining there's no hot bath?"

Ilena stepped forward. She gestured toward Ronny and Nancy while she spoke directly to Marta. "Look, Marta. Your kids are safe. We're all dry and warm. There's food in the pantry. This isn't a desert island. We're not shipwrecked. John's right. Arguing isn't going to get us anywhere."

"And who put you in charge?" Marta asked, hands defiantly on hips.

"Marta, please," Andy said calmly as he stepped between the two women.

"I'm only stating the obvious," Marta said.

"What's done is done," Andy told her. "It's history. We're here until morning. Let's make the best of it."

"History? What do you know about it? How can you make the best out of a divor . . . I mean a disaster like this?" Her face turned red as she realized what she was really angry about. Andy gestured toward the children. Marta really looked at them for the first time in several minutes and saw how upset they were. Ronny was kneeling on the floor with his eyes shut. Nancy, also kneeling, had her hand on her brother's shoulder and was tenderly rubbing his back. Marta immediately went to them.

"Ronny?" she said, kneeling beside him. She saw that he was trembling. "Ronny, darling." He opened his eyes.

"I'm scared, Mommy. I'm asking God to help us."

"Are we going to die?" Nancy asked, looking to her mother and then to the ceiling of the cabin as if she could look through it to the object of her own prayers.

"No. Oh no," Marta told her children. She put her arms around them. Tears filled her eyes. "No. No. Of course not. I'm sorry for, uh, for yelling. I was just . . ." She looked up. Everyone was watching her. Lisa knelt next to Marta and the children.

"Everyone is hungry and tired. No more arguing. We're going to help each other," Lisa said, "and get along just fine. Isn't that right, everyone?" They all quickly agreed.

"Good," Amelia said. "That's settled." She put her hand on Marta's shoulder. "Now, how about you and Nancy help me in the kitchen?"

CHAPTER 22

DRAWN CLOSER

Nancy stood up. She looked at her mother and whispered something to her.

"Why didn't you tell me right away?" Marta said. Nancy was embarrassed.

"Because there is no bathroom," she answered. Ilena, who was standing nearby, overheard.

"Actually, there is one, Nancy. I checked it out. It's in back of the cabin. It's called an outhouse."

"Is that because it's outside?" Nancy asked.

"Exactly."

"Is there paper in there?" Ilena wasn't sure.

"It'll be okay," Marta assured her daughter. She got up and reached for her coat. "I have a package of Kleenex. Okay?" Nancy shyly nodded yes.

"I've got my boots and jacket on already," Ilena offered. "Let me take her."

"Thank you," Marta said. "Nancy? Put your coat on and go with, uh . . ."

"Ilena. Ilena Burton."

"Yes. Of course. Ilena. I'm sorry I didn't introduce . . . This situation . . . I'm Marta Hood."

"That's okay, Marta. We're all a little strung out." Ilena reached out and took Nancy's hand. "We're gonna be fine. C'mon, Nancy."

Nancy put on her pink wool coat with a white faux fur collar. Marta helped her button it. When that was done she kissed Nancy on the cheek and wiped away the last trace of her tears. Ilena took Nancy's hand and turned on the flashlight. She saw that its power had faded considerably, so she turned it off and took one of the kerosene lanterns in hand.

"This will be better," she told Nancy and led the way through the rear bedroom and out onto the back porch. The two figures, one tall, with military bearing, and the other short, with tentative steps, made their way across a short expanse of snow that had been tamped down by Ilena and Andy when they scouted the outhouse and found the root cellar in the smokehouse. As they approached the smaller structure, Nancy shook her head.

"It really looks scary," she said, tightening her grip on Ilena's hand.

"It's only because the moon is behind a cloud right now. I'll be right outside all the time. Don't worry."

"About what?" Nancy asked. "Wolves or bears?" Ilena was surprised at the child's question. She had said nothing to anyone about her encounter with the red wolves and what she thought might be a bear when she had gone for water.

"Believe me, Nancy," Ilena told her cheerily, "the last place that wolves and bears hang around is an outhouse."

"What's that?" Nancy asked, pointing at the door.

"What?"

"It looks like someone cut a half moon in the door." Ilena smiled.

"Yes. It sure does. I think they did that to let the air out."

"Does it smell in there?"

"No. Not this outhouse, sweetie." Ilena laughed. "But there are some things in life you just have to hold your breath over, and most outhouses are that way. Think of our being here tonight as an adventure. You can tell your friends and classmates about it when you get home."

"That's right. I can. This really is an adventure. Okay, I'll be brave."

"Good."

The small outhouse, of indeterminate age, had cracks in the slatted sides. Dark moss was visible along the snow line. The wooden planks that made up the roof were slightly askew and covered with snow and ice. Ilena and Andy had cleared the snow away from the door when they'd opened it before.

"I'll wait for you here," Ilena said, opening the door and placing the lantern on the floor inside. "You have the tissues, right?"

"Yes," Nancy said tentatively as she studied the bare plank with the hole in the middle. "I sit there?" she asked.

"Yes."

"No flushing."

"No flushing."

"And you'll be right outside?"

"I promise." Nancy closed the door. Ilena heard her fumbling with her clothes.

"Oh! The wood is cold," she said. Then she giggled. "It doesn't smell. But it feels funny because there is no seat." Ilena smiled to herself. The moon came out from behind a cloud. Out of habit and training, she turned slowly in a circle surveying the terrain around her. She began close, then expanded her view outward. They were in a narrow, sheltered valley. The cabin, smokehouse, and outhouse occupied a slight knoll in the clearing. The heavily wooded Nantahala forest rose up toward the Great Smoky Mountains above. It was a good place to build a cabin, but who had done it was a mystery.

"How're you doing?" she asked.

"Almost," Nancy answered. The smell of smoke from both chimneys, and the silence of the winter night gave Ilena a comfortable, homey feeling. She imagined her Cherokee ancestors feeling the same way—a part of nature and filled with life.

Inside, the cabin was warm and fragrant with the scent of burning wood. The crackling sound was reassuring. Those inside gathered their dried clothing from the clothesline Ilena had rigged in the bedroom. Lisa and John had the fewest items of clothing. They were in the main room, repacking. Ronny was at the table, absorbed in his Game Boy.

Andy, Amelia, and Marta were in the bedroom attending to their dried clothing.

"I see Ilena had few things here," Amelia said.

"I like that soldier," Andy told her.

"A young girl like that, a soldier," Amelia said.

"Can you imagine what she's been through? In my day, women just didn't go to war. . . . I mean, like they do now."

"In my day, too," Andy answered. "I can imagine some of what she's seen." Marta, who was folding the children's dry clothing on the bed, listened to the conversation.

"You were in a war?" Amelia asked.

"Vietnam."

"Oh. That was terrible. My husband and I watched the news every night. He was in service. In Korea. A Marine. When we were walking through the snow I thought about him because he had frostbite on his feet. He lost two toes. It was December then, too. Nineteen fifty. A place called Chosin Reservoir where the Chinese came across the border and attacked. When he got home, he was very bitter. In the late sixties, we joined the antiwar demonstrations on campus." She saw Andy was looking away, far away, into the fire. "That must have been very disheartening to you. . . . I mean, so many people against the war while you were there. . . ." Andy looked at Amelia. He liked her. He liked her spirit. She was sensitive, and in the warm yellow glow of the fire and kerosene lanterns, she had a handsome aura about her. He imagined she must have been very beautiful when she was young . . . like his Maria. Maria. He smiled. Maria would have liked Amelia. He sensed great kindness in her soul.

"We heard about it," he told her. "A lot of us wondered what we were doing there. Why didn't they let us win? We figured the politicians gave up on us long before the people did. But you know, when you're there . . . in combat . . . it's day-to-day. You don't think about winning or losing, just staying alive, keeping your buddies alive; and getting back to the world in one piece."

"And you did," she said brightly.

"Yes. But I left a lot of good friends back there. And I found a world that did not honor our service." Amelia reached out and put her hand on his.

"Joseph and I did. Our demonstrations had nothing to do with our gratitude for those who served. Thank you." Andy was touched by her sincerity. He took her hand and gently kissed it.

"You know?" Andy said quietly. "You are the first person who ever thanked me. And I know you mean it." He took a deep breath and gathered up his dried clothing. "What say we pack this stuff away and get some dinner?"

When the two had left the room, Marta sat down on the bed and wiped away the tears she could not help shedding. Somehow, what she had just witnessed made her problems seem a little smaller and far more manageable. She shook out the quilt that the kids had been sitting on and spread it neatly on the bed.

Several minutes later, the door to the cabin opened, and Ilena and Nancy returned.

"Oh, Mommy," Nancy said, running to Marta. "You've got to try it. And you don't have to hold your nose because Ilena says it's old and not used and, anyway, it's too cold to be smelly." Everyone laughed.

"I want to go now," Ronny announced to more laughter.

"C'mon," Reggie told him. "I'll take you, little man." Ilena handed Reggie the lantern. Marta bundled her son up and looked gratefully at Reggie.

"Thank you." She handed him a package of tissues.

"My pleasure. Okay, tiger. Let's do the deal." Reggie headed for the bedroom and the rear porch. A gust of wind passed through the room as Reggie opened and closed the rear door. It caused the fire to surge and the lamps to flicker. For that moment, the room, the light, the rough-hewn furniture all seemed like a familiar, faded daguerreotype to Amelia. She felt comfort in these nineteenth-century trappings. The burden of her loneliness was lifted, and somehow the cabin, this night, these people, all felt like hearth and home.

"I'm going to get our dinner," she announced cheerfully. Lisa and Marta went into the kitchen area with her. Nancy followed.

CHAPTER 23

REMEMBER CHRISTMAS

The fixings were humble, to say the least: a thin carrot, potato, and beet soup and a few dozen small rolls. The blackberry preserves were going to be the special treat. Nancy was in the kitchen with Amelia, fascinated by the grandma-like lady's ability to make a dinner for nine people out of so little. Since Ilena had pointed out that what was happening was an adventure, it was now a point of view Nancy was eager to pursue.

There was a noise from the rear bedroom as the back door opened and Reggie and Ronny returned from the outhouse. Ronny was excited.

"Mommy!" he exclaimed. "You should see that place. I thought I was going to fall through the hole where you sit, but Reggie showed me how to do it. We had an adventure." That got a laugh from everyone. Reggie was smiling. Like Ilena had for Nancy, Reggie had removed the fear of the night and the unknown and turned the situation into an adventure for the boy.

As Marta and Lisa set the table with the aged utensils, bowls, and glasses they found in the cabinet, John and Andy gathered the stools and the few chairs and placed them around it.

"This stuff is really old," Lisa commented as she examined some matching stoneware pieces. She looked at the back of them. "There's a red-colored wing on them," she told Marta. John overheard.

"The Red Wing Company," he told Lisa. "My wife collects that kind of stuff. That could date back to nineteen hundred. We're going to eat on antiques." He went to get another chair.

Lisa looked over at Reggie, who was stoking the fire. Ronny was with him. "It's too bad the kids will miss Christmas with your family tonight," she told Marta.

"It's just my parents. I'm getting a divorce," she said softly.

"Oh. Sorry. I, uh . . ."

"Don't be. Ten years, and the rat takes off with a bimbo half my age, and his. Good riddance." Her jaw was clenched in anger. She looked at the children, then back at Lisa. Her eyes teared up a bit. She wiped them with her sleeve and smiled. "We're going to be okay."

Lisa nodded and smiled back. "I'm sure you are."

With the stools and chairs in place, Andy joined Reggie at the fire while John went over to his luggage.

"Getting colder out there?" Andy asked.

"Yeah. I was thinking that maybe spinning the wheels like I did melted too much snow. It'll freeze and lock the van in tight. Maybe I should go up there with the ax and try to dig out a little."

"I don't think that'll help much. We'll need a tow truck, anyway. Maybe in the morning—"

"It's buried steep and deep," Reggie interrupted. "If I don't loosen it, I think maybe we'll need a wrecker. Who knows if there's one around here. Maybe I should walk back to the town we passed through and see if I can find one now."

"That town is ten or twelve miles away!"

"So?"

"I took basic at Fort Dix, New Jersey. It was in the winter of sixty-nine. Record cold and snow. We were in the field for two weeks in this kind of weather. It's brutal, man. Wait till morning. We can go together."

John joined them. He was carrying an unopened bottle of Johnny Walker Blue Label Scotch. "A Christmas present for my father-in-law. I got it at the duty-free shop in Geneva. How about we crack it open now? He'll understand."

"Sounds good to me," Andy said. "I'll get some glasses and see if the ladies will join us." Reggie said nothing. His thoughts were still with the van.

Five minutes later they had all gathered around the fireplace. Five glasses had scotch in them for John, Reggie, Andy, Lisa, and Ilena. Marta, Amelia, and the children had water in theirs. John raised his glass.

"Well, here's to new friends and peace on Earth, good will toward men. . . ."

"And women and children," Amelia added. They all raised their glasses.

"Merry Christmas," Andy said.

"Merry Christmas," they all said. All except the children, Amelia noticed as the adults drank the toast. John refilled Andy and Reggie's drained glasses. Lisa and Ilena had only sipped theirs. Amelia studied the gathering: a band of strangers thrown together in this primitive, out-of-the-way place on a cold winter night. It was an extraordinary circumstance. Or was it? Lately, although she had never been a religious person, her loneliness had stimulated questions about human existence and God. Was there a grand cosmic plan? A life or existence beyond this one? Had this group of strangers come together for a reason? She wondered if all they had gone through this day—the airport, snowstorm, flight cancellation, Lisa's offer, the avalanche, the cabin, the van off the road, the trek through the snow, no fire, no food, freezing temperature—had it been for a purpose yet to be revealed? It was nearly Christmas Eve. They had forgotten Christmas Eve.

"Listen, everyone," Amelia announced loudly. "I have a thought." They all looked at her. "In an hour or so, it'll be Christmas." A few of them checked their watches. "None of us planned to have Christmas Eve out here in the . . . wilderness, much less with a group of strangers. But that's where we are, and so far, thankfully, we're safe and warm and . . . well, so I thought . . . The children . . . What I mean is, how about if we try to make Christmas here for them tonight? Surely you remember what this night meant when you were young."

"That's a really nice idea, Amelia," Ilena agreed immediately.

"Let's do it!" Lisa cried out, excited.

Andy held up his glass of scotch. "I'm in. John

already shared one of his presents with us. I have wine I bought in Atlanta, for my, ah, I was on my way to visit an old army buddy, George. It's really good wine."

"What about a tree?" Nancy asked.

"With lights and a star," Ronny added.

"There's no electricity, children," Marta told them.

"There's a few candles in the pantry," Lisa offered.

"And we can make a star from gift wrapping paper," Amelia said. The excitement in her voice was contagious.

"And ornaments from the ribbons," Marta blurted out. Even Marta, with the problems she faced, had somehow caught the spirit of the moment. Everyone became animated. Yes; they would have Christmas Eve. Excitement and hope had replaced the gloom of being stranded, and the absence of family.

CHAPTER 24

JOSHUA AND GOLDIE

A moment later, the cabin's front door burst open, striking the wall with a thunderous crack. Cold air swept through the room. A glass on the table fell, shattering on the planked floor. The fire rose up, blazing brightly out of the stone fireplace, reaching its hot, orange fingers toward the suddenly stunned occupants of the cabin. Instinctively, everyone braced and turned toward the door. Marta pulled Ronny and Nancy to her. Andy stepped protectively in front of Amelia. Reggie reached down for a log by the fire, clutching it tightly and raising it behind his back. Ilena spotted a knife on the table and swiftly grabbed it.

A tall figure, shrouded in the darkness of the frigid night, stood just beyond the frame of the door. The firelight, reflected in his eyes, burned as luminous orange specks. The amorphous shape became a man as he took a first step, then a second, from the darkness of the porch into the light of the cabin. A coarse, scraggly beard, gray with black streaks, covered his face. His nearly white, shoulder-length hair trailed out from under a well-worn beaver-fur hat with ear flaps. His intense gaze swept across the people gathered together in front of him. He wore a long, open, bearskin coat extending to his ankles. Deerskin leggings wrapped around his canvas trousers. Snowshoes fashioned from tough birch boughs and tied with deer tendons were strapped to his feet. Only his boots and the ancient Winchester long rifle in his right hand were factory-made. His hands were bare. Fur-lined buckskin gloves hung from thongs attached to his coat. Apparition or man? It was unclear at that moment to anyone in the room.

But all that they focused on was the old man's right hand that held the rifle. His finger was on the trigger as he brought the muzzle down in their direction and then lowered it to the floor. Then their attention was drawn to his left hand and that side of his coat that hid a large, shadowy object.

Outside the wind had suddenly picked up, rattling some loose wooden shingles on the roof. A gust forced its invisible tentacles through cracks in the clapboard, encouraging the fire and sending wisps of smoke twirling like spirits suddenly freed. Through the windows, tall pines were seen to be swept back and forth in great arcs, testing the strength of their narrow trunks. It was as though nature were announcing the arrival of the stranger.

No one spoke or moved. Since his entrance, what seemed like minutes had, in fact, been only a few seconds. His gaze passed from one to the other, taking measure of everyone in the cabin. His eyes, which were no longer glowing, but seemed a warm brown, settled on the children.

The shape behind him moved. The black nose, and then the kindly face of a large golden retriever appeared and stood next to the man. The dog's long coat was matted and wet from running in the snow. He growled with the intimidating low sound of a creature threatened. Without word or signal from the old man, the animal scanned the intruders for scents, signs, and sounds of danger. Seeing none, it stopped growling and cautiously sat.

"Easy, boy," were the man's first words. His voice was deep, but soft and without accent. His eyes remained on the children as he slipped his finger from the rifle's trigger and snapped on the safety.

"Mommy!" Ronny exclaimed. "That dog is just like Jake!" He wriggled out of his mother's grasp and stepped toward the large dog, whose shoulders were nearly as high as Ronny's. Marta protectively pulled her son back.

"He's a golden retriever, son," the man said as he stepped farther into the cabin. Now the fire and lamplight revealed his weathered face, pink from the cold. His brown eyes were even warmer and kinder. The dog also moved, wary but interested in Ronny and the other strangers around him. The man removed his hat, shook his long hair loose, and rubbed the back of his neck.

"We were just about to have dinner, sir," Amelia said warmly. She stepped forward and extended her right hand. "I'm Amelia McIntosh." He accepted her hand and nodded with a slight bow. Everyone waited for him to say more but he just smiled. Looking directly into the stranger's eyes, Amelia then said, "Would you like to join us?" He grinned broadly. The wrinkled corners of his eyes added to their kindness. "I would. I surely would, Amelia. Thank you kindly."

"No need to," she said. "We gather it's your food we're offering."

"Yes. That it is. But I don't consider you trespassers. Guests, is how I see it. Ain't had any in the cabin for a long while." Everyone relaxed as the old man set his rifle against the cabin wall and knelt to untie his snowshoes. They all watched him with great interest. When he was done he hung them on a wall peg, then hung his hat and great coat next to them. Last, he removed the deerskin chaps and hung them, too.

"There, that's better," he said. "You all are welcome. Sorry I wasn't here to greet you when you arrived."

"Your cabin saved us this night," Lisa said.

"Lord knows what would have become of us out there," Andy added.

"It's a hard night out there. But where are my manners?" the old man said. He stepped onto the porch and, bending over, lifted up a large object and brought it inside, closing the door behind him. He proudly held up a large, freshly killed, wild tom turkey. "I know there wasn't much to eat here, but I think this will make dinner a lot better." Everyone smiled and the children's eyes widened. "Here you go, young lady," he addressed Ilena, handing her the turkey. "You look like you might know what to do with this. But that knife you're holding won't do the job." He reached behind his back and produced a very large and very sharp bone-handled hunting knife. "This will." He flipped it gracefully in his hand and offered it to Ilena, handle first. "You'll find a butcher table out back."

Ilena took the knife and put down the turkey. She extended her hand.

"I'm Ilena Burton."

"I see you serve your country," he said, gesturing to her fatigues.

"Yes, sir. I do."

He nodded. "*Uganowa,* Miss Burton." Ilena frowned and cocked her head. Had she heard right? The others looked at her.

"*Uganowa?* You are wishing me good luck. You speak Cherokee?" she asked.

"That I do, Miss Burton. It also means 'peace.' " She nodded, picked up the turkey, and headed for the back porch. Andy stepped forward and extended his hand to the old man.

"My name's Andy, Andy Casiano," Andy said as they shook. "I'll go and help her."

"*Felice Navidad,* Andy. Nice to meet you."

"A linguist, huh?" Andy smiled. "Well, Merry Christmas to you, too." He left the room to find Ilena, who was already on the back porch looking for the butchering table.

"I saw your van," the man said to the rest of them. "I guess y'all had an accident." He smiled. "Not hard to do around here." Reggie self-consciously set aside the split he still held in his hand.

"It was my, uh, my fault. . . . The van. I was trying to turn it around, and the moonlight sort of changed. I missed the edge of the road." He extended his hand. "Reggie Howard." The man took it and shook it heartily.

"Yes, Reggie. It's like that sometimes. Moonlight on the snow can play tricks." The others stepped forward and introduced themselves, shaking the tall man's hand and thanking him for his hospitality. When they were done, he stepped closer to the fire. "So, how'd you happen to get up this way?"

"The airport in Atlanta was closed. Snowstorm," John began.

"So we decided to drive to Asheville," Amelia said. "Well that is—"

"The van is mine. I was driving to Asheville and offered them all a lift," Lisa interrupted.

"There was an avalanche," Marta chimed in.

"Avalanche," the old man said wistfully. "Been known to happen in these hills," he offered. "Storms can come on hard and fast. Wintertime can be mighty unforgiving sometimes."

"Well," John continued, "we were looking for a way around it."

"The avalanche had blocked the Parkway," Reggie said. "I was driving, and we went looking for a way around it. We tried Comfort Mountain Road."

"Ilena saw your cabin," Lisa said, "from the road. At first we weren't sure, but she and Andy had a look, and there it was."

"And at the same time, I, um, the van went off the road."

"So here we are," Amelia told him. "And most grateful your cabin was here."

"Well, you're welcome to it." The stranger suddenly shook his head and smiled. "Now, what's wrong with me? You've introduced yourselves and told me your story, and I haven't even told you my name. I'm Joshua, and that shaggy old beast is Goldie."

Goldie, tail wagging and smiling, sensed all was well. He trotted over to Ronny and Nancy, who immediately embraced and petted him. Ronny hugged his head, and Nancy hugged his torso. Goldie responded to the attention with licks.

"He's just like Jake," Ronny told his mother. The boy laughed with pleasure.

"Maybe they're brothers," Nancy said. Marta leaned over to Joshua and whispered. "My ex took the dog."

"Do you have a Christmas tree?" Ronny asked Joshua.

"Can't say as I do, son. Being alone and all, well, Christmas sort of sneaks up on me." Disappointed, Ronny looked down at the floor and shrugged his shoulders. He went back to petting Goldie.

"We were just talking about finding a tree when you came in," John reminded everyone.

"And making a star and ornaments," Lisa added.

"Well, I'd sort of like a tree, myself," Joshua admitted. "There's plenty of nice ones up on the ridge. Goldie can show you where the best are, can't you, old boy?" At the sound of his name, Goldie got up and stretched.

"Great," John said. "I'll go."

"Not in those city shoes, you won't," Joshua said. "You'll find a spare set of boots in the back room under the bed." John went to get them.

"Hey, Reggie," John said as he passed him. "How about giving me a hand finding a tree?"

"Sure," Reggie said half-heartedly.

"Can I go, Mommy?" Ronny asked. "Can I go with them?"

"Oh no, dear," Marta said. "It's freezing out there."

"I'll dress warm. My coat and boots are in the suitcase. Pleeeze, Mommy."

As Reggie put on his coat, John came back into

the room wearing a pair of heavy boots. Both men looked at Ronny pleading. They silently shared a memory of how, as boys, they wanted to participate in men's work. And this boy was without a father tonight. John was first to respond to the plea in Ronny's eyes.

"I'll keep an eye on him," John said to Marta.

"We both will," Reggie assured her.

"Please, Mommy, please," Ronny persisted.

"Well, all right," Marta relented. She went to retrieve Ronny's coat and boots while Lisa handed one of the kerosene lanterns to John.

"Stay with Goldie," Joshua told them, "and you'll be all right. He knows these hills." He opened a chest against the wall and took out two pairs of leggings. "These'll keep you dry," he said. Then he handed them each a set of iron cleats. "Strap these on. They'll keep you from slipping if you run into any ice."

While Ronny was being dressed, John and Reggie sat on the cabin floor and put on the gear Joshua had given them. The leggings were large enough to fit over their own clothes. When they got up and walked to the door, the cleats pressed into the wood floor. They stopped.

"Don't worry about them cleats," Joshua said. "Just join a fine company of scrapes already in the wood." Marta buttoned up Ronny's coat.

"Now be careful, and do what Mr. Sullivan—"

"It's John."

"Listen to what Mr. Sullivan and—"

"Reggie Howard," said Reggie.

"Yes, Mr. Howard, too. Listen to what they say. Do you understand me?"

"Yes, Mommy."

"Promise me."

"I promise."

Joshua walked to the door and gestured to Goldie. The dog trotted to join John, Ronny, and Reggie. As soon as they opened the door Goldie rushed outside. Joshua stepped out onto the porch. He went to the far corner and found a bow saw. He grabbed the small ax from the woodpile and handed both tools to Reggie, who wondered how he had missed seeing the saw earlier.

"Good huntin', gentlemen," Joshua said. "Okay Goldie. Go find us a nice tree."

Goldie trotted off ahead through the snow, then stopped and, with tail wagging, waited for John, Reggie, and Ronny to join him. John took Ronny's hand and walked toward Goldie. Reggie followed with the tools. Seeing them coming, Goldie started off at a steady trot across the clearing and into the woods.

CHAPTER 25

TRAIL OF TEARS

Ilena and Andy were so intent on how to deal with the wild turkey that they didn't hear Joshua step out onto the back porch. He stood silently watching as Andy held the bird firmly on a small table while Ilena plucked feathers from the bird's breast. There was a substantial pile of them on the porch already. The yellow light from the kerosene lantern they had hung was adequate, but barely.

"I figured you'd done this before, Miss Burton," Joshua said. His voice startled Ilena and Andy. They stopped their chore and looked up.

"Yes, sir. I'm half Cherokee. But you guessed that, didn't you?"

"Yes I did. From hereabouts?"

"No, sir. The Kentucky hills. My daddy had me skinnin' squirrels and dressin' out deer before I was twelve. My grandpa taught me the language." Joshua moved closer to them. Andy, a city dweller, was fascinated by the conversation. Ilena hadn't said much about her background before. But now, with this mountain man, she seemed comfortable and open, as though she were talking with someone she had known all her life.

"Do you have kin in these parts?" Joshua asked her.

"Not that I know, sir. Nearest is in Asheville."

"There used to be an orphanage here," he said as Ilena indicated for Andy to hold the turkey again. She began to pluck.

"I heard tell about that place," she said. "Kids whose parents had died on the Trail of Tears."

"Died on what?" Andy asked.

"It is called the Trail of Tears," Ilena said as she stopped plucking. "Most of these mountains were Cherokee lands. Here and in Georgia. In eighteen thirty-eight the U.S. Government, seven thousand soldiers led by General Winfield Scott, invaded the Cherokee Nation. Men, women, and children were taken from their land and forced to march a thousand miles to Oklahoma. Many of them died. The Trail of Tears. Some of the children were returned here, to an orphanage, where they were raised in the white man's ways."

Andy, whose ancestors were natives of Puerto Rico before the Spanish arrived, had never heard this story. But he understood the pain underlying Ilena's portrayal of the fate of the Cherokee Nation.

"The Spanish destroyed my people," he said. "The *Jibaro*." It was a statement he had never made to anyone before. Ilena nodded knowingly and went back to the turkey. Joshua watched them work together for a few moments.

"That orphanage was up top of this mountain. Comfort Mountain. The folks who started it meant well. There was some government money. Guilt money, I'd say. They kept the kids isolated until the tribal councils in Oklahoma demanded their return. By then most of the children had not only lost their families but their identity, too." There was sadness in Joshua's voice. Ilena nodded but did not comment. "Ah well . . ." he said softly, "Cherokee, *Jibaro*—another time, long ago." He took a deep breath and let it out slowly. "Well, there's hungry folks inside. I won't distract you anymore. I'm gonna go get me some nice hot tea from Miss Amelia." He went back into the cabin. For a long moment, neither Andy or Ilena said anything. The feathers flew expertly until the turkey was nearly naked.

"What happens after it's plucked?" Andy asked.

"We gut and wash it, sir."

"Andy. No more 'sir,' please. All I made was corporal."

"Two up. N.C.O., huh?"

"Yeah. Squad leader. I never thought I'd get this old. There were times I was sure . . . But you know all about that, huh?"

"Yes. I do," she said quietly.

"I sensed that back in Atlanta. At the airport."

"What?" she asked as she pulled out the last of the wing feathers.

"Where you've been. What you're doing. I've been there. Done that."

"I guess it shows." She took a deep breath. "This guy's ready to be gutted." They turned the large bird on its back. Ilena took Joshua's bone-handled knife and tested its edge. Razor sharp. She wasn't surprised.

"It's like I got old and became one of those

World War Two or Korean vets I knew when I was a kid," Andy said. "I couldn't imagine what they knew back then. And they sure weren't talking to me. Now, seeing you, so young . . ."

"Like you were?" she asked as she plunged the knife into the turkey, making an expert opening from the base of the breast to the tail.

"Yeah. So I, uh, I thought . . . Well . . . Maybe if we talked, things might be easier for you."

"And for you, too?" she asked, looking directly at him.

Andy nodded and looked away, up at the brilliantly starry sky. "Yes."

Ilena nodded and lifted the small ax up over her head. "Okay." She swung the ax and chopped off the turkey's head. "Let's take this guy down to the stream and clean him out. We can talk on the way."

They lifted the bird carefully so as not to spill any of the guts out and carried it across the clearing to the path that led down to the stream. Andy gathered his thoughts. He realized that they had already confirmed their common experience and camaraderie. Getting specific wasn't required. He knew she had made her peace with war and death. That was necessary. Worrying about dying was too much of a distraction from the business of staying alive and getting back to the world.

He laughed. "Okay," he began, "so, there I was, watchin' my third lieutenant in four months jump off the Huey with his pack and M16 . . ." Ilena stopped and looked at him. Andy was grinning, ear to ear.

"That's how they start war story movies, huh?" She laughed and set down her end of the turkey. He did likewise. She reached out, embraced Andy, and gave him a big hug.

"I really needed that," she said. "Thank you!" He smiled and nodded. They picked up the turkey and headed down to the stream quickly. They left a small pool of blood behind in the snow. When they had disappeared down the hill, the male red wolf stepped out of the woods cautiously and licked at the bloody snow. Then he stopped. His ears pricked up and his head turned toward a low, grumbling sound deep in the woods. He knew it as another, larger predator. But it was far off and presented no immediate danger.

CHAPTER 26

A PERFECT TREE

Goldie was still out in front. John, with Ronny now on his shoulders, and Reggie behind them, followed the retriever. As the terrain rose, thick firs were closer together. A hint of the presence of the moon was revealed by a gray cloud brighter than the others. Its light, reflected off the snow, was bright enough for them to see their way. The wind had lessened considerably, and only a slight breeze swept loose snow about in swirls. As they walked, they jostled clumps of snow from the overhanging branches, causing them to strike the ground with soft thumps.

Reggie took notice of animal tracks off to his left. He didn't know what they were, but he'd spent enough time in the Vietnam jungle to learn to pay attention to his surroundings. The tracks heightened his awareness.

"In the freezing woods, following a damn dog. Merry Christmas, ho-ho-ho," Reggie muttered to himself under his breath. *Okay, man,* he thought. *Just make the best of it, and don't freeze in the process. Tomorrow you'll be holding Yvonne in your arms, and all this will be a story for the Christmas dinner table. My son's table.*

Ronny was thrilled. Here it was, Christmas Eve, and he was in the woods, riding on a nice man's shoulders, having the adventure of his life! A white Christmas. And they were going for a tree, an actual, real tree in the woods! And a dog, just like Jake, was taking them to it. This was great! He then noticed that the snow was not deep in this part of the woods.

"Could I walk myself, John?" he asked.

John stopped. "Sure," he said, looking around. He lifted the boy from his shoulders, grateful to have his burden lightened. Ronny immediately ran on ahead to Goldie, who had stopped and waited. Reggie caught up to John, and they walked along together.

"He's a nice kid," John said.

Reggie nodded.

"So what do you do, Reggie?"

"I used to be an autoworker."

"Retired?"

"Hell, no. They closed the plant, shipped my job overseas and put my pension and medical in the toilet. Not exactly what you would call retirement."

"Jeez . . . That's tough," John said, truly concerned. "I'm sure something will turn up."

"Maybe in your world."

"My world?"

"Hey, man, get real. Don't patronize me. I'm not much for small talk. Just a tired, middle-aged black man gettin' screwed by the system ... again."

But John hadn't been patronizing at all. He was sincere and interested.

"What about retraining?"

Reggie stopped and glared at the other man. "Now what in the hell do you know about me or ... Look at you. Rolex, gold cuff links, Armani suit. Retraining? Who are you kidding?"

"Sorry. I didn't mean—" Reggie put up his hand to stop John from going on with this conversation.

"Look, man, let's get the tree, get through this night, and get on our separate ways." Reggie walked away. John caught up to him.

"Hey listen, Reggie. Wait a minute. I'm only trying to ..." Suddenly they were interrupted by loud barking. They looked ahead and saw Goldie sitting next to a small, full blue spruce. It had a light dusting of snow on it. The moon came out from behind a cloud, and the tree sparkled, as if beckoning them.

"Look what Goldie found!" Ronny shouted. "Our tree!" Reggie and John hurried to join the boy and dog. When they reached them, Ronny was jumping up and down with excitement. "Isn't it great?" Ronny asked.

"Perfect," John agreed. Reggie leaned the bow saw against a nearby tree. He hefted the ax.

"I'll chop the low branches so we can get underneath and saw it down," he said. He knelt in the snow and began to chop at the lower branches. John knelt on the other side of the tree.

"Look, Reggie. I'm not who you think ... I mean I know ..."

Reggie stopped working. "You know your watch costs more than I made in three months on the line?"

John looked down and unconsciously let his sleeve slide down and cover the Rolex.

"Two years and eight months from a pension, and it all goes away. I worked hard all my life. You understand? Hard. For my family. It's all gone. Don't tell me something's gonna turn up. You don't know nothin'."

John was frustrated. "You've got me all wrong. I run a business. I have employees. I understand what you're saying."

Reggie sat up and looked around. He raised his hand. "Hold it. Where's the kid?"

John got up and scanned the area. "He was right here. Ronny! Ronny?" John shouted.

Reggie got to his feet. "The dog's gone, too. Man! That kid gets lost, he could freeze out here. . . ."

"Stow it! No one's going to freeze." John took the lantern and circled the tree. He saw paw and boot prints in the snow heading off into the woods. "They went this way."

Reggie dropped the saw. "Okay. C'mon. Let's go!" Both men hurried off into the woods, following the tracks.

CHAPTER 27

EXCALIBUR

It had only taken ten minutes to wash the turkey in the stream. Before doing that, Ilena had carefully removed all of the innards and placed them in the snow at streamside.

"Don't we want some of those?" Andy had asked her.

"I think they'll serve us better this way," she told him. "When I was down here getting water I saw some wolves."

"Wolves?" He looked around nervously. "They didn't bother you?"

"No. They're red wolves. They vanished around these parts a long time ago. The park people reintroduced them. They have plenty of game to hunt." She didn't feel like getting into the Cherokee philosophy of the human's place in nature.

"So the turkey guts are for them?"

"Yes. In fact, they're watching us now." Andy looked around again, but saw nothing. He felt a nervous tingle run down his spine. He didn't like dogs. As a kid he had been bitten by a cousin's pit bull.

"And they won't bother us?"

"No. They were tracking us when we all walked down from the van."

"And you didn't say anything?"

Ilena stood at the edge of the stream and submerged the turkey, letting the icy water flow through the bird's now empty body cavity. A slick of blood flowed away from it, downstream.

"Why make people nervous? I saw how they were behaving and I knew they wouldn't harm us." She lifted the turkey and slid it toward the bank. "This is done. Give me a hand and grab it by the neck." Andy took hold of the turkey as she had asked. She then swung the rear of it onto the bank and got away from the stream. Her hands were bright red from the cold water and blood. She put her end of the bird down and blew on them.

"Put these on," Andy said, handing her his gloves. She took them without argument. Then he lifted the turkey onto his shoulder. They headed back to the cabin with Ilena in the lead. As they came to a rise in the path that led to the clearing, Andy looked back toward the stream. He saw three shadowy figures where Ilena had left the innards. They were devouring their Christmas gift.

Joshua brought an iron spit in from the smokehouse. Because the fire in the rear bedroom was blazing, he had to put on heavy leather gloves to set it in place. Lisa helped him. It fit nicely. Joshua then took it out, placed it to the side, and banked the fire, spreading the glowing, red hot coals evenly.

"This will work just fine," he told Lisa.

"I think we'll need more dry wood," she said.

"Did you use what was in the pantry?"

"Yes. For the stove."

"I have some covered up against the cabin out back."

Lisa grabbed her coat that was on the bed. "If you show me, I'll get on it."

He nodded and followed her out the rear door onto the porch.

The soup was ready. Amelia slid the pot to the rear of the stove where it would stay warm. She checked the rolls in the oven. The fire in there was small but steady. Andy had done a good job setting it up. The dough was baking slowly, just the way she wanted. She turned her attention to the turkey that was in the sink. She had to get it out and onto the worktable, but it was too heavy for her to lift. Amelia looked for someone to help her. Ilena and Nancy were at the cabin table, making ornaments. They had set aside some of the utensils and plates to make room. Andy and Marta were near the fireplace doing something else that she could not see.

"Andy," she called out. "Can you give me a hand for a moment?" He got up and came quickly to the kitchen.

"At your service, Madam Chef," he said cheerfully.

"It's the turkey. Could you put him on the worktable?"

"That would be my pleasure. This turkey and I are getting to be good friends. And the closer it gets to the dinner table, the happier I'll be." He went to the sink and lifted the bird out and onto the table in one swift and graceful motion. "What else can I do?" he asked.

"That's it, thank you. I have the salt and lard out already. And maybe I'll use some of those blackberry preserves in it, too. What do you think?"

"I think that sounds delicious. Sing out if you need anything else." He walked back to where Marta and he had been working. Amelia was feeling buoyant and, for the first time in a long while, useful. There was not a hint of loneliness in her life on this night. She went to work on the turkey.

The large ax was the only one around. Reggie and John had taken the smaller one to get the tree. Joshua had a canvas tarpaulin covering more than a cord of wood against the side of the cabin they had not explored. Joshua pulled a few logs from the stack and walked over to a large snow-covered stump ten yards away.

"I use this as a base to split 'em," he said as he dropped the logs and brushed away the snow. Lisa could see that the stump was dark and aged, and showed scars of many split logs. The tree had been cut down long ago. He placed one of the logs on the stump. Lisa stepped forward, tightened her grip on the ax, raised it high above her head, and swung it down with one swift, accurate chop. It was obvious she had done this before. But the log was large and damp, and the ax imbedded in it without splitting it. In fact, the ax was stuck. She struggled to free it.

"Problem, Lisa?" Joshua asked. His lips curled in a sly smile.

"You might say that. The wood was wet."

"Let me see it," he said. She stepped aside. He grasped the ax handle and with one mighty tug, freed it. "Excalibur!" he proclaimed.

"Excuse me?"

"Excalibur. The sword King Arthur freed from the rock to claim his royal birthright." He handed her the ax. "Did you know that took place on Christmas morning?"

"No."

Joshua looked up at the starry sky and around at the clearing and woods beyond. "Perhaps it was on a night like this, in a wood like this."

Lisa watched as he gazed around him. His expression was distant. He took a deep breath and exhaled slowly. His eyes, deep and dark in the moonlight, fixed on hers. "There is a poem about it." His voice was deep and strong, with an air of melancholy about it. It captured her complete attention and sent chills down her spine as he recited in a meter and tongue of a long time past:

"In clouds the Christmas morning dimly dawn'd; Grey gloom'd the minster aisles; but ere the mass was ended, an effulgent sunshine broke Through the east oriel, and all men were 'ware That by the altar stood a snow-white stone, Four-square."

He paused and smiled at her, then continued:

"And on its summit, in the midst, An anvil, holding in its iron bulk, a naked sword, along whose edges ran this legend: Whoso plucks me from my place is England's rightful king. Amen. Amen."

"That was beautiful," Lisa said respectfully, awed by his performance. "How did you . . . ?"

"I used to read a lot. Long ago, when things were less frantic."

"I remember a movie about King Arthur where he threw Excalibur away into a lake."

"Yes," Joshua said softly. "To the Lady in the Lake." Lisa turned away abruptly and swung the ax, shattering the log. She bent down to pick up the splits.

"Arthur threw away the sword because the responsibility it carried was too much to bear," Joshua said.

"Oh? Is that what happened? I forgot."

"What do you think she was doing there?"

Lisa stood up and glared at him. "Exactly what are you asking?"

"The Lady in the Lake. Was that someone you knew, Lisa?"

She reached for the second log and placed it on the stump. "It wasn't your fault. The lake. The lady," he said. For a moment Lisa was shocked and confused. Then she gathered her composure.

"I don't know what you're talking about." She lifted the ax again. "We'd better get this done and inside to dry if that turkey is going to get cooked." She split the next log with ease and unspoken anger. Joshua nodded and went to get more logs.

CHAPTER 28

DESCENT INTO DARKNESS

Reggie and John pulled their collars up as the temperature noticeably dropped. They were trudging through deep, blowing snow now, its icy touch melting against the exposed skin of their wrists, necks, and faces. Cold droplets of sweat coursed down their spines. The moon was behind clouds again. Reggie led the way, following the tracks, peering ahead by lantern-light, driven by the edge of panic that the blowing snow might obliterate the tracks and the boy might be lost.

"Damned moon's gone again," Reggie muttered. "I can't see much past the lantern." Then a shape emerged ahead. The dim light revealed Goldie at the edge of blackness. There were no trees or snow visible beyond him. It appeared the woods had suddenly stopped at the edge of night. Was it a clearing, a field, or an abyss?

"There!" Reggie cried out. "It's the dog." The men ran toward Goldie, who remained still. As they approached he moved forward a little and blocked their way.

"Easy," John said. "He's telling us something. I think there's a cliff or drop-off behind him." Goldie barked, as if to say, "That's right!" Suddenly, Ronny's voice rose up from the darkness.

"Help me! Help me!"

"It's the kid!" Reggie said. There was relief in his voice.

"Thank God," John added.

"Ronny? Where are you?" John called out, moving cautiously past Goldie. Reggie moved with him. The dog barked a warning again. Both men stopped. Reggie reached out the lantern and saw they were at the edge of a ravine. They peered over the ledge, lowering the lantern to illuminate what they could. They saw Ronny lying on a snow-covered ledge twenty feet below.

"How in the hell did he get down there?" John said to Reggie.

"No matter now. Thing is, how are we gonna get him up?"

"I'll go back to the cabin and—"

"There's not time for that. It's on us. We gotta do it. Now." Reggie took off his snowshoes, lay down on his belly and slid to the edge of the cliff. He looked down at Ronny, then around to the edge of the woods where Goldie stood watching. "Just be patient, son," he called to Ronny. "And don't move around. We'll get you out of there."

"So how do we do this without getting help?" John asked, slightly annoyed at Reggie's take-charge attitude. Reggie slid closer to the edge and checked the snow. "Damn rocks are covered with ice and snow. They're slippery." He sat up. "Here."

He handed John the lantern. "Take it. Go back and get the saw and ax. I'll stay with the kid. Make it fast." John grabbed the lantern and left Reggie in darkness at the edge of the cliff.

Looking down in the darkness, Reggie couldn't tell the difference between the solid rock beneath him and the chasm beyond him. He gazed up at the sky, hoping to see the moon come out from behind the clouds. But it was still hidden. Only a faint glow shone through. The wonder of how he got to this place, with the life of a stranger, a boy, in his hands, boggled his mind. All he had wanted to do was get to Asheville for Christmas Eve. He focused on the task ahead. "Okay, Reggie," he muttered to himself. "Don't you move until John gets back with the lantern. Just stay still and comfort the kid."

"Ronny boy, are you hurt?" Reggie called out in the most pleasing tone he could muster.

"I don't think so."

"Good. 'Cause you'd sure know it if you were. Now just be cool. John went to get the tools so we can get you back up here." The moonlight intensified for a moment, and Reggie leaned as far as he dared and saw the boy.

"I'm scared," Ronny said. He was close to tears. There was a rustling sound from down below and then the sharp clatter of rocks striking against the cliff face.

"Hey, Ronny. Don't you be moving around down there."

"Can you see me?"

"Not exactly. John has the lantern. But I can hear you, and I know where you are."

"I can see you a little, Mr. Howard."

"Reggie, kid. Call me Reggie. That's good. So tell me, what do you want for Christmas?"

"Christmas? I don't know. I'm just scared."

"That's why I'm talking about Christmas. So you won't be scared."

"It's not working."

"You got a girlfriend?"

"No," the boy yelled back impatiently. "Are you going to come and get me?" As he asked, the moon came out from behind the clouds, lighting the area so that Reggie could clearly see Ronny's situation.

"You bet I am. I can see you." Over his shoulder, Reggie heard sounds in the woods behind him. He turned to see John and Goldie making their way back, John carrying the needed tools.

"Here's John now," Reggie called down to Ronny. "We'll have you out of there in no time." John dropped the tools and knelt next to Reggie. "He's about fifteen, twenty feet down," Reggie told John. He pointed at a nearby half-dead pine. "That one looks good. Saw it down."

Driven by adrenaline, John quickly removed his snowshoes and sawed through the trunk. Reggie got to his feet, took the ax, and hacked the dead limbs away close to the trunk, making a rough pole ladder.

"We're almost ready," Reggie called out to Ronny. "Okay?"

"I'm okay," Ronny said. For that moment his voice sounded calmer.

"Grab the end," Reggie told John. They carried the tree to the edge of the cliff.

"You sure this thing's safe?"

"You got a better idea?"

John shook his head. "No."

"Where are you?" Ronny cried, panicky again. "I'm getting very cold. I can try to climb up."

"No!" Reggie shouted. "Just stay there. I'm coming." He looked past John. "Hey, where's the dog?"

"Took off, I guess."

"Great."

"Not to worry. I can find the way back. We left plenty of tracks."

"Okay. Ronny?" Reggie called out. "Now listen up. I'm lowering down a tree trunk. Just move back a bit against the rocks so it won't hit you. Okay?"

"Okay."

"If it gets too close to you, just yell, okay? Try to find something you can hang on to, but don't move around."

"Okay. Hurry up."

"Now, easy does it, John," Reggie said. "We don't want to knock the kid off the ledge or dump rocks and snow on him." The two men slowly lowered the makeshift ladder against the wet rock face of the ravine until its base rested on the ledge below with a dull thud.

"Okay, Ronny. Now, carefully push on the tree real easy and tell me if it's steady."

Ronny inched away from the rocks and pushed on the tree. "I think it's okay."

"Good boy. Just a minute now. John, give me your belt." Reggie took the belt and slipped it around his neck. "Hold the lantern over the edge," he told John. "I'm going down."

John held the lantern over the edge while Reggie backed down with one hand on the rock face and one on the tree. The rocks and the tree were slippery with water, snow, and ice. Reggie clutched hard with his bare hands. He felt carefully for a foot grip on the tree and found it. He began his descent, slowly but surely. His grip or footing occasionally gave way, but each time he recovered. The moon went behind a cloud again. His vision slipped from the lantern's yellow light into semidarkness. Reggie prayed softly to himself.

"Lord, I'm not saying I'm a good or deserving man. But You know I tried. All I'm askin' now is to please let me get this boy back to his momma."

CHAPTER 29

ONLY THE LONELY

Joshua left Lisa to chop more splits for the turkey fire while he took the ones she had finished inside and set them in front of the bedroom hearth to dry. He then picked up the spit and went into the main room to see how Amelia was doing with the turkey.

"That bird's lookin' mighty fine, Amelia," he said, admiring how she had prepared it. "Looks like I'm in for some real home cookin'."

"Well, I don't know. The lard and salt will help. And I put the blackberry preserves on it. I hope you don't mind. I used most of them. There's one jar left."

"That's fine."

"Well, then," she told him, "it is, as they say, good to go."

"Then go we shall," Joshua said. He slid the iron spit through the turkey's cavity and out the neck. Then he lifted it like a hobo might lift a very heavy sack of his belongings onto his shoulder and carried it into the bedroom. Amelia followed him.

She noted it was a Spartan room. No pictures. No clothes. No toilet articles. No sign of anyone inhabiting the room—just the rudiments necessary for their group, this night. She watched as Joshua fit both ends of the spit on two iron "Y"s on the sides of the hearth, placing the turkey near and above the hot coals.

"Mmm . . . I can taste it already," Amelia said.

"The coals are just right. Now it has to be turned once in a while. Everything in its time."

"True, true. I'll do that," she said. Amelia scanned the room again, looking for any evidence of who Joshua was. "Have you lived here long?"

"I come and go." Joshua banked the coals and checked to see if the new splits were drying. They were.

"Are you lonely with your husband gone?"

Amelia was surprised at the question for a moment. Had she mentioned she was a widow to him?

"You mean Joseph?"

"Yes."

"No. Not lonely. Just alone."

"Well, tonight you're not."

"Yes. It's very nice. This is going to be an old-fashioned Christmas Eve. How about you? Are you lonely?"

"There are things I miss, but no. I have Goldie and, well, as you say, this is Christmas." Joshua smiled warmly. Amelia smiled back. She closed her eyes and tilted her head as though she were listening to someone whispering to her.

"Yes. I see," said Amelia softly. "There is peace in

this home tonight." Suddenly they heard Lisa curse loudly.

"Sounds like someone needs help," Joshua said. "Just turn that spit some while I go see what's happened." He put on his coat and hat and went out the back door to find Lisa.

"Everything okay?" Joshua asked as he approached her.

"The darn ax is stuck again."

"Old Excalibur is stubborn tonight," he remarked.

"That 'Lady in the Lake' business again?" she asked sarcastically. He grasped the ax handle and freed it effortlessly. He handed it to her.

"Your sword, your highness."

"Are you mocking me?"

"No. No, my dear. Far from it. We were talking about responsibility that was too much for Arthur to bear."

"Oh? Is that what happened?"

"What do you think?"

Lisa's eyes narrowed. "What exactly are you implying?"

"The Lady in the Lake. Was that someone you knew, Lisa?"

Her lower lip quivered.

"It wasn't your fault. The lake. The lady."

Hurt and confused, she turned away, fighting to hold back tears.

"How do you know?" she asked softly as she turned back to him. Suddenly, there was a loud bark. Goldie rushed out of the woods and up to Joshua. A silent message passed between them.

"Goldie says your friends need help."

"The dog talks to you?"

"Goldie and I have been together a long time. I'll go help them." Joshua started for the woods, then stopped and looked back. "Maybe it's best if you don't say anything to the others. I mean about their needing help and about, ah, talking to the dog."

"Whatever . . . ," she said.

Joshua followed Goldie into the woods. Lisa looked after them, befuddled and concerned.

CHAPTER 30

COMPOUND
COMPLICATIONS

Reggie's feet touched the rock ledge while he clung precariously to the ladder, his shirt and underwear soaked with sweat, and the sweat seeping into his outer garments. He knew they didn't have much time to get Ronny to warmth and safety. The risk of exposure and hypothermia increased by the minute. He felt two small arms around his leg as Ronny hugged him.

"Okay, Ronny," Reggie said as he caught his breath and steeled himself for the ascent. "I'm here. Now be careful. You still okay?"

"Yes," said Ronny, clutching Reggie tighter. "I was afraid. Now I'm not."

Reggie looked below the ledge into darkness. Even the moonlight did not penetrate the void. He picked up a small rock and dropped it. He waited several seconds, but heard no sound of the rock hitting bottom. He knelt and held Ronny's shoulders as he looked into the boy's eyes.

"You trust me?" Reggie asked.

"Yes."

"Good. We're in this together." Reggie slipped John's belt through Ronny's belt, and then secured it through his own belt.

"What are you doing?" Ronny asked.

"Hooking us up. You're gonna' get a piggyback ride out of here." Reggie knelt and showed Ronny his back. He double-checked that the three belts were secure, then knelt down again. "Okay. Climb on, son." Ronny climbed onto Reggie's back. "Now, put your arms around my neck. Lock your hands together and don't let go. Don't let go for nothin'. You understand?"

"Yes. I'll hold on."

"Good boy." Ronny wrapped his arms around Reggie's neck. "Okay. Hang tight. Let's get out of here." Reggie looked up and shouted. "John? We're coming up! Hold the tree steady as you can. But don't push on it."

"Got it," John shouted back. "Bring it on."

"Thank you for saving me, Mr. Howard."

"No problem, son. And, like I said, my name is Reggie." Reggie started to climb. He carefully felt for handholds and footholds on the makeshift ladder. He gripped the highest branch he could reach, then placed his right foot on a branch. He moved hands and feet, one at a time, always keeping three of them secured to the tree. The moonlight glowed full, reflecting off Reggie's face. Beads of sweat glistened on his brow. His face was set with determination. His eyes were focused on the lantern that John offered, ahead and above him.

"Thank you," Reggie said quietly to himself each time he found a handhold and his grip didn't slip. "Thank you, Lord." Hearing Reggie, Ronny decided that it was a good idea to pray as well. His silent prayers mingled with Reggie's words as they ascended.

It was slow and treacherous going. Reggie made steady progress. He never looked down, but an image of them falling from the ladder into the abyss crossed his mind. He shook his head to clear that away. It worked. Slowly, they made progress up toward John and the lantern's light. Reggie felt the warmth of Ronny's breath on the back of his neck.

"How're you doing, son?"

"Okay, Mr., uh, Reggie."

"Right, Reggie," he said. "All the people I rescue call me Reggie." At that moment they emerged from darkness and John reached a hand over the edge to them.

"Can you reach me?" John asked.

"Not yet. Get back!" Reggie shouted. "Just keep the darn tree stable until we're closer." Reggie's tone of voice startled John and he quickly backed off the edge, but in doing so he slid on the snow-covered rocks and slipped precariously down the slope to the left, slamming hard into a boulder. He screamed in pain but was able to grab on to it. He wound up precariously holding on to the edge of the cliff by one arm.

"Ohhhh! Damn! Damn it!" John yelled.

Reggie heard John's pain and realized something bad had happened. He hurried to reach the top, sliding onto the flat, snow-covered ledge, pulling Ronny along with him.

"Hang on, John," Reggie shouted as he unhooked Ronny and shoved him clear of the ledge.

"Okay, Ronny. Now stay there. Don't move!" The boy nodded and sat still. Reggie slid back toward the edge where John held on by one arm. He saw the other arm was hanging loose and twisted. It was obviously broken. "Oh, man," Reggie muttered. "That's bad news." He carefully slid down to the rocks and grabbed John's good arm. "Okay," he said. "I've got you. Let go." Struggling with all of his strength against John's dead weight, he pulled him off the rocks onto flat ground above the ravine.

Both men were exhausted. John was shivering from shock and the cold. He moaned and sat up. His injured arm hung limp at his side.

"It's broken, for sure," Reggie told him.

"Yeah. I heard it crack. Boy, it sure hurts."

"I'm gonna open your jacket and have a look. Sorry, but it might hurt more." John nodded and gritted his teeth. Reggie carefully unzipped the Eddie Bauer jacket that John had unpacked from his suitcase, and slid it from his shoulder. John shivered. "It's not compound. No blood. Didn't break the skin." Reggie put the jacket back on.

"Thanks for small favors, huh?" John grimaced from the throbbing pain.

"Yeah. You think you can walk?"

John took a deep breath. "Got to, right? No taxis out here. Listen, Reggie. What you just did. That was no small favor. Thank you. I mean, you risked your own . . . Anyway, I owe you."

Reggie looked over at Ronny. The boy was shivering badly as the wind blew swirling snow around him. "Sure. I gotta get you both back to the cabin before somebody goes into shock or gets hypothermia."

"Help me up," John said, offering his good hand. Reggie pulled him up on his feet. John was momentarily unsteady.

"Wait, wait just a sec," John said, his words clipped by the pain as he saw Ronny sitting in the snow. "It's well . . . I mean after all this, I'd, uh, I'd hate to go back without that tree."

"Are you out of your mind?" Reggie said. "A broken arm? All of us freezing? The temperature dropping by the minute . . ."

"Yeah. Yeah. You're right," John said. "But it's Christmas Eve and the kids are all excited. . . . And now I can't feel the pain anymore," he lied. Reggie shook his head and smiled. This whole day and night was borderline insane. He shrugged.

"What the hell! Let me get the saw and ax, Hey, Ronny. Can you grab that lantern?" The boy got up and picked up the lantern as Reggie gathered the tools.

"Can we get the tree now?" Ronny asked.

"That we can, son," John told him. The boy was not aware John's arm was broken.

"I can carry the lantern," Ronny announced.

"All right, guys," Reggie said. "Let's move out—" Goldie's bark interrupted him.

"It's Goldie!" Ronny shouted. First they saw the big retriever, and then behind him, came the light from a kerosene lantern carried by Joshua.

"It's Joshua," Reggie said. "Great!" There was relief in his voice. Then Reggie and John exchanged a worried look.

"Listen, Ronny," John said. "I want you to do us a favor."

"What, Mr. Sullivan?"

"When we get back, don't tell your mother *you*

fell. We'll say it was me. I fell. Okay? It might worry her, and we don't want to do that. Right?"

"It'll be our little secret, son," Reggie added. "Okay?"

"Okay," Ronny answered. "I can keep secrets. My sister can't."

"Good. And now we have Joshua to help us get the Christmas tree," John said as Goldie and Joshua reached them.

"How's John's arm, Reggie?" Joshua immediately asked.

"Uh, it's broken," Reggie answered. He glanced at John, then back to Joshua. He was confused. "Now how'd you know about . . . uh?"

"Just look at it. Goldie came runnin' like you guys needed some help."

"Oh, yeah," Reggie said. "We had a little mishap. We were just heading back to get the tree."

"No need. Goldie showed it to me. I finished cutting it. It's just over there in the woods. A beauty, boys. Now let's see if we can get y'all back to the cabin, in one piece and pronto."

CHAPTER 31

CANDLES

While Amelia tended to the turkey, Andy and Marta sat at the kitchen table making candle lights for the tree. They cut the candles from the cupboard into pieces and melted them. Then they stripped some pine branches of their needles and dipped the ends into the wax, leaving the tips uncoated. Once the wax hardened, they dipped the exposed pine wood tips into kerosene. When lit, the kerosene-soaked tips burned slowly, melting the wax as they did.

"If you ask me," Marta said, "he's a real hermit, living like this, all alone out here."

"He seems content to me," Andy suggested. "When you think about some of the madness of the world today, then living out here must be peaceful."

"Maybe you're right," Marta responded. She looked over at Nancy, who was with Ilena, making ornaments. "The real world is pretty screwed." Andy studied her for a moment. From the time they first were thrown together, he had sensed she was unhappy. Unhappy and frightened. She was quick to anger and argue.

"I heard you are a single mom. That must be tough," he said sincerely. Marta was taken aback by such a personal remark. But his manner and tone sounded sympathetic, and he seemed a caring man.

"Yes, it is. I manage. I have to. But it's not easy. Our breakup was just a few days ago, and the kids are upset about it. . . ."

"Well, if it means anything, you seem pretty together to me."

"Thank you." She looked into his eyes and saw kindness, and something more. There was an aura of sadness around him that she had not noticed before. The room was quiet and warm. The crackling fire was comforting. They had food, and now everyone seemed to be pulling together to make Christmas Eve special for her kids.

"Do you have family in Asheville?" she asked as he finished making another light for the tree.

"No. An old army buddy. He's not well." Andy paused. "This will be George's last Christmas."

"I'm sorry. You must be close friends."

"He's the best. There was a time when we were welded at the hip. Inseparable. But now it's his time. He's known it was coming for a while."

"Oh?"

"He was never right after the war. Physically, I mean. His spine got all screwed up sliding down ropes out of helicopters with ninety pounds on his back. Had one operation after another, but the V.A. docs didn't get it right. And then there was Agent Orange. . . . Been a wonder he made it this far. Got a lot of extra years, he did." Andy looked away. "Me too. There was a time that either me or old George figured we weren't gonna make it much more than the next day. So the next day was always a gift."

"Did you have the, um, you know, Agent Orange problems?"

"So far, so good. A few small things, but nothing I can't deal with."

"And your family?" she asked, changing the subject to a topic she felt more comfortable discussing.

"Well, I'm originally from Puerto Rico. A small town called San Anton. Most of my family is there. You know that's where Roberto Clemente came from?"

"Who?"

"Roberto Clemente. He was a great baseball player. A truly great man. He was a real hero. His plane went down carrying relief supplies to earthquake victims in Nicaragua."

"I'm sure Ronny knows who he is . . . was. You're not married?"

"Maria, my wife, she died in May." He sighed. "Cancer." He wiped away a tear. "Sorry. We . . . I live in New York City. The Bronx."

For the first time in a while, Marta felt her tender side rise above her self-absorption with her own troubles. She saw Andy's loneliness and reached out to touch his hand.

"Don't be sorry to show emotion. I understand."

"Thank you." He smiled. "We had no kids. I was a transit worker. Retired. I drive a cab sometimes. I have a decent pension and a small army disability."

"You were wounded?"

"My shoulder. Shrapnel from a mortar. Me and George watched them across this rice paddy. They had us pinned down. First round struck on the far bank. Next round struck in the middle of the paddy, and, hell, we knew they had the range. I heard the next 'thunk' of the mortar. That's a sound like no other. You know it's coming your way. I looked at old George, and he looked at me. We knew it had our names on it. Nothing we could do but hunker down and hope they missed. Damn thing came in and hit the dike right in front of us." Marta was riveted. She had never experienced anyone telling such a story. This simple man, who had quietly helped all of them organize and survive this day, was openly sharing a deeply personal event in his life with her. "There's mud and water spiking up into the sky in a big old dirty plume. It sent old George flying through the air. He landed about ten yards away. Arms and legs flaying around, the back of his shirt ripped out, and there was blood, lots of blood, and bone." Andy did not look at Marta as he spoke. His eyes were on a scene from long ago and far away, a scene he had not dreamt of or visualized for a long time. He focused back on her. "I'm sorry. I didn't mean to—"

"Don't be foolish. I'm honored that you would share that with me. It puts my troubles, and our adventure here, in perspective. What happened next?"

"A gunship came in and took out the mortar. They got us onto a medevac. I was patched up and sent back into the bush. I didn't see George until I got back to the states. He was in the V.A. hospital in my neighborhood. To this day, he doesn't remember seeing me there. They had him doped

up, getting ready for his second or third operation. I forget." Marta realized she was still holding
his hand. He put his hand on top of hers. "You're
a good listener. So was my Maria."

"It's a pleasure to know you, Andy."

"Likewise, Marta."

"So where did you learn to make these candles?"

"My grandma. Years ago there was no electricity
in San Anton. She taught me. She's long gone
now, but she is with me, too."

Marta smiled and began to make another candle. "Well, tell her I am grateful to learn how, and
grateful for her kind and brave grandson, too."

CHAPTER 32

FOR MY COUNTRY

Across the room, at the table near the fire, Ilena and Nancy were busy finishing making ornaments for the anticipated tree. They were fashioned from the gift wrapping and ribbons that had been removed from presents the others had carried in their luggage. They had made colorful foil and paper stars, balls, triangles, and seven delicate angels Ilena had cut out of blue and silver paper with the scissors on her Swiss army knife. To get them ready for hanging, Ilena was cutting a piece of dried deerskin that Joshua had supplied into strips with her knife. As the strips were cut, Nancy attached them to the ornaments, leaving enough of the deerskin free to be tied to the tree branches.

"Do you think we'll have enough?" Nancy asked.

"I guess so. Unless they bring a really big tree."

"We have enough to make more."

"Okay, why don't you start some more?" Nancy gathered some of the leftover Christmas wrapping paper and began to fold it. She studied Ilena, who was cutting more strips of the deerskin. She watched how the pretty young woman, dressed in her army uniform, expertly handled the knife.

"May I have the scissors?" Nancy asked.

"Sure." Ilena handed Nancy the knife with the scissors open. "Be careful. Don't try to cut too fast. They're very sharp." Nancy took the scissors but kept her gaze on Ilena.

"Is it hard being a soldier?" she asked. Ilena looked up.

"Sometimes," she said, smiling warmly.

"On TV I see lots of soldiers. The announcer says they get killed and hurt. I see it every day, but they don't say who they are. Do you know them?"

"Some of them are my friends."

"Why do they have to die?"

"I uh, I can't say . . . I don't know. That's what happens in war."

"Aren't you afraid?"

"Yes," Ilena said softly. "Sometimes." Nancy placed the scissors on the table and folded her hands demurely as she looked into Ilena's face.

"If you're afraid; why do you do it? My daddy said no one really has to."

"Because I want to go to college. It's a way to get the money I need for that." Ilena paused, and looked directly at the child, realizing the falsity of her stock answer. Ilena had learned that it was the answer civilians expected to hear. They didn't really want to know why she was a soldier or where she'd been. That made them uncomfortable, especially since she was a woman. Hers was a road they had not traveled, and they were incapable of reading the road signs. But maybe Nancy deserved more than a flip answer. Maybe Nancy's directness and innocent curiosity warranted truth. She took a moment to gather her words.

"No. It's more than that, Nancy. I do it because I want to be there. Because I feel very alive when I'm there. Because I want to be a visible part of America. Because my best friends are there. And most of all, because I want to serve my country."

At that moment, Lisa came through the front door with an arm full of splits. She walked past the table. The cold air that clung to her jacket and the wood touched the ornament makers as she passed.

"Hi, guys," she said cheerfully. "Those ornaments look great." She set the wood down and spread it out to dry.

Ilena waited to see what Nancy might say to her honest response. The girl reached across the table and touched Ilena's hand.

"I really hope you don't get hurt before you get to college," she said. "I'm going to ask God to watch over you when I say my prayers every night." Ilena was surprised and profoundly moved by Nancy's words. She slid her trembling hand away from Nancy's and touched the young girl's shoulder. Lisa overheard the conversation and saw Ilena's reaction.

"Then I'll be safe," Ilena said. "Thank you, Nancy." She rose abruptly, a lump in her throat. Her movement knocked an empty cup off the table. Near tears, she quickly went out the front door onto the porch. Nancy watched and wondered what she'd said to upset her new friend so much.

Lisa saw the child's confusion and moved from the fireplace. She picked up the cup and placed it on the table, then took Ilena's place to help Nancy with the ornaments. The girl was close to tears.

"Did I say something wrong?"

"No, darling. She just needed fresh air. It's been a long day. She's tired. So let's finish these ornaments. The tree is coming. We want to be ready for it."

CHAPTER 33

MEDIC

Nancy's words echoed in Ilena's mind. She did not feel the cold, or the touch of the icy wind. Her thoughts were with her close friend, Beth Winters. Ilena pictured her in full combat gear and armor behind the wheel of a five-ton, driving hell-bent and balls-to-the-wall in the lead truck on the Highway of Death from the airport into Baghdad. Why did she leave her and her company? What was she doing in this frigid, lonely forest with a bunch of strangers? This wasn't her world. Not now, anyway. She felt empty and alone.

Her reverie was cut short as she heard a bark and saw Goldie emerge from the forest. Reggie came next, dragging a small, neat blue spruce. Ronny was next to him, carrying two lanterns. Joshua was the last to emerge, dragging something behind him. When she saw it was John, lying on a stretcher fashioned of saplings, she ran to help them.

* * *

The front door flew open, and Joshua backed in, pulling the makeshift stretcher into the cabin after him. Reggie had left the tree outside, along with the ax. Now he carried the other end of the stretcher. The two men brought it into the room and set it down near the fire. Ilena immediately knelt next to John and examined how his arm had been immobilized with belts.

"It's not compound," Reggie told her. Andy, Lisa, and Nancy gathered around. Marta immediately went to Ronny who was still holding the two lanterns. Goldie was next to him.

"What happened? Are you okay, Ronny?"

"I'm okay, Mommy. Mr. Sullivan fell and hurt his arm." The boy gave Reggie a quick look for approval. Reggie gave him a "well done" wink back.

Nancy watched as Ilena carefully unbound John's arm. He winced in pain. Ilena felt John's pulse while watching fifteen seconds count off on her watch, then multiplied the result by 4. "Well, you're not going into shock." She felt his arm through his jacket. "It's swollen. I'll have to cut the jacket off you."

"It's a new Eddie Bauer," John joked.

"Send the bill to my boss," Ilena answered. She turned to Lisa. "Can you hand me my knife. It's on the table with the ornaments." Lisa knew exactly where it was because she had been using it moments before. She got the knife and handed it to Ilena. Amelia, who had heard the commotion, came out of the bedroom.

"What's happened?" she asked as she rushed across the room. "Is someone hurt?"

Joshua met her halfway. "An accident, Amelia.

John fell and hurt himself. His arm may be broken, but he's going to be all right."

"Let me see," she said and went around him. Ilena was in the process of cutting away the jacket.

"I'll have to cut your shirt, too," Ilena told John. She looked up and saw Amelia had arrived. "Can you get me some hot water, Amelia?"

"Yes. Right away." Amelia hurried to the kitchen.

"I'll need something to use for a bandage and sling," Ilena announced as she carefully removed the sleeve from John's jacket and began to cut away his shirt sleeve. "And two strips of wood for a splint."

"I have two fleece sweatshirts in my bag," Lisa said, and went to get them.

"I'll get the wood," Andy announced. "There's some nice smooth ones in the pantry." As everyone sprang into action, Joshua stepped back and watched with great interest. Nancy went over to her brother.

"Did you find a tree?"

"Yes. A beauty. It's on the porch." She smiled and went back to watching Ilena minister to John. Marta stood with her. They watched as Ilena cut away John's shirt sleeve, revealing his swollen arm. There was a bump below the elbow where the bone was broken. Ilena touched it.

"Ow!" John said. "That hurts."

"Sorry," Ilena said. "What I'm gonna do will hurt even more. Are you up to it?" John looked into her eyes. He saw her steadfast confidence.

"Do what you have to, doc. I've got insurance."

"Not necessary. This one's on the taxpayers."

Andy was back with two smooth splits about a foot long. "How are these?"

"Perfect," Ilena told him. "Now, let's get at it."

"Do you know what you're doing?" Marta asked in a loud voice. Her tone silenced the room. Everyone looked at her and then at Ilena. Reggie shook his head and backed away. Instinctively he was ready to tell Marta off, but he didn't want to get into another confrontation with her.

"For God's sake, Marta," Andy said. "She's a soldier. She's trained to do this. Reggie and me, too, but what she knows is a hell of a lot more current than what we know."

"I've done this before, Marta," Ilena said softly, but with deep conviction. Moisture welled in her eyes. "I've seen worse, much worse than this in Iraq. And not just our people. Civilians. Children." She looked directly at Marta. "Trust me. I'll take care of John. But he'll need to see a doctor when we get out of here."

Realizing her error, Marta was embarrassed. "Yes. Of course," she said softly. "I'm sorry. I truly am. Let me help Amelia with the hot water." She went into the kitchen.

"I'm going to have to reset the arm," Ilena told John. "It's gonna hurt when I do it, but it'll feel better after. Okay?"

John smiled. "No pain, no gain, huh? Okay. Hey, Andy? How about a shot of that Blue Label first."

"You got it, pal." Andy poured a triple shot of the amber liquid. He handed it to John, who drained it in one long gulp as Lisa came over with the sweatshirts.

"Smooth stuff," he said. "Okay, doc," he told Ilena, "do your thing." Amelia and Marta arrived with the hot water.

"Okay. Now I want you to lie as still as you can," Ilena told John, whose face was flushed red from the scotch and the heat from the nearby fire. He smiled bravely, but it was clear he was nervous. "Andy, can you hold his shoulders?" she asked. He nodded and took up a position at the head of the make-shift stretcher. "Lisa, can you hold his feet?"

"Sure." She moved to the foot of the stretcher and put her hands around his ankles.

"I saw this in a movie once," John said, grinning. The effects of the belt of scotch had him relaxed. "But they were cutting off an arm then."

"Not today," Ilena told him. "Maybe in the morning," she joked. With that, she nodded to Andy and Lisa. They gripped John tightly. Then, kneeling closer to John, Ilena slid her left hand under his arm and gripped the crook of his elbow firmly. John looked away, into the fire. She grasped his arm just above the wrist with her right hand and took a deep breath. Marta turned Nancy and Ronny away. She did not look, either. Amelia knelt on the other side of the stretcher and held John's other hand. She smiled at him. He squeezed her hand. Then, in one expert motion, Ilena twisted with her right hand and pulled with her left. There was a popping sound and the lump in John's arm, made by the broken bone, disappeared.

"Whoa!" John said as his body stiffened. But then he relaxed and smiled. "All right!" he said. "That really does feel better."

"Good," Ilena told him. "I think I got it right. Now let's get that washed down and secured. Please don't try to move it or twist it. Okay?"

"Whatever you say, doc. Just one thing."

"What?" she asked.

"Bend over here so I can thank you properly." Ilena smiled and bent close to him. He raised his head slightly and gave her a warm kiss on the cheek. "Thank you!"

"You're most welcome," she said. "Now let's get you another shot of scotch and into bed."

CHAPTER 34

SILVER LININGS

Satisfied that everything was under control, Joshua moved away from the activity and went out to the front porch. Goldie followed him. Reggie, still wary of Marta, and feeling out of place among these white folks, saw that Andy, Ilena, and Lisa were moving John to the bedroom. They didn't ask for his help. The fact that he had saved John, and Ronny, from a very dangerous situation was never brought up or discussed. He understood that John was in pain, and that Ronny had been told not to mention he had fallen off the cliff. Still and all, he was angry. Reggie put on his jacket and went outside.

The moon was bright—out from behind the clouds again but lower in the sky. Its light cast long shadows on the snow in the clearing. Reggie saw Joshua and Goldie standing on the porch. He walked over to them.

"Beautiful night," Joshua said. "Brilliant." He looked up. Reggie followed the old man's gaze up to the sky. He immediately thought of Van Gogh's painting, *Starry Night,* but all he did was nod his agreement. He then noticed the tree they had left in the snow.

"Time to bring the tree in?" Joshua asked.

"Not yet," Reggie said. "Let them get John settled in." Joshua nodded and patted Goldie's head. The dog looked up and licked his master's hand.

"You did a brave thing out there, Reggie."

"I did what I had to."

"Makin' that ladder out of that pine was darn smart."

Reggie reached for the cigarettes he had bought. He realized he had given them to Andy and was sorry about that for a moment. Then he smiled.

"I once had a fishing cabin up on Lake Huron. Near a town called Alpena. In Michigan. Wasn't much, but it was mine. Did a lot of work on that place." He smiled again and stretched his arms. "Chopped a lot of wood. Cleared a lot of brush. My son, he lives in Asheville now, fell into a tight ravine one day. I couldn't reach him, and he was crying. Didn't want me to leave to go get a rope. So I did the same thing. Made a ladder from a downed tree."

"But this time you had to go down and get the boy. That took a lot of guts."

"How'd you know my son climbed up himself? I didn't say that," Reggie blurted out.

"I thought I heard you just say that."

"I didn't."

"Well . . . My hearing's not what it used to be. Anyway, John told me you climbed down for Ronny."

"When'd he say that?"

"On the way back."

"Hey, man. I never told John about my boy and the ladder. I wasn't far behind you."

"Well, maybe it was Ronny," Joshua said as he turned and faced Reggie. The broad smile on Joshua's face disarmed Reggie. "No matter." There was something comforting in Joshua's voice and manner. Reggie was suddenly bone tired from the long, stressful day and the physical strain of saving Ronny and John. His knees felt weak.

"Let's sit a bit," Joshua suggested, pointing to two small log benches at the far end of the porch. They sat down. Goldie settled at their feet and closed his eyes. "So what happened to that fishin' cabin of yours?" Joshua asked.

"I had to sell it to help pay to send my boy off to college."

"You do what's necessary."

"I hated to do it . . . I mean sell the place. But to give my son the opportunity I never had? No, man. I don't ever regret that. Still 'n all, there was a lot of me in that old cabin."

"Your boy's grown now. Why not get another one?"

"You kidding? I'm laid off and heading to Asheville to work for him. The old man working for his son. Funny, huh?"

"No. I don't think so. Seems he's successful because you made that sacrifice. You know? What goes around comes around."

"An overrated truism. I remember, 'As GM goes, so goes the nation.' Now they're closing assembly lines. Put thousands like me out of work.

Shipping jobs off to Mexico, Japan, China, India, and Lord knows where else. Damn. That's just plain wrong."

"Yes. Hard to see any right in a wrong like that."

"There is none. Not for the working man, anyway."

"In my time they said that if you work hard enough and believe—"

"Hey, man," Reggie interrupted, "I don't know what plane of existence you're living on out here." He gestured out to snow glowing dully in the moonlight and the distant, dark woods. "I mean, there aren't exactly a lot of folks out here. No people, no right, no wrong. But where I come from there's people, there's right, and there's wrong. They usually aren't mixed up together."

Goldie stirred and shifted his position at Joshua's feet. The man instinctively reached down and gently stroked his dog's head. "Well now, son, I'm not so sure about that. Long as we're tradin', what was it you said, truisms?"

"Yes. I said that."

"What's that old one about a silver lining behind every cloud? Like the sky tonight. Maybe you got a silver lining in front of you and you ain't seen it yet."

Reggie shook his head and smiled. "That's what my wife says. Think what it would be like if you didn't have Donald—he's my boy—to go to work for? But . . ." Reggie shrugged. "Taking away a man's job, well, that's taking away his pride."

"Only if you let them."

Reggie laughed. "Only if you let them? Doesn't that beat all? Who were your people, Joshua?"

"My people?"

"Yeah, your people? Scotch, Irish, Dutch? Who settled up here way back when?"

"They were from Glasgow. Scotch, and fierce Calvinists that lot was. Predestination. God's will. To them, it was all written." Joshua waved up to the night sky in a grand flourish. "What you were going to be, what you were going to do; it was in the hands of the Good Lord."

"What's predestined about when a man can't make a living for his family? Man, you know how hard *we* had to fight for the right to work good jobs?"

"You mean against the unions and bigots?"

"I mean being a *black* man in *white* America. Just when we move up and grab a piece of the pie, we get knocked down again. Like being on a merry-go-round your whole life, and just when you think you're going to reach out and grab the brass ring, somebody knocks you off the horse, or moves the ring farther away, or in my case, shuts down the damned carousel."

"That's true, Reggie. I said they were Calvinists. I'm not. I was tellin' Ilena about the Cherokee orphanage that used to be on Comfort Mountain. Run by the church."

"Right here?"

"Up top. They were so self-righteous they believed it was their mission to destroy the culture and beliefs of those unfortunate children. This so-called God-fearing, Christian country darn near destroyed the entire Cherokee nation. I understand what you're sayin', son. All I'm sayin' is that's your lot, and do what you have to do. But keep your dignity, and never despair; do like you did tonight for Ronny and John."

Reggie felt a strong kinship with this strange old man. He seemed a hermit, a wild mountain man, and yet he spoke simple wisdom that was not only true, but gave Reggie uplifting comfort. Joshua was like a long lost relative who had returned from traveling the world, learning its secrets, and finding peace.

"I suppose you've got a point there, Joshua."

"You have a son and daughter-in-law, and two fine grandchildren who love you and want to help. It's something to treasure, Reggie."

"Who *are* you, man? How'd you know about my family and my grandkids? I *never* mentioned them to you." Reggie stood up. His movement woke Goldie, who got up and stretched. "And back there by the cliff . . . How'd you know John broke his arm?"

"I saw it, like I told you."

Reggie shook his head. "I don't know. You and this dog; this place; what's going on here?"

Joshua got up from his bench with the slow movement of an aged body. "Just an old man sharing his hearth and home with a bunch of people who seem to be a little lost this Christmas Eve."

"Lost?" Reggie was about to confront Joshua for answers to his questions when the cabin door opened and Andy stepped out, interrupting Reggie's quest. Goldie barked.

"There you are," Andy called out. "Listen, John's asleep. The turkey's about done. We're all starving, and the kids are asking if we can bring the Christmas tree inside now."

"That's why we're out here," Joshua answered quickly. "Right, Reggie?" Reggie cocked his head and squinted at Joshua questioningly.

"Merry Christmas, Reggie," Joshua said, extending his hand.

"Merry Christmas, Joshua," Reggie said reflexively. He squeezed the old man's hand tightly, and in return felt the strength of Joshua's hand.

"You're going to have a great year, son."

Reggie found himself believing Joshua's words. For a brief moment he wondered if this old man was truly someone out of the ordinary. Or was he being hustled by a white man one more time? Feeling the spirit of Christmas, Reggie patted Joshua on the shoulder and smiled.

"Thanks," was all he could muster, knowing this was no hustle.

"C'mon, guys. Give me a hand!" Andy shouted as he grabbed the base of the tree.

Reggie and Joshua came off the porch and joined him. Reggie reached inside the branches for the trunk in the middle, and Joshua took the top. Together, they shook off the snow that had stuck to the branches where the tree had lain. Andy backed up onto the porch and opened the door. "Here comes Christmas," he called out to those inside. Goldie, who took up the rear, barked, ruf-ruf-ruf-ruf, four times, as if to say his own "Merry Christ-mas."

CHAPTER 35

CHRISTMAS TREE, O CHRISTMAS TREE

Ronny and Nancy clapped their hands and jumped up and down as the men brought the tree into the cabin. Ilena and Lisa moved the meager furniture aside to make room for the five-foot, and very full, blue spruce. Once Andy, Reggie, and Joshua had the tree upright in the corner of the room adjacent to the fireplace, everyone marveled at its perfect shape.

"Oh my!" Amelia exclaimed. She had been in the bedroom, turning the turkey. "That tree was made for this cabin," she said.

"Hold it there," Joshua told Andy and Reggie. He opened a wooden toolbox in the corner where he kept the snowshoes and took out a hammer and several nails. Selecting two of the smaller splits that were drying near the fire, he nailed them crosswise. "Tip the tree over," he told Andy and Reggie. When they did, Joshua nailed the splits to the sawn base of the tree. "Okay, raise her up."

Reggie and Andy raised the tree until it stood level and steady.

"Won't it need water?" Ronny asked.

"No, son," Joshua said. "It only needs to last for Christmas Eve."

"Speaking of which," Amelia said. "Our Christmas Eve dinner is just about ready. I'll just need a little help getting it off the spit so it can cool a bit."

"I'll do that," Joshua said as he took off his coat. "Why don't the rest of you get this tree lookin' like Christmas?"

"Right," Lisa said. She went to the table to get the ornaments. Nancy and Ilena went with her.

"Come and help Andy and me with the candles," Marta said to Ronny. The three of them went to the kitchen table to get them. Reggie watched everyone get busy. He saw Joshua looking at him, and though no words were spoken, he knew the old man wanted him to help with the turkey. Reggie nodded and followed Joshua and Amelia into the back bedroom.

Six eager hands decorated the tree. The ornaments, made with Christmas gift-wrapping paper and foil went on first. Lisa held them; Nancy chose where they would be hung; and Ilena, who was tall, carefully tied them in place. When that was complete, Marta and Ronny carefully carried the makeshift candles to the tree. One by one, the pine and wax candles were attached and securely tied to branches of the tree where they would not catch fire. In a few spots, Andy had to cut away the branches above some of the candles just to be sure.

Meanwhile, Reggie and Joshua wrapped heavy

pieces of canvas around the ends of the spit and then carefully lifted the turkey, firmly speared on the iron spit, away from the fire. Amelia had prepared another piece of clean canvas, wrapped around a wide, wooden plank, to hold the turkey for carving. The men set the bird, now brown and steaming, on the plank. Amelia covered it with another piece of clean canvas.

"Let's leave it a little away from the fire," she whispered, keeping her voice low so as to not wake John, who was asleep in the bed. The men did as she asked.

"I'll bank the coals," Reggie offered, and using a log, pushed the red hot coals back against the rear of the hearth. Amelia tiptoed over to the bed and checked John. Satisfied that he was sleeping soundly, she signaled for the men to leave with her.

In the main room, Lisa had found three long ribbons on some of the gifts in the luggage and draped them on the tree as the finishing touch. One was bright red, another was silver, and the third one gold. All that was left was for the candles to be lit. Andy took a long, narrow split from the wood that was drying near the fire and lit it. One by one he touched the flame to the kerosene-soaked pine stems. They immediately caught fire and settled down to small, bright, conical flames that were contained by the wax. Everyone's spirits, already kindled with the Christmas cheer, grew brighter with each candle lit. Goldie sat close to the tree and watched. The dog's mouth was open, and he panted rapidly.

"Look," Ronny said. "Goldie is smiling." And so it seemed to everyone that he was.

Amelia, Reggie, and Joshua came into the room

just as Andy lit the last candle. He found himself the object of a warm, approving smile from Amelia. Lisa, Ilena, and Reggie selected a few gifts they were bringing for kids in their families in Asheville and placed them under the tree for Nancy and Ronny. Everyone stepped back and gathered to admire their work.

"It's wonderful," Lisa said.

"It's a real Christmas tree, Mommy," Nancy told Marta.

"Beautiful," Ilena added.

"But where's the star?" Ronny asked.

"Don't have a star exactly," Joshua told them, "but I got somethin' I think'll do just fine." He walked across the room to the small pantry in the kitchen and went inside. Everyone watched with anticipation. A moment later he came out carrying something in his hand that they could not immediately see. "I found this a while back in the ruins of an old huntin' cabin that burned down," he said as he joined the group. "Struck by lightnin', it was." He held up an opaque, white angel. It was about ten inches long and hollow inside. It had delicate wings spread out behind it. The face appeared to be that of a young girl. She was smiling. Her arms were spread in a welcoming way.

Joshua walked to the tree and placed it carefully on the very top. The angel fit perfectly with the size of the tree.

"Always been partial to angels," Joshua said softly as he stepped back.

"She's really pretty," Nancy told him.

"Perfect," Marta said. Then, the bright, full moon, now low in the sky, sent a shaft of moonlight magically through the cabin window directly on the angel.

"Look!" Ronny exclaimed. The moonlight caused the angel to glow radiantly.

"Oh my," Amelia declared. "That's lovely."

"Sensational," Andy said.

"Miraculous," Ilena added in a whisper.

"Now we have a real, official Christmas!" Ronny announced, beaming.

Everyone laughed and applauded except Reggie. He studied Joshua with suspicion. The old man caught Reggie's gaze. He smiled and winked. Like a novitiate among Druid elders, Reggie thought he was beginning to see something magical and powerful in Joshua, the cabin, Goldie . . . the whole day and night, though he wasn't certain what exactly it was, or what it meant. Then there was silence as they all took in the wonder of the moment. Amelia broke the silence as her beautiful and heartfelt voice sang:

> O Christmas tree, O Christmas tree,
> of all the trees most lovely.
> O Christmas tree, O Christmas tree,
> of all the trees most lovely.
> Each year you bring to me delight,
> meaning in the Christmas night.
> O Christmas tree, O Christmas tree,
> of all the trees most lovely.

Her beautiful soprano voice filled the cabin. Everyone joined in the singing. Joshua slipped away, unnoticed, to the back bedroom as the singing continued around the tree.

O Christmas tree, O Christmas tree,
with faithful leaves unchanging.
O Christmas tree, O Christmas tree,
with faithful leaves unchanging.
Your boughs are green, in summer's glow,
and do not fade in winter's snow.
O Christmas tree, O Christmas tree,
with faithful leaves unchanging.
Each year you bring to me delight,
meaning in the Christmas night.
O Christmas tree, O Christmas tree,
of all the trees most lovely.

Then they repeated the song with even more spirit and harmony. It grew joyously, echoing into the rear bedroom where John slumbered.

CHAPTER 36

HEALING

Alone in the back room, with the door shut, Joshua went to the window and pulled the faded curtain aside. Starlight fell upon Joshua's face as he looked up and nodded skyward. Then, as if called to a mission, a narrow beam of silvery moonlight passed through the window and shone on John's broken arm. John stirred from his sleep, rubbing his eyes with his left hand and then tousling his hair. He sat up, swung his legs over the side of the bed, and stretched. He looked around and saw Joshua standing next to the window.

"Hi," John said.

"Hello, John," Joshua answered. "Have a good sleep?"

"Yes," John said. "That second drink of scotch put me away."

"How do you feel?"

He moved his arm hesitantly within the splint. "Hey, this feels good." He slipped out of bed and stretched again. "Real good."

"Ilena did a fine job," Joshua said as he moved to where the turkey had been put. "She's a good soldier."

"Is that the turkey I smell?"

"That it is. We're about to eat."

"Then I'm glad I woke up. I'm famished." John walked to the end of the bed. He looked around the room.

"Can I ask you a question, Joshua?"

"Please do."

"This place," John began. "The life you lead. It seems like, well, like you're a real hermit. How come? I mean . . . if it's not too personal, why?"

"We can't always control where life takes us, John, or certainly how much time we've got. I just decided to live life one day at a time, try to do the right thing, and let the rest sort itself out."

John shook his head. "I'm just the opposite. I've been trying to control mine. Maybe you've got it right. Maybe a natural life is better. I mean, compared to mine. You've got a home here. I've got one, too, but truthfully, I'm never there."

"Out makin' a buck? What's it called? The rat race?"

"I make a lot of money."

"Sounds important."

"I thought so. Then today happened. These people. This place. You. What happened out there on that ledge. How everyone pitched in to help. Even Goldie."

"So what do you think it all means?" Joshua asked.

"I think maybe I've been chasing the wrong dream. Here I am, stuck in the middle of nowhere with a bunch of strangers, and we're all . . . I don't know. That guy Reggie. He's had a bad time. But when it came to saving the kid . . . I figure you know he was the one who fell."

"Yes. I knew that. From Goldie . . ." John wasn't listening. He was too wrapped up in his own revelations.

"Well, out there in the cold and snow watching Reggie save the kid, and then me. I mean, I could easily be at the bottom of that ravine. Then you show up, and everyone here pulling together. Ilena setting my arm. I guess what I'm saying is that this feels right. The way things should be. The way to live with one another. I was thinking how great it would be if my family . . . if they were here now with me, with us, to have this experience. Together. You know what I mean?"

"I do," Joshua said. "I surely do."

"I've never really seen where strangers can become like close friends, if only for a moment in their lives."

"It's there for the taking every day. Sometimes folks focus so much on their work, careers, things, that they forget to live. They don't see there are people to love and nurture. They put that part of being human out of their lives."

"You're absolutely right. We all need that."

Joshua knelt down to check the turkey. It was warm and ready. He stood up.

"I know you love Anne and your twin girls. But they don't hear it enough, and the clock's running. Be more than a shame if you'd gone into that ravine and Kate and Carly never knew how much you really loved them. That is the only gift you alone can give them. Be proud of what you've built, but know that they need you, too. Maybe what you're feeling is not to live a life like mine, but to bring balance into your own life." Joshua knelt again, picked up the board with the turkey on it, and walked to the door.

John followed Joshua. Realizing what he had heard, he reached out to stop him. "Hold on. My wife and twins? How did you know their names? How did you know I had twins?" As he grasped Joshua's arm with his left hand, he was aware that he could move his injured arm as though it were not broken! He let go of Joshua and stared at his right hand. He flexed it and twisted his arm. There was no pain.

CHAPTER 37

HOW'D THAT HAPPEN?

"**H**eeeeecrrrree's Johnny," John exclaimed, emu
lating Ed McMahon's classic introduction of Johnny
Carson on *The Tonight Show*. He followed Joshua
into the main room.

"Hey there, John! How're you feeling?" Andy
asked.

"Amazingly good," John answered. His voice was
strong and bright. "I had a great nap and woke up
to angels singing."

"Did we really sound that good?" Amelia asked.

"Oh, yes. Especially you. I think there's a whole
bunch of angels around here." The group looked
at John quizzically. Ilena thought he was probably
suffering from delayed shock. "Lisa gave us a ride
here," he continued, "Reggie saved my life, Joshua
here dragged me home, Doctor Ilena patched me
up . . . . All of you."

"Not angels," Ilena said. "Just friends."

"Oh yeah? Well, check this out." John carefully

began to unwrap the bandage and splint around his right arm. Ilena became alarmed.

"Whoa. Don't do that!" she cried. John stopped, smiled, and held up his other hand.

"Take it easy, doc. I know what I'm doing." Impetuously, he untied the rest of the bandage and began removing the splints.

"I wouldn't do that," Andy said, moving to stop him. But before he could, John had freed his injured arm. He waved it over his head.

"Look! It's healed!" No one spoke. They could not believe their eyes. A shockwave of disbelief passed through the group. Spines shivered. Hairs stood on end. Only Joshua remained calm, waiting for the moment to pass. Finally, Reggie broke the silence. He spoke to John, but looked at Joshua.

"How in God's name did that arm heal so fast?"

"I don't know," John said.

"Maybe it was just badly dislocated," Joshua speculated as he returned Reggie's gaze. "Not broken at all. What do you think, Ilena?" She was stunned. But what other explanation could there be? She had seen far too many injuries and wounds in Iraq. Maybe she had just assumed it was broken. Maybe it had been only dislocated.

"It's possible," she said. "Let me have a look." She examined John's arm, rubbing, twisting it slightly, and then squeezing where it had seemed to be broken. She let go and shrugged.

"Is it healed?" Marta asked.

"I, uh . . . yes," Ilena said, dumbfounded. "Healed for sure. It must have been a dislocation. A break just couldn't . . . wouldn't . . ."

"Hey there, folks," Joshua interrupted. He held

the board with the turkey up for all to see. "Our Christmas Eve dinner is gettin' cold."

"And I'm famished," John announced. "I've been sleeping next to that tasty bird, just smelling it and dreaming of how good it's going to taste."

"Well, let's stop dreaming and get to it," Amelia said. She took over. "Marta? Why don't you and Lisa get the bread and the rest of the plates? Ilena can put the chairs and stools back around the table. Joshua, you take that lovely bird out of the canvas and put it on the table. Andy, you and Reggie take the soup off the fire and bring it to the table. Be careful. It's hot! Children? Take a seat at the table. John? Why don't you join them?" As people moved to their assigned tasks, Amelia oversaw everything, directing where things were placed on the table and where everyone was to be seated.

CHAPTER 38

MERRY CHRISTMAS

Just as everyone was settled in at the table, Andy got up and snapped his fingers.

"I've got something this table needs. Almost forgot." He quickly went to his suitcase that was against the wall and took out two bottles of wine. He fumbled through the suitcase and found a corkscrew, too. "These were a gift for my buddy, George, in Asheville. He's what you call a wine connoisseur. But it's Christmas Eve. So I figure they should be part of this fine dinner with my new friends. I'm sure George will understand. I even brought a corkscrew 'cause George is in the V.A. hospital, and we'd have to drink this on the sneak." He opened one bottle and poured it for the adults. "Everybody has some," he said cheerfully. "No designated drivers tonight." When Andy finished pouring, Lisa stood up. She looked at her wristwatch.

"It's midnight, everybody," she announced, raising her cup of wine. "Merry Christmas!" Everyone wished each other "Merry Christmas" and took a drink. The kids toasted with water.

"There is no Pepsi for us," Ronny said. "But it's still a Merry Christmas!" Everyone laughed at his childish enthusiasm.

"I'd like to say grace," Amelia offered.

"Please do," Joshua said, speaking for all of them as they bowed their heads.

"We are thankful, Lord, for the warmth and safety of this generous home, for new and good friends, for the meal we are about to have, and for Your blessing on this Christmas night. Amen." As she spoke, the group collectively recalled their long and arduous day and the life-threatening situations they had endured. After Amelia said, "Amen," they all responded, "Amen," and looked around at the blazing fire and the tree decorated with homemade ornaments and flickering pine-branch candles. They breathed in the familiar, re-assuring aroma of roast turkey and marveled at the camaraderie at the table. The expressions of joy and anticipation on the children's faces lifted the adults' spirits and bestowed a peace in their hearts that had been absent earlier that day.

Amelia had placed Joshua at the head of the table. The turkey, now without its canvas covering, stood warm and brown, waiting to be carved. Joshua picked up the large hunting knife and fork he had placed on the table.

"Now, who's carving?" Joshua asked.

"It's your house, sir," Andy said, respectfully.

"Well, tonight it's home for all of you. Choose someone besides me." There was a long moment of silence.

John stood up. "If I may suggest," he said, "I think Reggie has earned the honor."

Lisa stood and raised her glass. "Absolutely! To Reggie, the carver."

Everyone stood and raised a glass. "To Reggie, the carver." They all drank a toast. Reggie was overwhelmed. He stood up and walked to the head of the table. Joshua handed him the knife and fork. Reggie took it, avoiding eye contact with anyone. He stood over the turkey for a moment, then looked up. He struggled to control his emotions as he spoke softly, and from the heart.

"Thank you. All of you. Look, I, uh, well . . . I guess I've been a little, no a lot, I guess, sometimes rude and grouchy. I just want to . . . That is . . . I just . . ." He was about to break down. He lowered his eyes and stared at the table. Andy jumped up.

"Here's to Reggie!" he shouted. "Merry Christmas!"

"To Reggie! Merry Christmas!" everyone shouted. They drained their glasses and cups. Reggie smiled and nodded.

"It's time to open the other bottle, Andy," Marta said, grinning. She was feeling warm and a bit dizzy from the wine.

"The other bottle!" they all exclaimed. Andy began to open it, and Reggie began to expertly carve the turkey. He glanced over at Joshua, who smiled and winked.

"While Reggie's doing that, let's start passing the soup and bread around," Amelia suggested. Plates were passed, cups and bowls were filled, and the happy sounds of a good meal with good friends and family filled the cabin.

* * *

Outside, the sky was cloudless, starry bright. The moon remained low in the northern sky, casting its silvery glow, but it was not bright enough to dim the stars. The wind had stopped. The forest was still.

After scraping away the snow, three does nibbled on moss at the base of a tree. A ten-point buck watched over them from within the woods. The deer looked at the warm light emanating from the cabin windows when the sound of human laughter filtered out into the night. Across the clearing, the small pack of red wolves had been drawn to the odor of the turkey roasting over the fire. They, too, listened to the human sounds that filled the wintry night. They saw the deer, and the deer saw them. The red wolves settled to the ground, indicating they posed no danger to the deer. The buck stepped out and joined his does. It was Christmas.

CHAPTER 39

GOLDIE'S CONSTITUTIONAL

It was a Christmas Eve dinner they would remember the rest of their lives. The turkey was properly roasted and exceptionally tender for a wild, winter bird. Amelia's stuffing, that she had crafted from some of the bread she had baked and the wild blackberry preserves, was the hit of the dinner. Both bottles of wine were consumed. The conversation centered mainly on the day's events and how they had all pulled together.

"We dodged a bullet," John summarized, "and in my case, thanks to Reggie, Ilena, and Joshua, I dodged two bullets."

"I helped," a full and sleepy Ronny insisted.

"That you did, and you have my never ending gratitude, young man."

Ronny smiled and puffed up with pride. But no one at the table was prouder than his big sister and mother.

At the point when it was clear that dinner was over and the hour very late, a long moment of silence settled on the room. The fire, fed by Andy during the meal, was high and crackling. Goldie lay asleep in front of it, his golden coat hot to the touch as though he were storing up warmth for the rest of the winter. Joshua sat at the head of the table, Amelia at the other end.

"I'd like to say something," Ilena announced, breaking the silence. She slid her stool back a bit but did not stand. "Where I came from, just two days ago, is about as far removed from this cabin and table as I can imagine. I didn't want to come home for Christmas. Andy and Reggie understand how hard it is to leave your fellow soldiers, especially when there is so much danger. Over there, we live in a very different world. And sometimes, actually almost all the time, we forget about this other life—a table like this, good people, a safe, warm room. . . . What I'm trying to say is thank you. No one spoke of the politics of this war, and I appreciate that. We don't in-country, in Iraq. We volunteered, and we understand what our job is. Being here with all of you and sharing Christmas Eve, especially in Joshua's home, well, it gives me hope and, in a very positive way, strength to go back and fight for my country—for all of you and our right to gather like this in peace and friendship. So, Merry Christmas, and thank you." Her eloquence touched everyone. Even the children, who were not old enough to understand all of the consequences that Ilena faced in Iraq, understood that she had expressed something very human and important.

"And we all thank you, Ilena dear, for your courage and for your service," Amelia responded. Everyone agreed with a loud, "Hear, hear!"

* * *

A while later, in the wee hours of the morning, the table had been cleared. The dishes and utensils were washed and put away. Joshua, Ilena, and Reggie cut enough splits for the rest of the night. They were drying in front of both fires.

On one trip out to get wood, Ilena had taken the turkey carcass and set it at the edge of the clearing. As she walked away, the largest of the red wolves came out of the woods and picked it up. Joshua observed what had happened.

"I see you have made other friends," he said as she stepped up onto the front porch.

"They are my brothers. But of course you know that, don't you?"

"Yes," he said. He put his arm around her shoulders. "You're going to be all right, young lady. You have powerful spirits watching over you."

"Yes. Thank you," was all she had to say, because deep in her heart she knew it was true.

The children were asleep in the bedroom, tucked in warm under the quilt, with a nice fire crackling at their feet. Marta checked on them and then joined everyone gathered around the fire and Christmas tree in the cabin's front room.

"Are they asleep?" Amelia asked.

"Yes. With visions of sugar plums, thanks to all of you."

"They can open their gifts in the morning," Lisa said.

"No. Please," Marta said. She sat on a chair near the fire. "Look. Thank you all for thinking of them, but they told me they would rather you bring the gifts to the kids you bought them for. When we get

to Asheville they'll get plenty from my parents."
John, Ilena, and Andy nodded a silent "okay."

"You've got two great kids in there," Reggie told
her.

"That's for sure," John added.

Joshua stoked the fire and then turned to face
them all. His gaze drifted across the group as he
smiled and nodded slightly with a look of deep satisfaction.

"Well," he began, "it's been quite a fine Christmas Eve for all of us. Goldie and me, we, ah, we
enjoy the company and take pleasure in sharing
home and hearth with y'all. Now it's time for
Goldie's nightly constitutional." He took his coat
and snowshoes from the wooden pegs on the wall
near the door.

"Going out at this hour?" Lisa asked.

"We do it all the time. Goldie's gettin' on in
years and likes to take his time. Maybe chase a rab-
bit for fun or run with the deer."

"I thought dogs *chased* deer," Andy remarked.

"Not my Goldie. He's like kin to just about
everything that walks, flies, or swims out there."
On hearing his master say his name, Goldie got up
from his place near the fire and went to Joshua.
The big golden dog lingered for a moment, looking around at what he knew to be his houseguests.
He wagged his tail rapidly and then nodded his
head, as if to say, "It's good that you're all here."
Joshua stroked the back of his neck. Goldie looked
up at the old man. He nodded back at the dog,
then stepped into his snowshoes, strapped them
on and reached for his rifle. "We'll be a while. You
folks just settle in and get some sleep." He opened
the door. "I'm sure it'll be a well deserved and

peaceful one." With that said, he stepped out onto the porch. Goldie rushed by him out into the night. "Good night, then," Joshua said. "And a very Merry Christmas to y'all."

"Merry Christmas," they all said.

Joshua closed the door behind him.

CHAPTER 40

TRACKS

Nothing was said for several minutes. The fire crackled. Amelia leaned back in her chair and closed her eyes. Marta stared at the tree, her gaze drifting up to the white angel on top. The moon no longer made it glow, yet it still seemed bright. Lisa and Ilena stared into the fire, sitting side by side, two young women living worlds apart, but now brought close by unexpected events on this special night. Andy checked to make sure that all of the pine-branch candles in the tree were extinguished, while Reggie stacked the dried splits. John took some of them into the back bedroom and promptly returned to the group. He sat down near Marta.

"Joshua's one special guy," John said, breaking the silence.

"Yes," Ilena agreed. "Is it just me, or do any of you feel like, well, like you've known him all your life?"

Amelia, who had not been sleeping, opened her eyes. "That, and more," she said.

"What do you mean?" Reggie asked.

"There's something about the way he looks at you and the way he talks. It's comforting, isn't it? Like he knew what we needed to hear before we ever said a word."

"Yes," John said. "I felt that. But there's even more to it." He stood up. "When Reggie got Ronny up from that ledge—"

"Ronny? The ledge?" Marta asked. John realized his error and sheepishly looked at Reggie for help.

"The truth be told, Ronny sort of wandered off," Reggie said, taking on the uncomfortable task of explaining, "and got himself in sort of a little trouble. We . . . John and I, took care of it."

"Exactly what is 'sort of a little trouble'?" Marta asked. She stood. Her body language made John move a step away to the left.

"You seemed upset before," John began, "about getting stuck here, and the van and no food and all . . ."

"I wasn't upset," she told John, looking directly at him. "I was worried. Concerned for my children."

"Right. Yes, we saw that . . ." John said awkwardly, "so we didn't want you to get, you know, more, uh, you know, concerned."

"That's how you broke your arm, isn't it?" she asked.

"After Ronny was safe. It was my own fault."

Marta was not smiling.

"Ronny is a brave little guy," Reggie said, hoping to soften her annoyance at not being told the truth.

"And Nancy is a wonderful child, too," Ilena said. "You should be very proud, Marta."

"I am. And I'm also not so happy about being lied to."

"I don't think it was exactly a lie, dear," Amelia interjected. "If you think about it, they were concerned about your feelings, and the boy was all right. No harm done." She looked at John, then back at Marta. "Not to Ronny, anyway."

"And not me anymore," John added, flexing his arm. Marta relaxed and sat down. She shook her head and looked into the fire as though she were trying to rid herself of something very unpleasant by casting it into the flames.

"Things have been hard for us lately," she said. "I've not been very pleasant company here." She looked at Reggie. "Especially to you. I am sorry. Please forgive me."

Reggie nodded and spread his hands, indicating the apology was accepted. "No problem, Marta. It's in the past."

"Thank you. Like Ilena said," she continued, "I feel the same way. You've all made this night so special. It's given me hope." Tears came to her eyes. "I had so little this morning . . . yesterday morning, that is, at the airport. Now I have enough hope to last me a very long time."

"You said something before about the way Joshua talked to you," Reggie said to Amelia. "What happened?"

"Oh . . . He knew I was alone," she answered. "Lonely. Missing my husband. He comforted me."

"He made you feel at peace, right?" Reggie asked.

"Why, yes, dear," she said. "Peaceful. That's it."

Lisa fed a few logs onto their fire and stoked it. Then she went to the window and looked out. In the moonlight she saw three does at the edge of the clearing, striking through the deep snow with their sharp hooves in search of food.

"When he spoke to me," John said, "I felt as though he knew everything about me. And Goldie . . . the way he led us to the tree, and then when I had the trouble he went to get Joshua. Right, Reggie?"

"Yes," Reggie agreed, reflecting on his own experiences with Joshua and Goldie. Lisa turned away from the window, but stayed there, listening.

"Like Joshua knew I'd broken my arm and needed help?" John asked.

"Yes," Reggie answered.

"Exactly," John added.

"We're all talking about the same thing," Andy said.

"I think Joshua," Ilena chimed in, "is very special."

"I think what he was trying to tell us all was to break free from whatever stone we've tied around our necks," Reggie said. "Like my anger and bitterness about being laid off and all."

"Or my guilt," John admitted shyly, "at being away from my family so much."

"Yes," Amelia agreed. "After we spoke, my loneliness left me. It was as though a great weight had been lifted, almost magically, from my heart." They were all struggling to understand what kind of magic, if that was the word, that Joshua had worked in his small, neat cabin in the woods.

"Andy and I were talking before," Ilena said, "about the army—his war and mine. Like I said, I've just come from . . . Well, two days ago people were shooting at us." She took a deep breath and glanced over at Andy. He gave her a nod of encouragement. "My friend Rosa was killed by an RPG," she continued. "I've lost some good friends. That's hard. But being here, meeting Andy and Reggie, who have been where I am, helped me a lot. And Joshua? It's like Amelia said. Somehow he brings your heart peace."

"I hear that," Andy said. He reached over and took her hand in his. "Mine too." He looked around the room. "And I want you to know you guys have made this a Christmas Eve I never expected this year."

John got up from his chair and took a deep breath. "I guess we're all searching to express something pretty profound. Joshua's presence seems to have been a catalyst for us. In the bedroom before, when I awoke and he was there, it was like Joshua was in my head and I didn't hear what had happened. I just accepted that somehow I was healed."

Lisa, who had been listening to everyone talk about Joshua, stepped away from the window and stood behind Amelia's chair. "When I was fourteen," Lisa began, "we went sailing, my mom and dad and me. On Lake Superior. We had our summer vacations there. There was a sudden thunderstorm and we got caught." Amelia reached her hand up to Lisa, who held it tightly. "The boat swamped, and we . . ." Tears misted her eyes. "We went overboard. My father got to me, but my mother . . . I panicked and struggled. I held on to him. I almost drowned him." She paused and looked away, into the fire. "I kept him from saving my mother, and she . . . She was there and then . . . and then she was gone." Ilena came over and put her arm around Lisa.

"I'm so sorry, dear."

"She just disappeared," Lisa said in a choked whisper.

"It wasn't your fault," Andy said. "We all fight to live."

"And that's what Joshua told me," Lisa explained. Tears were running down both cheeks. "He called her the Lady in the Lake."

"What a strange way to put it," Marta said.

"Well, no. Not really. We were talking about King Arthur and—"

"Excalibur!" John interrupted. "King Arthur breaks the sword free from a stone and claims his kingly birthright."

"Yes. He recited a beautiful poem. Did you know King Arthur did that—extracted Excalibur from the stone—on Christmas?"

"No, I didn't," John said.

"Well, Joshua said he did."

"What I think is that Joshua was telling you to break free and claim your own Excalibur," Amelia said. "When Arthur couldn't bear the burden of his birthright he threw the sword into the lake. The Lady sent it back. My dear Lisa, Joshua was telling you that your mother would want you to live your life without this burden you have put upon yourself."

"I believe you're right," Lisa said, squeezing Amelia's hand. "You're very wise. Like Joshua."

"So what's going on here?" Andy asked. "I mean, what is this place? And who is Joshua that he has so much to say to us . . . about us, I mean?"

"The only Joshua I know of was the one Moses appointed to lead the Hebrews across the Jordan River into the promised land, Israel," Reggie said.

"The Bible, Old Testament, says God forbade Moses from entering himself."

"And in that Holy Land, from the Israelite tribes and the House of King David, Jesus was born. . . . On a starry winter's night, just like tonight," Amelia said.

"Joshua was a leader of his people," Ilena added.

"It's like our compasses were broke, and our Joshua knew the way," Reggie said.

Marta said, "He surely did show us the way." They all became silent as they tried to absorb what they had just discussed about Joshua, and the night, and their most unexpected Christmas Eve.

Lisa walked back to the window and stared out again. There was something out there that bothered her . . . that wasn't right, or in place. She stared and wondered, scanning the clearing and the edge of the woods. Suddenly, as if through an out-of-focus camera lens that came into sharp focus, it registered.

"Come on, everyone!" she shouted. "Outside!" She ran to the door and opened it. Everyone was startled by her insistence. They got up and went to the door, not bothering to get their coats or boots. Lisa held the door open. They gathered together on the porch.

The moon was low in the sky, but still bright. Its light illuminated the porch and the clearing, throwing very sharp shadows across the snowbound landscape. They all stood close together: Lisa, Amelia, Reggie, Ilena, Marta, Andy, and John.

"Do you notice anything?" Lisa said, pointing toward the clearing in front of them. Everyone looked across the snow toward the woods.

"What are we looking for?" John asked.

"Wait a minute," Andy said, pointing. "I see some deer over there." Ilena looked for the red wolves, but they were gone.

"Not them. Joshua came out this way with Goldie," Lisa said.

"Yes," John said, "and we came and went, too. From the van. Back for the luggage. For the tree, for wood. . . . So?"

"So where are our tracks?" Andy asked, staring at the snow. "There are no tracks."

"Maybe the wind blew them away," Marta suggested.

"The wind has been down for a long time," Reggie said, "since we dragged John back on that makeshift sledge."

Ilena's mind was racing as she took in the scene. "He had on snowshoes. He's a big man. Goldie ran out here, too. We saw that. Maybe a half hour ago. There are no tracks!"

"Right!" Lisa exclaimed. "None at all. Not ours, not his. Not Goldie's. So where did they go?"

"Not where," Amelia said. "The question is how?"

"And why?" Reggie added.

The group stared out into the night, so in awe and confusion that they did not feel the cold. Though it was unspoken, they all knew in their hearts that Joshua and Goldie would not return, and that whatever answers they sought, they would have to find them themselves.

They filed back into the cabin in silence.

CHAPTER 41

A MOST UNEXPECTED GIFT

Reggie was the first to wake up. He rubbed his eyes and noted the gray morning light seeping in from the windows. He checked his watch. It was 7:22 A.M. Christmas Day—time to get back to his family in Asheville. He stretched; set aside the jacket and coat he had used as a blanket, and quietly sat up. The others were asleep.

Andy, John, Ilena, and he had camped in the cabin's main room near the fireplace. Their beds consisted of clothing they had removed from their luggage. The fire was banked; the coals still glowed red and gave off warmth. Reggie stood up and stretched again. Ilena stirred. Andy opened his eyes. Reggie waved good morning to them. Then, while they were getting up, he went to the fireplace and added four heavy splits to the coals. The wood caught immediately, sending out heat and an orange glow that illuminated the room. As Ilena and Andy stood up and stretched, John stirred and awoke.

"Hi, everybody," he said cheerfully. "Merry Christmas." He set aside the clothing he had used as a blanket and got up. The first thing he did was check his arm. It was a little sore, but in one piece and operating perfectly. The other three, who had gathered close to the fire, watched him. He saw them staring and gave them a thumbs-up, indicating that his arm was okay.

Amelia, Lisa, and Marta were in the back bedroom with the children. Ilena tiptoed to the door, which was partially open, and looked in. The three women were fast asleep on and under their assorted clothing. Nancy and Ronny were dead to the world, sharing the bed and quilt. Marta had piled some of their clothing on top of it for additional warmth. The fire had dwindled to a bed of hot coals above which a blue and white flame danced and spread its heat. Ilena closed the door and joined the men.

"They're all asleep. The room is warm. No need to stoke the fire."

"Okay," Andy said. "Let them sleep. Now, what about the van?"

"Let's have a look at it in the daylight," Reggie suggested. "I was thinking that we could get some logs or pine branches under the tires and with a push, maybe horse it out."

"That might work," Ilena agreed. "We've got Joshua's axes and saw here." The mention of Joshua's name brought back last night's events sharply. "I dreamt about him," she said.

"What was the dream about?" John asked. "If you don't mind sharing."

"It's okay. I don't recall much except that he was happy and smiling. He was talking to someone—I don't know who. Maybe Goldie. Walking along. But not on the ground. Sort of floating, and as he did, there was snow, but as he passed, it melted and flowers grew. All kinds of animals appeared and followed him." She stopped and smiled. "That's about it."

"Sounds happy," Andy observed.

"Oh," Ilena said, "it was very pleasant. Like him."

Reggie bent down and put two more logs on the fire. "What say we get moving?" he suggested. "The sun's up." They looked at the windows and saw that they were glowing with dawn. "If we can't get the van out ourselves, it's going to be tough finding a wrecker on Christmas Day."

As they got ready to go, Ilena put her arm on John's. "I'd feel better if you didn't push things, John," she said. "Not until you see a doctor and have an X ray."

"But it's fine," he said, flexing it. "Really."

"Still, it might need attention. Please."

John shrugged. "Okay. I'll hang here and start to pack."

Before they left, Ilena said she wanted to make a trip down to the stream so that there would be fresh water when the others got up.

"I'll go with you," Andy said, remembering their encounter with the red wolves.

"I'm going to go ahead and start to check out the damage," Reggie told them. He was anxious, worried about how they would get help getting the van back on the road and whether or not it would be able to travel after that.

Ilena and Andy went out the front door and around the cabin to the rear so as not to wake their friends in the back bedroom. Reggie put on his boots and jacket and headed across the clearing toward the woods.

The rising sun, still below the tree line, had yet to vanquish the last remnant of night from the forest. Once they left the clearing, which was still devoid of footprints of any kind, they set out in different directions—Andy and Ilena toward the stream, Reggie toward the van and the road. The footprints they now made were the only ones visible. But once they reached the woods they noticed that the paths they had made the night before were still there. Ilena also noticed wolf tracks alongside their own leading to the stream.

The water was high from the runoff of yesterday's storm, but it was clear. Ilena quickly filled the soup pot with water and handed it to Andy.

"Looks like your wolf friends were here," he said, pointing to a small pile of bone fragments.

"It's the turkey carcass. I gave it to them."

"That was nice of you," he said, lifting the pot of water.

"They are my brothers and sisters," she said. She took one of the pot handles.

"Really?" was all Andy could muster.

"It's a Cherokee thing. We'd better get a move on. I imagine Reggie is going to be upset when he sees that wreck in the daylight."

Reggie was extremely anxious to see what damage he had done to the van, and if it was possible to get it out and onto the road without a wrecker. He moved quickly through the woods and saw the road ahead in what seemed a much shorter trek than the night before. He stopped for a moment and looked back, but there was no sign of Ilena and Andy. A few minutes later, Reggie stepped from the woods into the ditch that ran below the shoulder of the road. He looked toward where he had backed the van off the road and gotten bogged down. But the van was not there! He checked where he was and where he had come from and was sure he was looking at the right place. The van was gone!

Ten minutes later, as Ilena and Andy hurried to catch up to Reggie, they heard him hooting and hollering loudly. They ran to the road.

"Hey! Hey, guys. Come and look at this," he cried out when he saw them coming. His shouts reverberated through the forest. They ran faster, thinking he had "lost" it.

When they emerged from the woods, Reggie was standing on the road above them. "Hurry on up here," he said, as excited and animated as they had ever seen him. They hurried up the incline to the road. "C'mon," he urged. "You gotta see this!"

Ilena came on up first on Reggie's right. Andy was right behind her to his left. Reggie offered his hand to each, pulling them up onto the road. He placed his arms on each of their shoulders as they stared in disbelief.

"After everything that happened to us yesterday, this just blows my mind!" Reggie said.

The van was on Comfort Mountain Road, parked on the other side, facing down the mountain toward the Great Smoky Mountain Parkway.

"How in God's name did it get there?" Andy asked.

"That, my friend, is the sixty-four-thousand-dollar question!" Reggie said.

"Now that's what I call one heck of a Christmas present!" Ilena exclaimed.

"C'mon," Reggie said happily. "Let's check it out." They spent the next ten minutes inspecting the van, inside and out.

"Everyone ought to be up by now," Reggie said when they had seen enough; and what they had seen had disturbed and elated them. Anxious to get back to the cabin, they trotted across the road and quickly slid down the embankment to the ditch.

"Just a sec," Reggie said. "Come with me." Just to be sure they weren't dreaming, they ran over to where the van had been stuck the night before. They all agreed this was the place. There was no evidence that it had ever been there. The tree that it had hit was intact; the snow was undisturbed; there were no tire tracks leading from there to the road above them.

"What happened?" Andy asked.

"Like I said," Ilena told them, "it's a Christmas present."

"You'd better believe it, bro," Reggie answered. He reached his clenched fist in the air to Ilena and Andy. They both made a fist and touched Reggie's together. A three-way Dap. Then they took one last look at the pristine "accident" scene. Their eyes scanned the untouched tree and the virgin snow leading up to the road. Ilena grinned. Andy shrugged his shoulders. Reggie grinned.

"It sure is something," Reggie said. "Well, okay, then. Let's go get everybody and be on our way."

CHAPTER 42

AN ANGEL LEFT BEHIND

As Ilena, Reggie, and Andy hurried back to the cabin, everyone there was awake and on the move. Amelia was in the kitchen putting some of the water Ilena had left on the stove for tea. Lisa was setting a plate of leftover bread and blackberry preserves on the table near the fire. John had finished his packing and was arranging the luggage for the others. Marta was in the bedroom helping the children get dressed. They came out into the main room carrying their clothes.

"Where is everybody else?" Ronny asked.

"They went up to have a look at the van," John told him. "They should be back soon." Ronny went to the front door and opened it.

"Don't let in the cold," Marta scolded. Ronny looked outside and saw the tracks that Reggie, Ilena, and Andy had made earlier. His eyes followed them to the woods and there, up above on the bluff, he caught sight of the three heading toward the cabin.

"They're coming back!" Ronny cried out, excited.

"Joshua and Goldie?" Amelia asked.

"No. It's Reggie, Andy, and Ilena."

"Well, I guess now we'll find out if we can get out of here in time for Christmas," Lisa said. She went to the doorway and joined Ronny.

"Did they go to the gas station?" Nancy asked.

"Not yet," John told her.

"Maybe they got a ride there," Amelia said hopefully.

"There wasn't time," John said.

Five minutes later, Reggie, Ilena, and Andy arrived at the cabin. They were a little out of breath from hurrying back through the snow. They went to the fire to warm themselves and were strangely silent.

"What's wrong?" John asked.

"The van," Reggie said. "It's on the road."

"You got it up there already?" Lisa said, excitedly. "That's great!"

"We didn't do anything," Andy said.

"At first we thought maybe someone . . . The road is plowed. . . . Maybe they pulled it out," Ilena said.

"But there's not a scratch on it," Andy said.

"And," Reggie announced emphatically, "believe it or not, it has a full tank of gas!"

"How is that possible?" Lisa asked.

"Good question. It's like the accident never happened!" Ilena exclaimed, spreading her hands in the air.

Everyone was confused and stunned.

"I don't understand," Marta said. "Are you telling us that we can just walk out of here, get into the van, and go to Asheville?"

Reggie, Andy, and Ilena nodded.

"That's what we're saying," Reggie told Marta.

"I'll bet Joshua did it," Nancy suddenly said. "He's our friend."

"And Goldie helped him, too," Ronny added.

"Yes, children," Amelia said. "I wouldn't be the least bit surprised if that's exactly what happened."

"Right," Reggie said. "Old Joshua hooked up a harness on Goldie, and he just pulled that big old van up onto the road. Then Joshua hammered out the dents, painted it, drove it to town, filled it with gas, and brought it back."

"And?" Amelia asked with a knowing smile.

"And . . ." Reggie took a deep breath. "And you and the kids are probably right. Except . . . I don't know. I guess some things . . ."

". . . passeth all understanding, bro," Andy said, finishing Reggie's sentence. "That's one I know. Philippians four, verses six and seven. 'And the peace of God, which passeth all understanding, shall keep your hearts and minds through Christ Jesus.' "

"Amen," Lisa said. "Maybe we shouldn't question. Maybe we should accept this as a gift on His birthday."

"Like this cabin," John suggested. "Like our Christmas Eve dinner. Like my arm healing."

"Perhaps some healing for all of us," Amelia offered with a quiet smile.

"And a Christmas gift of safe passage," Ilena concluded.

"Yes. Safe passage from Joshua," Marta said wistfully, nodding and closing her eyes as if to say a silent prayer.

"And Goldie," Ronny added.

"Right you are, Ronny. That Goldie is one fine mechanic," Ilena told the boy. They all laughed. Ronny understood it was a joke and laughed too.

"Well then," Andy said, "if we're going to get to Asheville for Christmas, we'd better get moving."

"Right," agreed Lisa. "We've still got to find a way around that avalanche."

"At least Comfort Mountain Road is plowed," Andy announced.

"Maybe we should continue up the road and see where it goes." The mischievous glint in Amelia's eyes was caught by everyone but Reggie.

"Oh no, we don't," he said emphatically. Then he saw everyone was looking at him and grinning. He smiled and raised his hands in surrender. "Okay. You got me."

Everyone packed hurriedly, anxious to be with friends and families in Asheville on Christmas Day. The kitchen and pantry were put in order. The plates, cups, glasses, and utensils were put away in the cupboards. Ilena volunteered to make one last trip down to the stream for water so that they all could wash and brush their teeth. Meanwhile, as soon as the suitcases were packed, the men began to carry them up to the van.

Their last act was to extinguish the fires that had kept them warm, cooked their food, and in a very real sense kept their spirits alive and hopeful. When the final flame had been snuffed out, and the last smoldering log removed, the finality of a very magical night was clear. They all knew their time in this place was over.

They left the cabin without ceremony, forming a single file as they walked across the clearing through the path made by the men carrying luggage. Ilena led them. Lisa helped Amelia as she had done on their trek to the cabin the night before. Marta and the children were next. John took up the rear. Only Reggie and Andy remained behind to make sure the fires were out and to carry the last few pieces of luggage up to the van.

"Keep on the path we've made," Ilena called to everyone as she entered the woods. She observed fresh wolf tracks and beyond them, on the bark of a thick white birch, signs of a bear. Stepping aside, she let John take the lead. After the others passed, she went to the white birch and removed the glove on her right hand. She respectfully fit her fingers within the fresh marks on the trunk. The sign of the bear. She traced the scrapings, made by the bear's claws, with her fingers. Through them, her grandfather's words came back to her again. She was indeed a warrior who made her people proud.

She caught up with the group and trotted past them to the head of the line, setting an easy pace that did not put a strain on Amelia. They reached the ditch below the road in twenty minutes.

As Lisa helped Amelia up the incline to the road, Ilena, already there, took the older woman's hand and helped, too.

"My God," Lisa said at the sight of the intact van. She walked over to it and traced where the dents had been with her hand. The others got up onto the road and also studied the van.

John and Ilena loaded the luggage they had just

carried on top of the van while Marta, Amelia, and the children got in. The morning was sunny but still bitterly cold. Lisa started the engine and turned on the heater.

Back at the cabin, Andy carried two suitcases out onto the front porch and set them down. Reggie followed him with Marta's largest, heaviest suitcase. He put it down and closed the front door as tightly as possible.

"I left Joshua a note on the table with my phone number in Asheville," Reggie said. "I'll be living there now. I have a job with my son." He sounded positive about moving. He realized that it was the first time he had mentioned the move in a positive way.

"That's good," Andy said. "I'll be there for a week or so with my buddy. I hope Joshua calls you."

"Yeah . . . Sure he will," Reggie said sarcastically as he picked up Marta's suitcase.

Andy smiled and nodded. "I hear that, bro," he said as he picked up the two suitcases.

A few minutes later they had crossed the clearing and plunged into the woods. When they reached the knoll above the cabin Andy stopped and put down the heavy suitcases.

"Let's take a break," he said. "I'm not as young as I used to be." Reggie put his down as well, glad to have a rest. He laughed.

"I guess we're both in that boat," Reggie said. Andy laughed with him.

After a few moments, they were ready to press on. Without saying anything, they both felt the same pull and looked back at the cabin one last time. What they observed froze them in wonder and disbelief, sending chills down their spines and their mouths agape.

The cabin was slowly disappearing from sight, fading away like a memory of long ago; though still in their conscious minds, it was soon no longer visible. Only the clearing was left, and that now had trees and brush throughout. In the center, where the cabin had stood, was a tall, perfect blue spruce. At the very top of it the men saw something white and shiny, waving in the breeze: the angel Joshua had provided last night for their Christmas tree. Reggie and Andy looked at one another.

"Lord!" Reggie exclaimed. "What in the world?"

"It's Christmas," Andy said. Further words were unnecessary. They picked up the suitcases, glanced back at the clearing one last time, then continued on their way toward the van.

CHAPTER 43

THE STATUE

"What's up?" Lisa asked when she saw the odd expressions on Reggie and Andy's faces. "You guys look like the cat that swallowed the canary."

"Nothing," Reggie said, smiling.

"Just glad to be on the road again," Andy said. On the way up to the van, both men had decided to say nothing about what they had just seen. They felt there would be disbelief, or worse, confusion. Some might want to go back and see. The children might not understand. They would be delayed and miss Christmas with their friends and families. Andy suggested that perhaps they could all get together in a few days, and maybe then Reggie and he would tell the story. Some might doubt it, thinking Reggie and Andy had simply been tired and looking in the wrong direction. Others might accept it, but they both agreed it would be best if the kids weren't told. Marta could decide whether to do that later.

The last of the luggage was secured on top. Reggie

and Andy got into the van. Lisa was behind the wheel, announcing she had mapped out a route around the avalanche. They would go back through Bryson City, maybe stop there for breakfast. From there it was west on County Route 28 to State 129 into Maryville, Tennessee. Then they could pick up State 321 to Interstate 40, which would take them into Asheville.

"It's roundabout," Lisa said, "but the only sure way around the mountains."

"How long will it take?" Marta asked.

"It's about one hundred miles," Lisa said. "It's only eight-fifteen now. Even stopping for breakfast, I'd imagine we'll be there by noon."

They drove the mile and a half down plowed Comfort Mountain Road to the Great Smoky Mountain Parkway and came to a stop. There they waited as several cars and trucks passed in front of them, going in both directions.

"It looks like the road has been cleared," Lisa said. "I guess that avalanche wasn't that big, after all."

"Great," John said. "That'll get us to Asheville in an hour or so."

Across from them, a state trooper sat in his cruiser, pulled over on the side of the road. Its engine was idling, sending a wisp of condensation up from the exhaust into the frigid mountain air. John checked his cell phone.

"No signal yet," he said.

"Before we head up the road, I'm going to check with the trooper," Lisa said. "Just to be sure."

She got out and looked both ways across the Parkway. All clear. She trotted across the snow-caked road to the North Carolina State Trooper's car. As she approached, he rolled down his window.

"Good morning," Lisa said, waving a hello.

"Good morning, ma'am," he said. He got out of the cruiser and put on his hat. "How can I help you today?" He was an older man, in his late fifties, she guessed. His ruddy, weathered face wore a pleasant smile. His uniform was immaculate.

"Has the avalanche been cleared up ahead?"

"What avalanche might that be?"

"About two miles up north. We ran into it late yesterday afternoon. The road was blocked. We thought there was a way around it up Comfort Mountain Road, but we got stuck."

"Comfort Mountain dead-ends up top. There's only an old abandoned Cherokee orphanage up there, and we had no avalanche."

"Oh," Lisa said. "No avalanche? You're sure?"

"Yes, ma'am. Might have been a snow slide, but nothing to block the road. I came on at two A.M. No avalanche here." Lisa was confused, but saw that the trooper was telling the truth. Maybe the avalanche had been just a temporary thing, and the plows had pushed the snow aside. But they had gotten out of the van and stood there! Snow had completely blocked the road and was more than six feet high. Even Joshua said there were avalanches. But maybe it had just looked that way. It had been late in the afternoon when the light was failing.

"Well, okay, then," she said. "And thank you."

"Yes, ma'am." He tipped his hat. "You say you were stuck up there?"

"Our van went off the road."

"You stay in it all night? That can be dangerous, you know. Especially in this cold weather."

"No. We found a cabin up there and spent the night with an old man and his dog. He was very hospitable." The trooper frowned. "Thank you, Officer. Merry Christmas."

"Yes, ma'am. You're welcome. And a Merry Christmas to y'all, too." Lisa turned to walk away. "Old man and his dog?" the trooper said, smiling. "The boys at the barracks put you up to that?"

"No," Lisa said. "Put me up to what?"

"That statue across the road by your van?" he answered, pointing. "It's not the first time that old story's been told around here." Lisa looked across the Parkway. Everyone was out of the van and gathered around a statue. She couldn't see what it was. Confused, she shrugged.

"Well, okay. Whatever, then . . . Bye."

"Yes, ma'am. Take care."

Lisa crossed the Parkway quickly and approached the group now clustered in a semicircle before the statue. As she joined them she remembered seeing something that they had passed yesterday, but it had been growing dark and the object had been covered with snow. *It must have been this statue*, she thought.

"According to the trooper," Lisa said as she joined everyone, "there was no avalanche. What's going on here?"

"Come here, my dear," Amelia told her. "Come and have a look at this."

CHAPTER 44

CHRISTMAS 1907

Beginning in late October 1907 the snow and frigid weather had come on early, hard and unrelenting. Descendants of those who lived during that fall and winter would often recount the many tragedies of that harsh time in the Great Smoky Mountains. The creeks, tributaries, and eventually the major rivers had frozen solid. By Thanksgiving, river traffic had ceased. By December, farmers, trappers, hunters, and the Cherokee children at the orphanage were shut in. The only ones who would profit from the cold were the harvesters of ice, who carved the river into large square blocks, covered them in sawdust to keep them cold, and waited to sell them to people in nearby towns during the hot summer months.

Many villages and mountain hamlets of hill people, Scottish settlers, and descendants of the Cherokee who had eluded the federal army seventy years before were also snowbound early that year. All were on their own. There was no state or federal relief. For the lonely Cherokee orphanage, on the top of Comfort Mountain, that winter was an especially severe hardship.

Residents of the orphanage were the tragic legacy of the forced acculturation of the Cherokee. Their parents had died during the infamous Trail of Tears, the mandated migration of the Cherokee from their eastern mountain homelands to the western territories.

Love and family was not in abundance in the orphanage. The children were fed a mixture of basic skills and strict discipline to develop what was termed "their respective stations in life." They were taught not to expect much. That way they would have few disappointments in the future.

Located at the top of Comfort Mountain, a small mountain surrounded by larger, darker ones, the orphanage had two barns sheltering milk cows on the eastern side of the compound. Barracks-style dormitories for the children were next to them. A rustic schoolhouse with rooms heated by small wood-burning stoves was used only after the morning chores of the farm that supported the orphanage were completed. At times of planting, harvest, milking, and haying, there was no school. Small, tidy cabins were built on the warmer southern side of the compound for the teachers and staff, who were all women.

The headmistress, Elmira Ferrarri, was the daughter of Italian immigrants. She was a graduate of City College of New York, originally founded as the Free Academy of the City of New York in 1847. A combination prep school and college, it provided children of immigrants, and the poor, access to free higher education based on academic merit alone. Elmira carried this philosophy to the orphanage but was hamstrung to carry it out with these unfortunate children for lack of funds and the corruption and bigotry that existed at the time in the Bureau of Indian Affairs.

The only man who lived on the property was Hans Bjenndik, a widower who had lost his farm to drink and gambling and now served as foreman overseeing the work of the children.

The orphanage was for the most part self-supporting, with a few northern patrons, friends of Elmira, and a small federal stipend that had to be squeezed annually from the Bureau of Indian Affairs budget. The children's labor saw them through the necessities for most of the year. They were a hard-luck bunch, and they knew it, as much from their Spartan surroundings as by the lessons stressing their inferiority that were imparted to them daily by their teachers. They were rigorously taught "useful" skills such as farming, blacksmithing, cooking, mending, and sewing.

Once a year, though, even the most hardbitten of the mostly spinster faculty allowed one small glimmer of joy into the children's lives. The kindness of the local community, in the spirit of Christmas, manifested itself by bestowing handmade and second-hand, but genuinely appreciated, gifts to the orphans. Warm jackets, mittens, and socks were especially welcomed. Occasionally a broken toy or one poorly repaired was donated, and the surprise was even more appreciated because of the rarity of that event.

During the winter of 1907 there had been few visitors to the orphanage because of deep snow and frigid temperatures. Once a month, the county postman managed to get up to Comfort Mountain.

But then fate intervened when the postman stopped in at Tucker's General Store, a small clapboard structure on the lone, dirt road that ran from Bryson City to Waynesville through the Great Smoky Mountains. That road would eventually become the Great Smoky Mountain Parkway.

Old Man Tucker, as he was called, was Joseph Palmer Tucker, formerly a corporal in the Fifth North Carolina Regiment. He was six feet, five inches tall, gray-haired, and slender as a rail. His forehead retained the thin scar of a Yankee saber at Antietam. Memorabilia from the Confederate States Army occupied niches in the general store that he had run for forty years—a rebel cap, an old musket, and several faded daguerreotype images of young men at war during America's bloody Civil War. Nearly every inch of floor space and shelf space held the hundreds of sundry items that rural mountain life required in the recently arrived twentieth century, and many from the century past.

An ancient Ben Franklin stove, its metal skin flaked by years of winter fires, sat in the middle of the store on an iron sheet that kept sparks from setting the store afire. A scarred pinewood counter ran along one side of the store, with tall shelves filled with dry goods behind it. Locally produced cheese, pickles, and crackers, stored in wooden barrels, were arrayed along the front of the counter. Several gunnysacks tied at the mouth with rope sat in the far corner of the store. The black, block-letter imprint of the Hubbard & Millsop Feed Company of Charlotte was visible on them. Ironically, most of the seed was derived from those plants developed by the Cherokee Nation.

That winter's day, with late afternoon's long, deep shadows falling across the rough-hewn floor, an elderly man with a coarse, scraggly beard, gray with black streaks, and shoulder-length white hair sat by the stove. His long-haired dog, a large golden retriever, lay at his feet. He was whittling a piece of maple with a long-bladed hunting knife. Slender, curled strips of wood were piled at his feet. The dog slept soundly, his back resting against the man's boot ensuring that he would awaken, were his master to go anywhere.

With a rattling of a loose-fitting door and a tinkling of the brass bell affixed to it, the snow-drenched postman, William Cathcart, entered the store. Billy, as he was known, was a short, stout man with strong arms and back developed from thirty years life of delivering letters and packages throughout the Carolina hills. He brushed snow from his shoulders and tapped his woolen hat, brushing the snow from that, too. He stamped his boots on the plank floor, then greeted Old Man Tucker with a grin that exposed several missing teeth.

"Mornin', Tucker," Billy said. "Colder than a well digger's a—"

Tucker raised his hand to silence Billy, nodding toward a woman and child in the back of the store.

"Uh, colder than a well digger's, uh, knees," Billy said. Tucker nodded his approval. The old man whittling near the stove smiled.

"Hot coffee's on the stove. Welcome to it, Billy," Tucker told the postman.

"Afternoon, Billy," the man by the stove said.

"Good to see y'all, Joshua. You too, Goldie." At

the mention of his name, the dog looked up, saw an old friend, wagged his tail, and then nodded off back to sleep.

The postman poured himself a cup of hot, black coffee, cradling the cup in his cold hands. He took a quick, mouth-burning sip and smiled.

"That'll warm a body down to the soul, Tucker."

"Surprised you're out," Joshua said.

"Wanted to make one last trip up to the orphanage."

"Oh?"

"Some of the folks in Waynesville were a little late with the presents this year, the weather bein' what it is and all. . . ." The postman gazed outside through the store's only window to distant hearths. "And there's times a distant relative or do-gooder sends the poor unfortunates a card or gift late. I have a few in my sack on the mule outside."

"Wish I'd known you were makin' a trip today," Tucker said. He nodded toward a burlap sack in the corner of the store. "Townsfolk pulled together a few presents for them poor kids, too." The postman looked out the window again. It was snowing heavily and the sky was darkening.

"Yup. I hear ya, Tucker," he said, pointing outside, "but ain't nobody getting up Comfort Mountain through that storm today. We tried. Me and the mule barely made it t'here."

A young sandy-haired boy, Tommy MacGregor, seven years of age, with wide, inquisitive eyes, stepped to the stove. He wore an unbuttoned, thick, navy blue coat that was several sizes too large. It had been patched and mended many times. His mother, Elizabeth, a thin woman in her thirties with hair turned gray prematurely from the travails of the harsh mountain life, stood next to him. Her threadbare cloth coat covered a faded print housedress. She had heavy workboots on, probably her husband's, and a wet, gray, rough woolen shawl on her shoulders that served as headwear outside.

"Are there presents in that sack?" the boy asked Tucker.

"Yes, son. For the children at the orphanage."

"Tonight's Christmas Eve," the boy said, turning to the postman, "if'n you don't bring 'em, how they gonna git 'em? Ain't they gonna be sad tomorrow on Christmas mornin'?"

Tucker leaned down on the counter, cradling the boy's head in his long, gnarled hands. "I suppose you're right, son," he said. "That's a kindly thought, but sometimes you just have to abide by things the way the Lord makes 'em."

A blast of icy wind rattled the faded cedar shingles on the roof of the store. Joshua looked up and listened to the melancholy sound they made.

"Lord's will, Tommy," Billy said. "Many things passeth all human understanding."

"Amen," Elizabeth said, fingering her worn shawl and stepping closer to the stove.

"But, why?" Tommy asked.

"Only for the Lord to know," Billy answered.

"But the Indian children. They have no kin, and now they'll have no Christmas."

"You have a kindly heart, Tommy, but there's no way I can do it," the postman told him. The boy's shoulders sagged. He looked at his mother, hoping she might help convince the postman to bring the presents to the orphanage.

Joshua ceased his whittling, bent down, and patted Goldie. He whispered something to the dog that none in the store could hear. Goldie got up and stretched. Joshua then rose to his feet with deliberate dignity, and the slowness of an aged and arthritic back. A sharp pain shot down his legs until his first few steps chased it away.

"I'll take them," he said softly.

"Now that's plumb crazy, Joshua. You can't make it," Billy warned. "I was up the road a might, and had to turn back. It's gettin' worse out there by the minute."

"So you said. Well, Billy, I know these woods better'n most. And our cabin's halfway up Comfort Mountain anyway. Right, Goldie?" The dog barked and wagged his tail, eager for another adventure with the only master he had ever known. Goldie was aware of all the man's mannerisms and of how they had changed as he had painfully aged lately. He always fed his canine companion before he fed himself. At night, the dog lay by Joshua's side, and Joshua always gave him three pats on the rump, and told him, "Good night, boy. God bless." Theirs was an unbreakable bond.

Joshua nodded to Elizabeth, then knelt in front of Tommy. "Don't you worry now, son. Goldie and I'll get them gifts up there before Christmas."

"Then you'll be their Santa Claus," the boy said.

"Maybe so. Me and Goldie, we've been a lot of things in this life. Never been a Santa before. Seem's a proper thing to be on Christmas Eve." Joshua stood up and took his heavy bearskin coat from a peg on the store's wall. He pulled a beaver-fur hat with earflaps out of the coat's sleeve and put it on, tying the flaps tightly under his chin. Before he closed the coat he tied deerskin leggings around his canvas trousers. His high snowboots, store-bought, were laced up. He opened the knots and pulled the laces tight.

"I'll take that sack now," he told Tucker. Then he turned to Billy. "The gifts you have are out on the mule?"

"That they are, Joshua, but I'm agin you totin' them up there."

"Is that official, Billy?" Joshua asked.

"'Course not. You're on a fool's errand, Joshua, but Godspeed to you."

Joshua took the sack and walked to the door, where his snowshoes were leaning against the wall with his Winchester long rifle. His hands were bare. He checked to see that his fur-lined buckskin gloves were in his coat pocket.

"Well, that's about it," he said to Tucker, Billy, Tommy, and Elizabeth. "Have a Merry Christmas, y'all."

Once outside, Goldie ran into a snowdrift and rolled around in it, as if he were preparing himself for the cold journey ahead. Joshua went to Billy's mule and removed the sack of toys and mail. It was larger than the sack Tucker gave him, so he put that sack into it. He then slipped on his gloves and lifted the heavy bag to his shoulder. He held his rifle in his other hand and stepped out onto the snow covered road.

As if it were an omen, the snow let up and a weak sun shone slightly above the treetops as he and Goldie made their way toward the path up Comfort Mountain. Old Man Tucker, Billy, Elizabeth, and Tommy watched through the store window until Joshua and Goldie were out of sight.

*   *   *

Trudging on in the failing light, the pair reached the orphanage by dusk, where, to the surprise and delight of the children, Headmistress Elmira Ferrarri, and Hans Bjenndik, the farm foreman, they delivered the sack of presents and cards. That Christmas Eve the younger orphans believed they saw Santa Claus, and for the rest of their lives they would tell their children and their grandchildren the tale. The older children, pessimists seasoned by experience with the white man, saw Joshua and Goldie's feat as a simple fact that someone cared about them. It brought them the beginning of hope about their future.

The headmistress offered Joshua Christmas Eve dinner in the dining room of the children's dormitory. They sat at a well-made plank table in front of the room. Elmira Ferrarri sat on his left and Hans Bjenndik, on his right. The children, all forty-six of them, sat at long tables in front of the adults. The staff and teachers had gone home for the holiday, so Miss Ferrarri had prepared the modest dinner of soup and sourdough bread herself.

"Mighty nice, what you done, Joshua," Hans said.

"My pleasure," Joshua told the widower, who was older than Joshua by ten years. "Seemed a righteous thing to do."

"It's a blessing," the headmistress added. "God will reward you."

"Thank you kindly, Miss Ferrarri. And this soup is also a blessing. It is the best I can ever remember tasting." Joshua wiped his mouth on the back of his hand. He dipped a piece of the crusty bread into the soup and reached under the table, placing it into Goldie's open mouth.

When he had finished, Joshua pushed his chair back from the table and patted his belly. "A fine, fine meal, Miss Ferrarri."

"It has begun to snow again, Joshua, and the temperature is well below zero. Perhaps you should stay the night," she suggested.

"I thank you, ma'am, but I think not. I reckon Goldie and me'll be home in no time, no matter the weather." Joshua felt a tugging at his hip. He looked down to see a young boy wiping his straight coal-black hair from his eyes with one hand while he held something concealed behind his back with the other.

"Merry Christmas, sir," the boy said politely, as he had been trained to do.

"Merry Christmas, lad." The boy looked at Goldie, who was now out from under the table and as anxious to be going as his master.

"May I give him a present?" the boy asked, pointing to Goldie.

"Of course you can." The boy moved his arm from behind his back and offered a small object wrapped in faded newspaper. Gently, he placed it on the floor. Eagerly, Goldie tore back the paper, revealing a hefty soup bone. He took up the bone with his teeth and wagged his tail. "Now, that's probably the best present old Goldie ever got. We thank you, son. What's your name?"

"Red Wolf," he said proudly. "I am Cherokee!" he added, looking defiantly at the headmistress. Goldie, clutching the bone in his mouth, nuzzled the child.

"His name is David," Elmira said, glaring at the boy. "David Theodore Roosevelt. He's named for our president." Joshua saw the boy shake his head but remain silent.

"You know, son," Joshua said, kneeling down to the boy's level. "Once, when I was a young man, I saw a play in Asheville. *Romeo and Juliet*, by William Shakespeare. It was something. And I remember Juliet. She was a young girl in love with Romeo. She said, 'What's in a name? That which we call a rose by any other name would smell as sweet.'" The boy smiled. Joshua looked up at Miss Ferrarri. "Now ain't that a right smart comment about names?"

"Yes," she answered. "Of course."

No one saw them again until early spring, when, as the deepest snows melted, Joshua's and Goldie's bodies were discovered at the foot of Comfort Mountain, about a hundred yards from the road that would one day become the Great Smoky Mountain Parkway in the Nantahala Forest. They were frozen together as one.

CHAPTER 45

A GIFT TO REMEMBER

Lisa joined the group around the life-size, weathered granite statue of an old man and his dog. The man was tall, wore a beaver-fur hat with earflaps and a long, flowing bearskin coat. The dog was a golden retriever with long matted fur. On the stone pedestal, on a bronze plaque weathered to a deep green patina, was an inscription.

Joshua Baker and Goldie. Lost in an avalanche on Christmas Eve, 1907, after bringing presents to the Comfort Mountain Cherokee Orphanage. True heroes of these mountains who now rest here in peace, together and forever.

Everyone stood there speechless. Joshua's likeness looked out benignly on the world, with Goldie, faithfully forever by his side. Both were very familiar to those now gathered. Amelia was the first to speak.

"Wasn't it wonderful?"

"Wonderful and beautiful," Ilena agreed, as she wiped a tear from her cheek.

"I feel blessed," Marta said, hugging Nancy and Ronny close to her.

"We all are," Andy said. They nodded one to the other and then slowly walked back to the van.

Everyone was silent as Lisa started the engine and they pulled away. She waved to the state trooper as they made the turn out of Comfort Mountain Road onto the Parkway, and headed north toward Asheville.

Words were unnecessary to share their profound experience. Each knew something momentous had happened. As if they were dizzy from suddenly rising too fast, or abruptly awaking from a dream that was not a dream, each in the van was changed. Each felt an inner glow growing inside until it filled their humanity with hope, love, and joy.

Amelia smiled radiantly, recalling Joshua's words that had lifted the pain of her husband's loss, dislodging that pain with the overwhelmingly happy memories of their love and life together.

Andy felt renewed hope and deep gratitude for having loved Maria so deeply in the time that they had together. For the first time, he'd been able to unburden himself of some of the dark experiences of war by helping a young soldier, Ilena, to understand their common pain and pride. He couldn't wait to share the experience with his buddy George in the V.A. hospital in Asheville.

Marta was relaxed. Her thoughts were positive as she looked ahead, excited to be free of a domineering, cheating husband, and hopeful about her family's future. She turned and smiled at her children.

Ronny and Nancy, in the backseat with Ilena, saw their mother's warm, loving smile and were happy. Their mother was back, the way she used to be, and they knew that things would be all right.

Lisa drove carefully as she finally knew absolution for a crime she had committed only in her mind, and through Joshua's metaphor of King Arthur, had received the commutation of the sentence of guilt she had imposed on herself.

John knew what he needed to do, and he prayed silently, among the reassuring presence of the others, that he could indeed make the effort to be a better father to his children, and a constant, present, loving husband to his wife. Joshua had healed more than his arm last night.

Reggie, seated between Lisa and Amelia, vowed to never forget what he had seen happen to the cabin in the clearing when they left. Joshua had subtly set a stage that showed him that everything was going to be all right in his presently confusing, topsy-turvy world—not that the old man could make it so, but that Reggie had the power and strength to accept change and recognize it was out of love he was being offered a helping hand. The old man and these strangers had given him that precious gift when the knife and fork were passed to him to carve the turkey.

Ilena, seated in back with the children, mulled over Joshua's words to her. "You're going to be all right," he had said. That gave her some comfort but did not take away the deep concern and fear she carried for the others in her unit in Iraq. As if he sensed Ilena's quandary, Andy, who was with

John and Marta in the middle seat, turned and offered Ilena his hand. She leaned forward and took it, feeling the care and strength from someone who had walked in her boots and understood the emotions she was feeling and would feel for perhaps all of her life. In that moment of camaraderie peace came into her heart.

When Ilena leaned forward, it gave Ronny more room, and something drew him to turn in his seat and look out the rear window. He wiped the condensation from the glass with his hand. He leaned closer when he saw something come out of the woods on the side of the road. He strained to see. As the van pulled away he realized it was Joshua and Goldie, standing side by side. They were faint, translucent shapes against the dark pine trees. Joshua waved. Goldie wagged his tail, and Ronny thought he could hear the dog's bark over the sound of the van's engine. Ronny waved back and smiled.

"Merry Christmas, Goldie," he whispered to himself. He turned and saw Nancy was kneeling on the seat beside him, looking back down the road. She was smiling and waving, too.

If you enjoyed A CHRISTMAS PASSAGE,
be sure to look for
David Saperstein and George Samerjan's
wonderful first novel,
A CHRISTMAS VISITOR.
Inspired by the popular
Hallmark television movie starring
William Devane and Meredith Baxter,
it is a moving and magical story about
a father who struggles with the past,
a daughter who fights for the future,
and a mother who searches for answers.
The Boyajians have not celebrated
Christmas in eleven years.
They lost their faith when they lost their son to
the Persian Gulf War.
Now a stranger has joined them—
around the same age the boy would have been.
Is he a con artist?
Or is this young man the miracle their family has
been waiting for?

Read on for a special excerpt from this powerful
tale of a mysterious young man who brings the
family out of sadness and mourning and into the
warmth and joy of the Season once more.
This holiday, a stranger will change them forever.

A Christmas Visitor

Available from Kensington Publishing Corp.

CHAPTER 1

IN MEMORIAM

Each year brought a different perspective. As with changing seasons, the passage of time revealed different hues of color, from bright to muted to bright again, reflecting the loss he carried deep inside. The emptiness seemed not to diminish, nor ease, though thirteen years had passed.

The cold, threatening November day had kept people indoors. As the crisp autumn night rapidly descended, the Town Square was deserted. George Boyajian stood motionless on the narrow, gray stone sidewalk that led to the town's War Memorial. His six foot, sixty-year-old frame was erect; shoulders square—the physique of a man twenty years younger. George's full head of brown hair gave no hint of age, though some gray flecks had begun to appear at his temples. Under his weathered leather jacket, and fleece-lined gloves, were powerful, sinewy arms and hands—the result of a life's work in the building trades. He was a master carpenter.

George Boyajian had, for the past thirteen years,

observed a private ritual on the night before the somber public assembly took place at the memorial. He moved forward down the walkway toward the five polished native granite columns, which formed a circle of honor. Each column was fronted with a brass plaque. His heart pounded. A chill ran down his spine as he heard the rattle of the rope tapping against the lit hollow flagpole, and the crack of the American flag snapping briskly in the breeze above. It caused him to gaze up at the stars and stripes, illuminated against a brilliantly starry sky.

The sound and image transcended time, stringing his memories of this place together like dark pearls in an endless necklace. He did not feel the chill wind. The acuity of his vision was almost surreal. He could see every broken blade of grass along the path, every stone, and every patch of earth— all fitting together in a sentient mosaic.

George stopped again. It was 1966 and he was standing at attention in his fatigues in Vietnam at a jungle base camp as the chaplain read the names of that week's fallen. In that faraway, long-ago place, he might well have been one of the names announced . . . names recorded on lists of wars—wars begun millennia ago with rosters of the dead in the millions. And still there was no end to them in sight.

His memory and reflection was but a momentary diversion. He walked on, wanting to be strong for John's sake. It was the reason why George Boyajian would come to this place the night before the annual ceremony—to inoculate himself against any public display of hurt and loss, his private emotions locked away while he performed his public duty.

"Oh dear God," George whispered inside him-

self. "My dear God . . ." Gathering courage, and remembering his pledge to honor John, he reverently
walked into the circle of the five stone columns.

The names of deceased servicemen from New
Chatham were displayed on the columns' brass
plaques. The Great War, the one they said was to
end all wars, contained eight names; World War II
listed twenty soldiers, sailors, and marines who
had fallen; five men had been killed in the Korean
Conflict—a "police action" they called it; the Vietnam
War plaque listed twelve men who had made the
supreme sacrifice in South Vietnam, Laos, and Cam-
bodia. George shook his head in somber disbelief
at the number of souls his small town had offered
to America. He paused briefly before the Vietnam
plaque. It listed the names of his schoolmates and
friends who had died in Vietnam. He knew them
all. It still amazed George, after nearly four decades,
that his name was not engraved there. He was here,
living and breathing. Yet part of him had been left
behind, forever entwined in the souls of those who
fell beside him.

The last plaque, memorializing the first Iraq War,
contained only one name, his son, John Boyajian.
He removed a small plastic baggie from his pocket.
In it was a cloth he had partly dipped in Brasso. He
gently rubbed the brass letters of John's name with
the caustic fluid and then wiped it dry with the rest
of the cloth.

"There you are, son. All spit and polish." George
knelt. First with his eyes, then his heart, and finally
his hand, he reached out across a lifetime. With a
tender touch, more an embrace, his finger found
the name, John's name, shining in moonlight that
gave the brass a blue patina. He stared at the

raised characters, and then through them, seeking to catch a glimpse of John on the other side. He closed his eyes and remembered a place nearby. The New Chatham train station . . .

John, a strapping twenty-five-year-old, stood before him, tall and slender, exuding the easy, wiry, physical presence of youth and the deep inner confidence of a man who knew who he was and where he was going. John had completed his training and was a proud member of the elite 5th Special Forces Group. He wore his Class-A uniform. Black spit-polished boots were bloused in the distinctive custom of the Airborne. His Green Beret proudly displayed the Special Forces insignia.

Clutching John's right arm tightly was Elizabeth Meyers, Lizzie, his girlfriend since junior high. Her sandy blond hair, tossed by a gentle breeze, fell across John's shoulder as she rested her head there. John squeezed Elizabeth's hand and kissed her softly on her forehead. It was a hard moment for them, but there were things George needed to say.

"So remember . . . stay in the middle. Never volunteer for nothing . . . and don't let 'em get to know your name too easy," he told his son.

"Yes, Dad," John said, laughing. "That's the same thing you told me when I enlisted, and it's the second time you told me that this morning."

George smiled and nodded. "A senior moment, huh?"

"Hey . . . you made it back from Vietnam okay. I'll make it, too. Six months in the Gulf, and I'll be home. Piece of cake." John looked down the platform toward the parking lot. "I wish they would have come."

George felt impotent, unable to change events. He glanced around nervously. A scattering of men in business suits stood waiting for the train. Another day at the office for them.

"They love you, son. You know that."

"Yeah."

"Your mother's scared to death. You're her baby, you know. First born. It's how women . . . how mothers get." George glanced at Elizabeth. She smiled shyly. "Just look at you, son. You're a man, now." George smiled. "A warrior."

John laughed, and slapped his father on the shoulder.

"Yeah. I know. Just like you were. Lean, mean, and almost bulletproof."

A woman with a young boy at her side approached them. The child tugged at his mother's sleeve and pointed.

"Look Mommy. A soldier!" The boy threw a child's salute at John, who smiled and returned the salute. The mother pulled her son away.

George saw John glance away again toward the parking lot, hoping that his mother and sister might magically appear. But they didn't.

"Nothin's going to happen to me, Dad. I'll . . ." The sudden wail of a train whistle turned their attention away. Up the tracks a bright headlight signaled the approaching train. The wooden platform trembled slightly beneath their feet. John pulled Elizabeth close to him. The moment George dreaded was here. The three of them stood frozen as the train pulled in, and with a final creak and bang, it stopped to gather the travelers. Sensing the moment, Elizabeth disengaged and George stepped forward to embrace his son. Around them, the other passengers hurriedly boarded the train. For them it was just a little trip into the city. They would return later that evening. For John it was the start of a journey into an unknown fraught with danger.

"I love you, Dad," John whispered as his father held him close, closer than he ever had in his life. George tried to speak, but no words formed. His throat was dry. John pulled away gently and smiled. George nodded and placed his hand on his son's cheek, then stepped back to allow the few moments left to be between John and Elizabeth. Tears welled up in Elizabeth's eyes and spilled out. Her body trembled. Wisps of her hair matted on her wet cheeks. John gently stroked the hair away and kissed her. He tasted her tears on the softness of her lips and inhaled the scent of her love. Embracing Elizabeth tightly, he kissed her neck and whispered, "I'll be back. Let's surprise everyone at Christmas and get married."

Elizabeth looked into his eyes. "You really mean that?" She felt lifted and thrilled.

"Yes." His voice was hoarse. He swallowed hard.

"Oh, John, I love you. I don't want you to go. I'm afraid and . . ."

"I'll be fine . . . And home for Christmas." He kissed her quickly, hard on the mouth, then picked up his duffel bag and hefted it onto his shoulder. Smartly, he turned away and walked toward the train. Once aboard he looked back and waved one last time. Moments later, as the train disappeared down the track, George and Elizabeth were alone on the platform.

"God love you, son," George whispered as he placed his arm around Elizabeth. She got weak in the knees and sagged a bit. George held her close while she wept. She did not see or feel his tears as they melted into her golden hair.

The vision faded. George Boyajian was at the monument, his finger still pressed against the name he loved, but his expression was now serene.

Behind George, three grungy, drunken teenagers sauntered into the park toward him. They wore black engineer boots with dog chains strung around them, loose fitting blue jeans, and overly large, heavy plaid shirts. Two sported baseball caps cocked sideways. Their moonlit shadows moved along the deserted walkway, spilling onto George's as they stopped close by him. The leader of the motley group smeared his finger on the Vietnam War plaque.

"Hey man, where's Rambo? Like Rambo's gotta be here, man." He chuckled at the wittiness of his remark. The others laughed with him.

A sudden hot rush of anger made George shake his head rapidly to clear away this rude intrusion into his privacy. He strained to ignore the young barbarians; to recapture the serenity of the emotional moment they had interrupted. A second teenager did an insulting mimic of "Taps."

"For God's sake," George said with precise pronunciation of each word, "This is a cathedral! Have respect!"

The leader looked at George with a cynical smile. He glanced at his cohorts for support. "You got a problem, old dude?" He chuckled. "Yo, man—

We just looking for Rambo. With all these here dead mothers . . . Hey, gotta be Rambo, too. Ain't that right, old dude?"

Rising to his feet, George eyed the leader and then the others. He figured he could take down one big mouth before the others got him. If that was the price of protecting John's sanctity, he was ready to pay it.

"If you can't show respect, please leave."

"Yo, man . . . You're the one who needs to show respect," another boy said, opening his shirt and revealing the butt of a 9mm Glock automatic pistol.

"School the old dude, Frankie," said the leader.

"Yeah. Show him who we are, man," the third kid chimed in. They moved threateningly closer to George.

"Hey there old man," the leader said with a wide grin, "it's showtime!" They closed in slowly, like a pack of hyenas on the savannah, cornering what they thought to be an easy victim. George quickly glanced over his shoulder at John's name, as if to gather strength or perhaps to say good-bye. He saw the shadows of himself and his tormentors on the brass and granite. As he turned back to the confrontation, the indistinct shadows of two more men appeared from behind. A clear, deep voice cut through the tension.

"Is there a problem here?"

"Something we might help with?" the second man asked. George kept his eyes on the gang leader, now assuming that whatever the punks tried to do the strangers behind him would help. The expression on the gang leader's face changed as he looked beyond George. The young man's eyes grew wide and afraid, unable to comprehend. His bravado was gone as a great danger was suddenly staring him in the face. A cold blast of wind blew his arrogantly placed baseball cap off his head. It pushed him backward. He shuddered. His skin, a moment before flushed red with heated blood and arrogance yearning for action, had now turned a deathly gray.

"No. Uh . . . No man. No problem." George watched in confusion. The leader was responding to something the stranger had said, but George had heard no words.

"Yes, sir," a different gang member said, hearing another voice that escaped George's detection. Respectfully, the frightened kid bowed his head.

"No problem, sir," the leader said again, his voice now thin and fearful. "We uh . . . we didn't mean . . . What?" A flash of pain twisted his face in anguish, yet George didn't see anyone touch him. "No, man. We . . . we're sorry." The leader backed away. "Like really sorry, man . . ." He then turned and ran. The others quickly followed.

George turned to thank the strangers. But they were gone. He looked all around the memorial park, then up and down the Town Square. But not a soul was in sight.

"I'll be damned," he muttered as he returned to John's plaque. "If that doesn't beat all." He knelt again. "Listen Johnny . . . I'm gonna talk to your mother and sister. Get them to come. To understand . . ." He felt a chill though no breeze had blown. "Oh God! Yes. I know you can see me, son."

He touched John's name again, this time with the palm of his right hand. "You're here, aren't you . . . just on the other side. You know they didn't come to say good-bye at the station. But here . . . maybe . . . Maybe I can get them to understand. It's time. Maybe tomorrow."

CHAPTER 2

VETERANS DAY

George stood in the warm kitchen with his back to his wife and daughter. The aroma of pancakes on the griddle blended with brewing coffee and the tang of freshly squeezed oranges. His gaze was fixed on the rolling fields between the old farmhouse and the distant foothills. He was rehearsing his lines as though he were an actor in an impossible play, about to step on stage to face an unwelcoming audience. Yet he had no choice but to perform. After the events of last night at the monument George felt he was driven by a force he could not resist. He was a strong-willed man but now something compelled him to act.

He sipped from his gray ceramic coffee mug, then turned his gaze away from the outdoors, over his shoulder, to his daughter, his "baby," Jennifer. But Jenny was grown up. She was now in her late twenties—grown, married, divorced, and a single parent. A woman. Where had the years gone? She had George's brown hair, but not his blue eyes. Hers were duplicates of her mother's—brown, warm, bottomless pools that drew you into her soul. Jenny sat slumped at the oak butcher-block kitchen table that George had built five years ago when they'd remodeled. Nicks, scars, and stubborn stains on the table bore witness to the kitchen being the center of life in their home—a locus of all good, bad, joyful, and tragic events that had befallen the Boyajian family. It all seemed to have centered around this sturdy, serviceable table in the kitchen.

Jenny cradled her coffee mug between her delicate hands as if it were an offering to some deity and she the supplicant seeking an answer to her prayer. She wore a loose fitting pale blue sweater and jeans. Her pretty features bore the same troubled and distracted look George had observed for months. But it had become more pronounced over the course of the last few days. George's wife, Carol, a stunning woman in her early sixties, sat next to Jenny.

George had fallen in love with Carol the first time he had seen her, and though heated passion had abated over the years, there was no diminishing of his deep and total love for her.

Carol sat pensively with her left hand on Jenny's. She sensed George's mood. Thirty-five years of marriage will do that. Her eyes narrowed. Her head tilted slightly to the right.

George read the suspicion on her face; she knew him too well, and all of his moods and methods.

"Listen, guys," he began, "I uh . . . Last night I had this experience. I can't explain it exactly, but it was, well, something." Jenny now looked at him, too. Daughter and mother—a pair of skeptical bookends. "What I want . . . I mean what I'd like is for you two to come to town with me today . . . to—"

"Don't start, George," Carol curtly interrupted. "We settled all that long ago. Jenny's home to be with us. We're not going to the ceremony. And that's that!"

"But if you'll just . . ." he said stubbornly.

"For God's sake, George!" Carol grasped Jenny's hand. "Don't you think we have enough to deal with without your raking up more pain?"

George moved to the table and took their clasped hands in his. "Jenny? Honey? Please. It's been so many years. Too many. It's time we . . ."

"No," Carol said as she pulled her hand away. "It was like yesterday. It will always be yesterday for us." She extricated Jenny's hand from his and stood up.

"Please . . ." he begged.

Carol shook her head slightly and looked away. She was making an effort to control her emotions. She took a deep breath and looked at her husband.

"You're the one who let him go. He's a man, you said. He wants to serve his country, you said. You're the one who took him, in his uniform, to the American Legion Hall. You—the proud father! I don't need to see his name on that cold plaque. I buried my son next to your parents. His name is on the family stone. That's more than enough for me."

"No dear . . . It's not about that."

"What else is there but names?" she said sarcastically. "Lots of names. Others we knew and grew up with. Will seeing them bring them back to us? What is the point in going there again, and again, and again?"

George knew that when Carol dug her heels in like this, nothing could move her. His only hope to get them to town was Jennifer.

"Please, Jenny. Please trust me on this."

"Maybe I should go," Jennifer said bitterly. "After all, it may be my last chance before I'm in the ground next to Johnny."

"No! No . . ." George quickly said. "That's not what I meant, sweetheart."

"We have a living child here who needs us," Carol announced, wanting no more of this talk. "Jenny has to concentrate on only one thing—getting better."

"Well, damn it, I'm going. I haven't missed a year since . . ." George plucked his brown tweed sports coat from its peg on the nearby pine coatrack, thrusting his arms through the sleeves. He paused before the mirror above the coatrack and adjusted his collar. He stared at the reflection of the Combat Infantryman's Badge on his lapel. He looked at Jennifer one more time, asking with his eyes for her to go with him. She turned her head away. Carol's gaze stayed locked on him, showing neither anger nor compassion.

George left, shutting the kitchen door gently behind him.

More by Bestselling Author
Hannah Howell

More by Bestselling Author

Janet Dailey

Bring the Ring	0-8217-8016-6	$4.99US/$6.99CAN
Calder Promise	0-8217-7541-3	$7.99US/$10.99CAN
Calder Storm	0-8217-7543-X	$7.99US/$10.99CAN
A Capital Holiday	0-8217-7224-4	$6.99US/$8.99CAN
Crazy in Love	1-4201-0303-2	$4.99US/$5.99CAN
Eve's Christmas	0-8217-8017-4	$6.99US/$9.99CAN
Green Calder Grass	0-8217-7222-8	$7.99US/$10.99CAN
Happy Holidays	0-8217-7749-1	$6.99US/$9.99CAN
Let's Be Jolly	0-8217-7919-2	$6.99US/$9.99CAN
Lone Calder Star	0-8217-7542-1	$7.99US/$10.99CAN
Man of Mine	1-4201-0009-2	$4.99US/$6.99CAN
Mistletoe and Molly	1-4201-0041-6	$6.99US/$9.99CAN
Ranch Dressing	0-8217-8014-X	$4.99US/$6.99CAN
Scrooge Wore Spurs	0-8217-7225-2	$6.99US/$9.99CAN
Searching for Santa	1-4201-0306-7	$6.99US/$9.99CAN
Shifting Calder Wind	0-8217-7223-6	$7.99US/$10.99CAN
Something More	0-8217-7544-8	$7.99US/$9.99CAN
Stealing Kisses	1-4201-0304-0	$4.99US/$5.99CAN
Try to Resist Me	0-8217-8015-8	$4.99US/$6.99CAN
Wearing White	1-4201-0011-4	$4.99US/$6.99CAN
With This Kiss	1-4201-0010-6	$4.99US/$6.99CAN
Yes, I Do	1-4201-0305-9	$4.99US/$5.99CAN

Available Wherever Books Are Sold!

Check out our website at **www.kensingtonbooks.com**